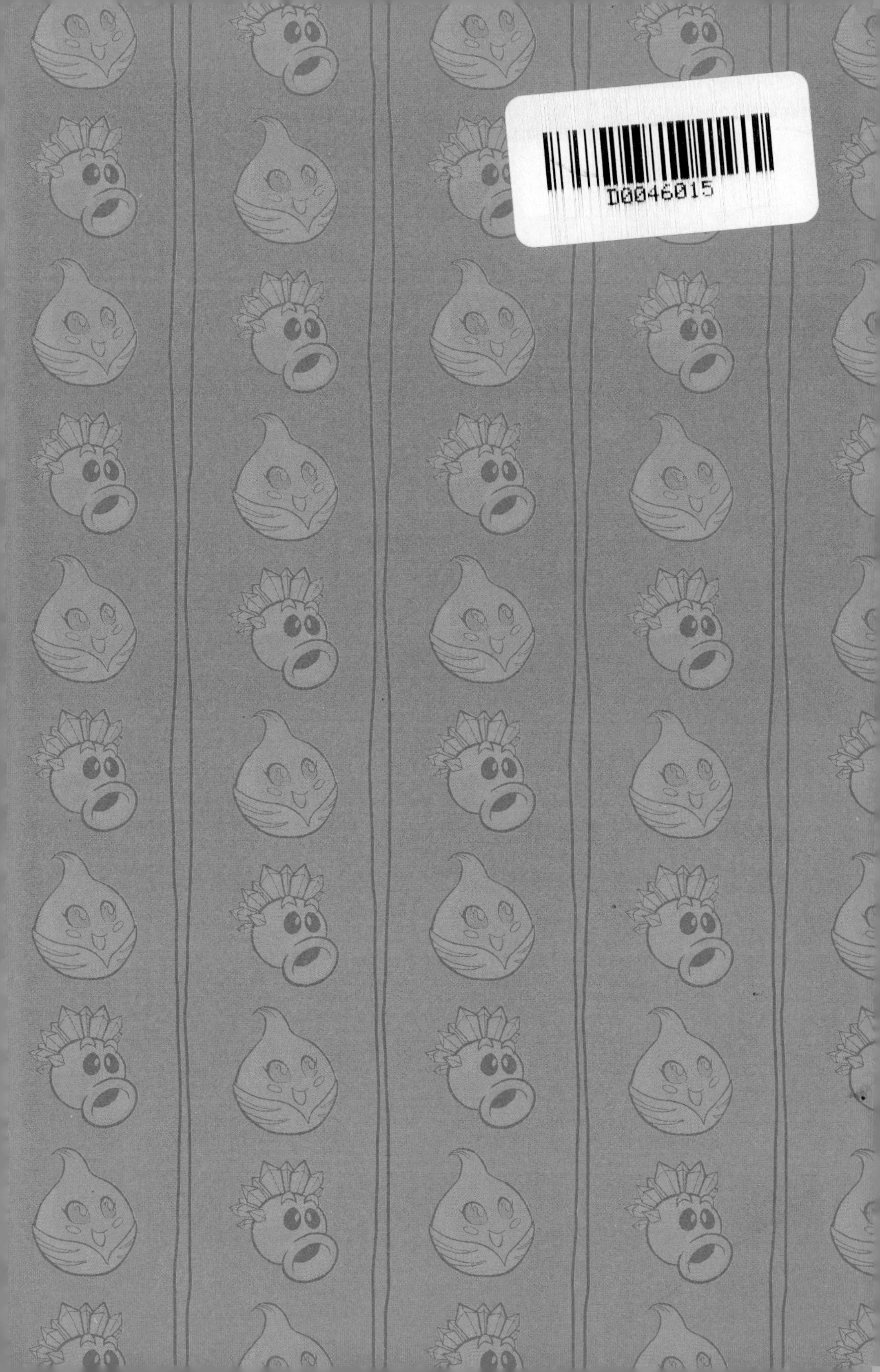

PLANTS VS. ZOMBIES

THE GREATEST SHOW UNEARTHED

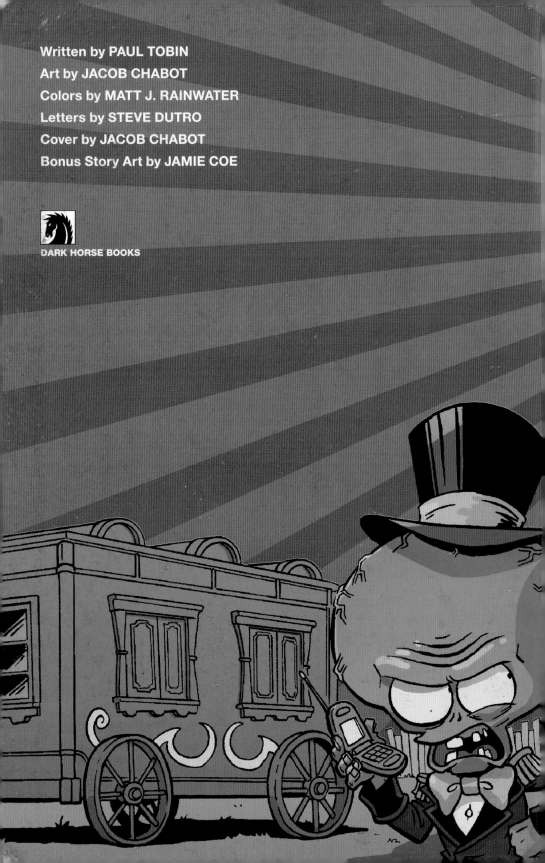

Written by PAUL TOBIN
Art by JACOB CHABOT
Colors by MATT J. RAINWATER
Letters by STEVE DUTRO
Cover by JACOB CHABOT
Bonus Story Art by JAMIE COE

DARK HORSE BOOKS

PLANTS VS. ZOMBIES

THE GREATEST SHOW UNEARTHED

I AM A BEAR.

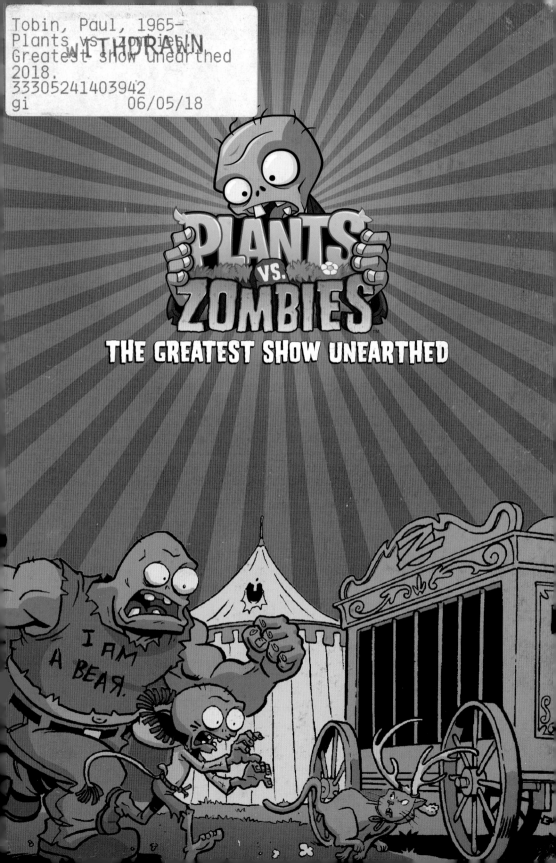

Publisher **MIKE RICHARDSON**
Editor **PHILIP R. SIMON**
Assistant Editor **MEGAN WALKER**
Designer **BRENNAN THOME**
Digital Art Technician **CHRISTINA McKENZIE**

Special thanks to Leigh Beach, Rachel Downing, Alexandria Land, A.J. Rathbun, Kristen Star, and everyone at PopCap Games.

First edition: February 2018
ISBN 978-1-50670-298-8

10 9 8 7 6 5 4 3 2 1
Printed in China

DarkHorse.com
PopCap.com

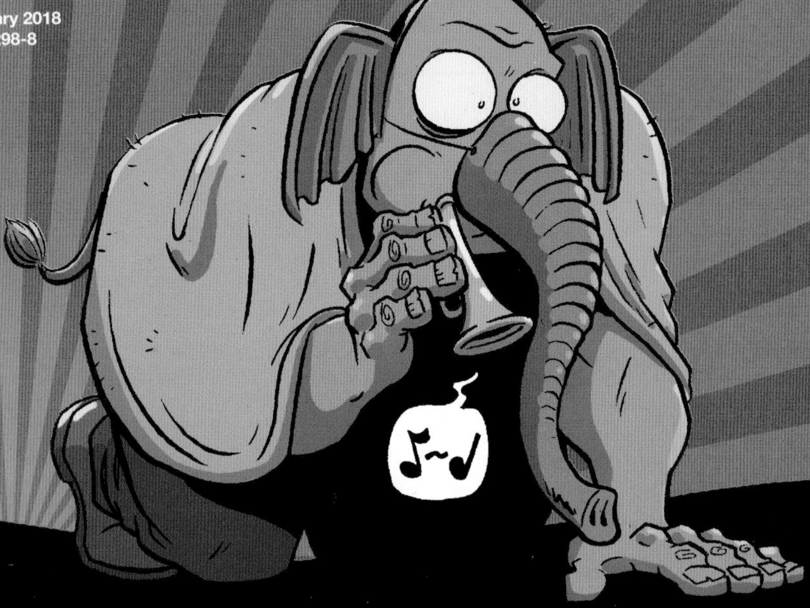

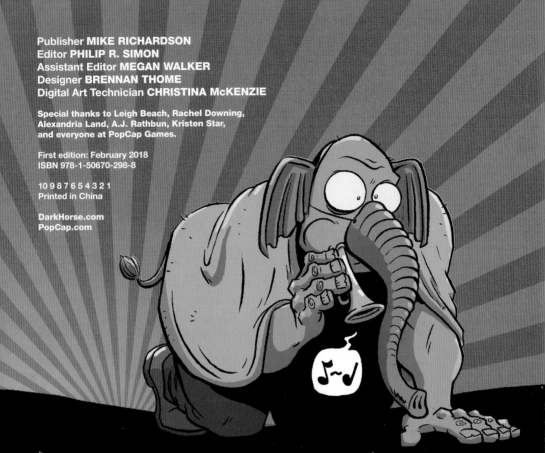

No plants were harmed in the making of this graphic novel. However, Dr. Zomboss did try on many different circus top hats before he found just the right one that fit his glorious, oversized head.

PLANTS vs. ZOMBIES: THE GREATEST SHOW UNEARTHED | Published by Dark Horse Books, a division of Dark Horse Comics, Inc., 10956 SE Main Street, Milwaukie, OR 97222 | International Licensing: (503) 905-2377 | To find a comics shop in your area, visit comicshoplocator.com |

Library of Congress Cataloging-in-Publication Data

Names: Tobin, Paul, 1965- author. | Chabot, Jacob, artist. | Rainwater, Matthew J., colourist. | Dutro, Steve, letterer. | Chabot, Jacob, artist. | Coe, Jamie, 1990- artist.
Title: Plants vs. zombies. Greatest show unearthed / written by Paul Tobin ; art by Jacob Chabot ; colors by Matt J. Rainwater ; letters by Steve Dutro ; cover by Jacob Chabot ; bonus story art by Jamie Coe.
Other titles: Plants versus zombies. Greatest show unearthed | Greatest show unearthed
Description: First edition. | Milwaukie, OR : Dark Horse Books, 2018. | Based on the video game Plants vs. Zombies. | Summary: "Dr. Zomboss erroneously believes that all humans hold a secret desire to run away and join the circus, so he aims to use his new 'Big Z's Adequately Amazing Flytrap Circus' to lure Neighborville's citizens to their doom! Once plant-friendly neighborhood defenders Nate and Patrice infiltrate his show, Ringmaster Zomboss is in for a garden-ful of trouble!"-- Provided by publisher.
Identifiers: LCCN 2017037809 | ISBN 9781506702988 (hardback)
Subjects: LCSH: Graphic novels. | CYAC: Graphic novels. | Zombies--Fiction. | Plants--Fiction. | Science fiction. | BISAC: JUVENILE FICTION / Comics & Graphic Novels / Media Tie-In.
Classification: LCC PZ7.7.T62 Pj 2018 | DDC 741.5/973--dc23
LC record available at https://lccn.loc.gov/2017037809

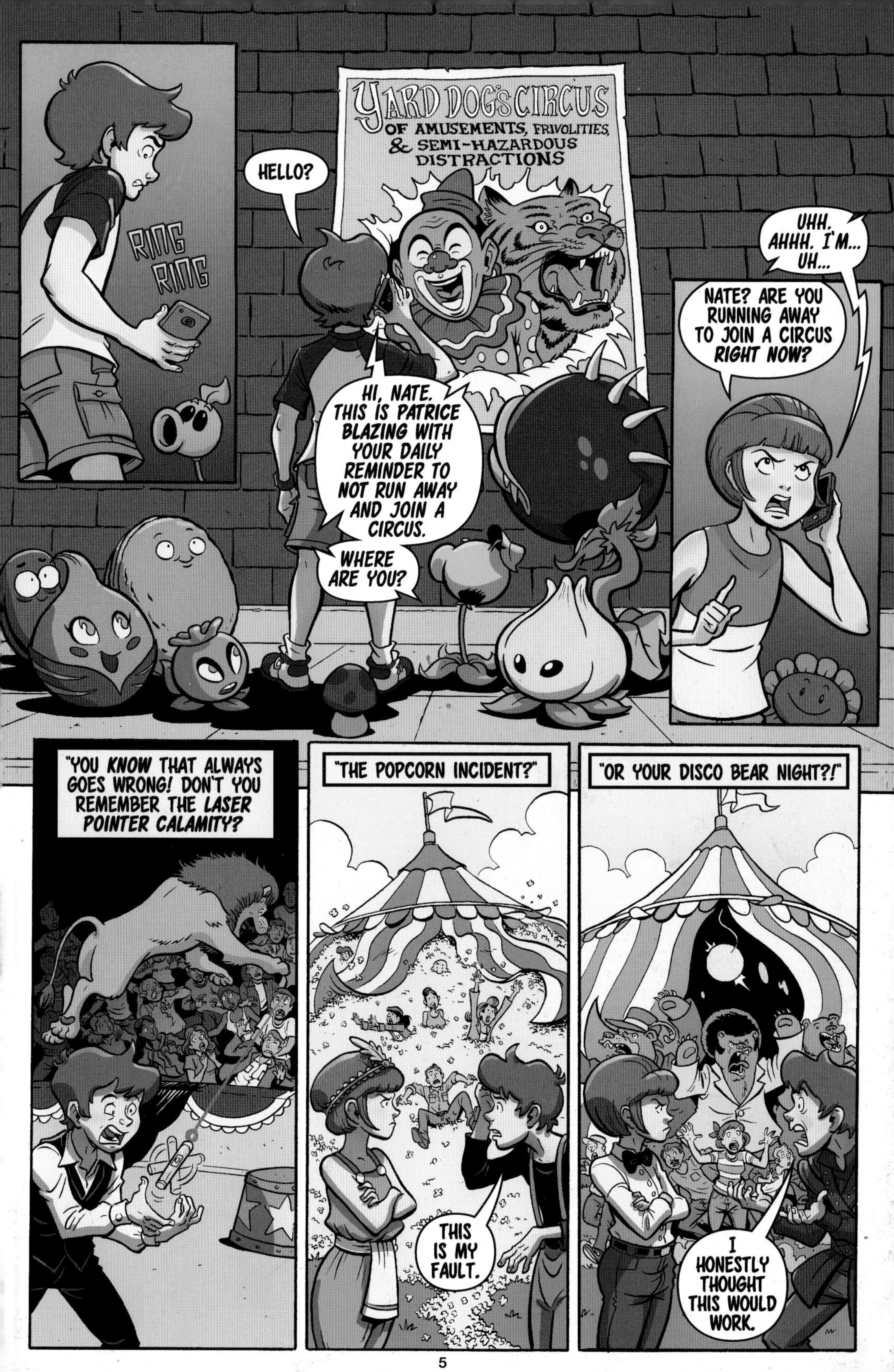
RING RING
YARD DOG'S CIRCUS OF AMUSEMENTS, FRIVOLITIES, & SEMI-HAZARDOUS DISTRACTIONS
HELLO?
HI, NATE. THIS IS PATRICE BLAZING WITH YOUR DAILY REMINDER TO NOT RUN AWAY AND JOIN A CIRCUS.
WHERE ARE YOU?
UHH. AHHH. I'M... UH...
NATE? ARE YOU RUNNING AWAY TO JOIN A CIRCUS RIGHT NOW?
"YOU KNOW THAT ALWAYS GOES WRONG! DON'T YOU REMEMBER THE LASER POINTER CALAMITY?
"THE POPCORN INCIDENT?"
THIS IS MY FAULT.
"OR YOUR DISCO BEAR NIGHT?!"
I HONESTLY THOUGHT THIS WOULD WORK.

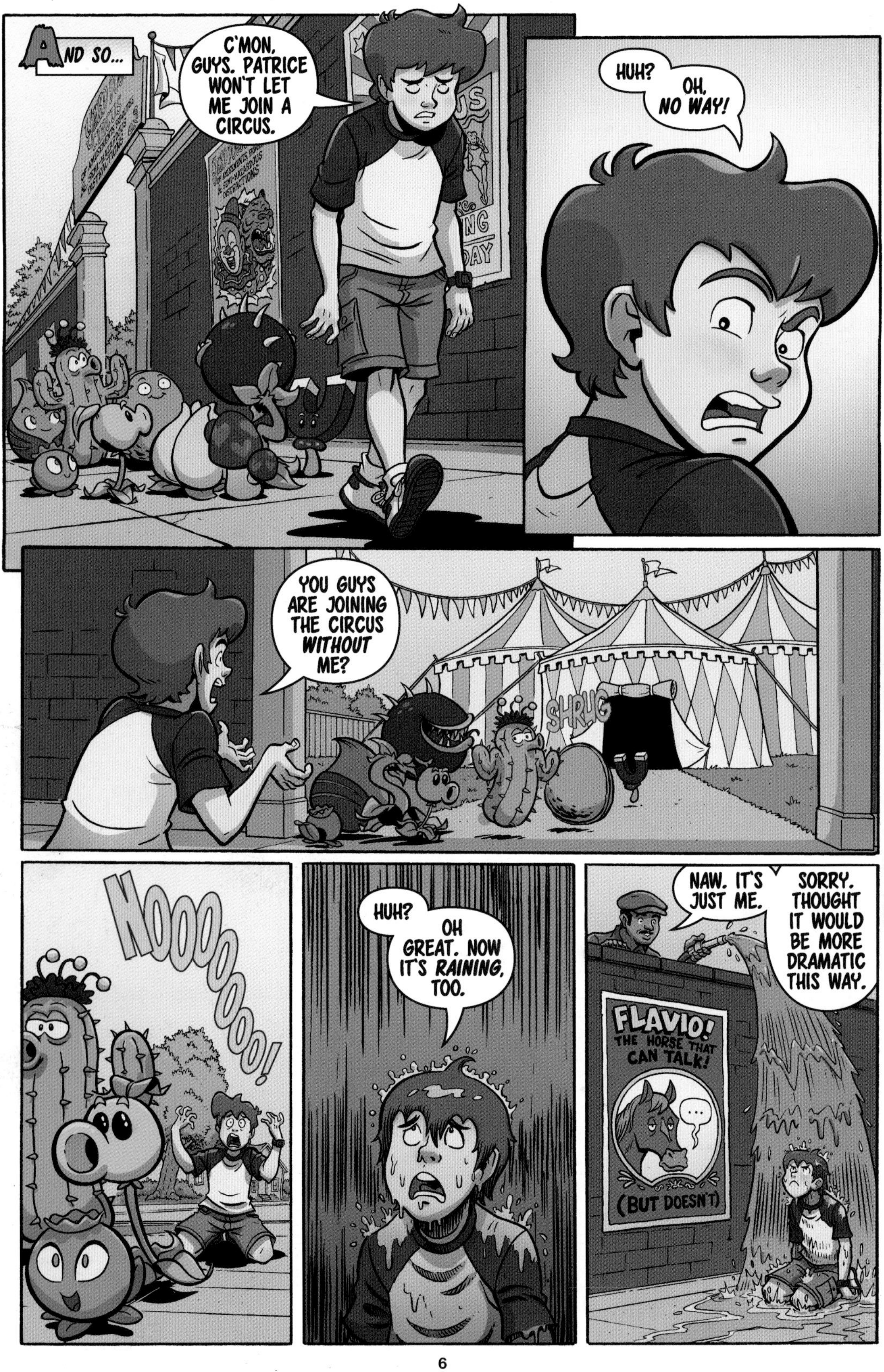
AND SO...
C'MON, GUYS. PATRICE WON'T LET ME JOIN A CIRCUS.
HUH?
OH, NO WAY!
YOU GUYS ARE JOINING THE CIRCUS WITHOUT ME?
SHRUG
NOOOOOOOOO!
HUH?
OH GREAT. NOW IT'S RAINING, TOO.
NAW. IT'S JUST ME.
SORRY. THOUGHT IT WOULD BE MORE DRAMATIC THIS WAY.
FLAVIO! THE HORSE THAT CAN TALK!
...
(BUT DOESN'T)

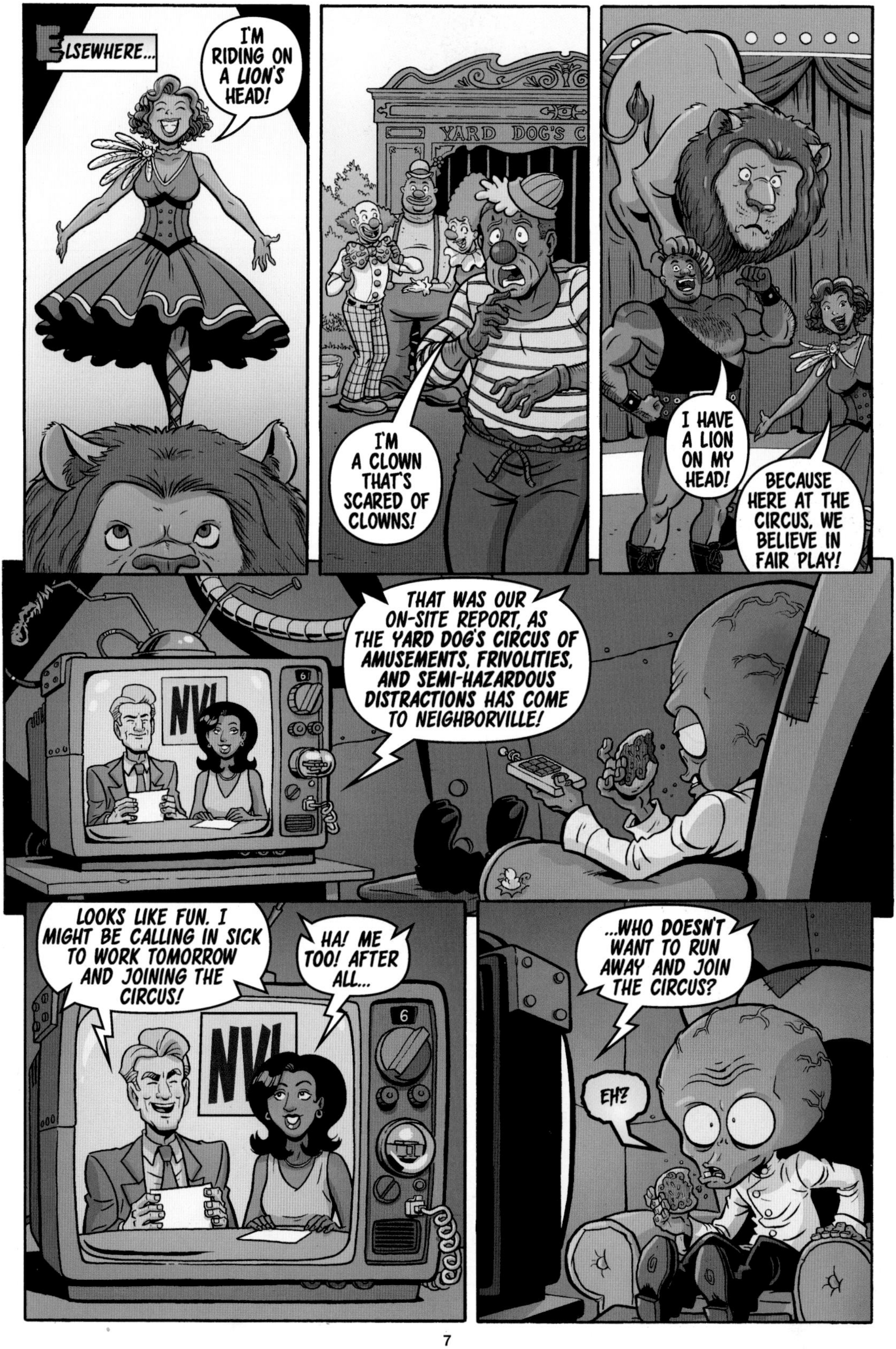
ELSEWHERE...
I'M RIDING ON A LION'S HEAD!
YARD DOG'S C
I'M A CLOWN THAT'S SCARED OF CLOWNS!
I HAVE A LION ON MY HEAD!
BECAUSE HERE AT THE CIRCUS, WE BELIEVE IN FAIR PLAY!
THAT WAS OUR ON-SITE REPORT, AS THE YARD DOG'S CIRCUS OF AMUSEMENTS, FRIVOLITIES, AND SEMI-HAZARDOUS DISTRACTIONS HAS COME TO NEIGHBORVILLE!
NVL
LOOKS LIKE FUN. I MIGHT BE CALLING IN SICK TO WORK TOMORROW AND JOINING THE CIRCUS!
HA! ME TOO! AFTER ALL...
NVL
...WHO DOESN'T WANT TO RUN AWAY AND JOIN THE CIRCUS?
EH?

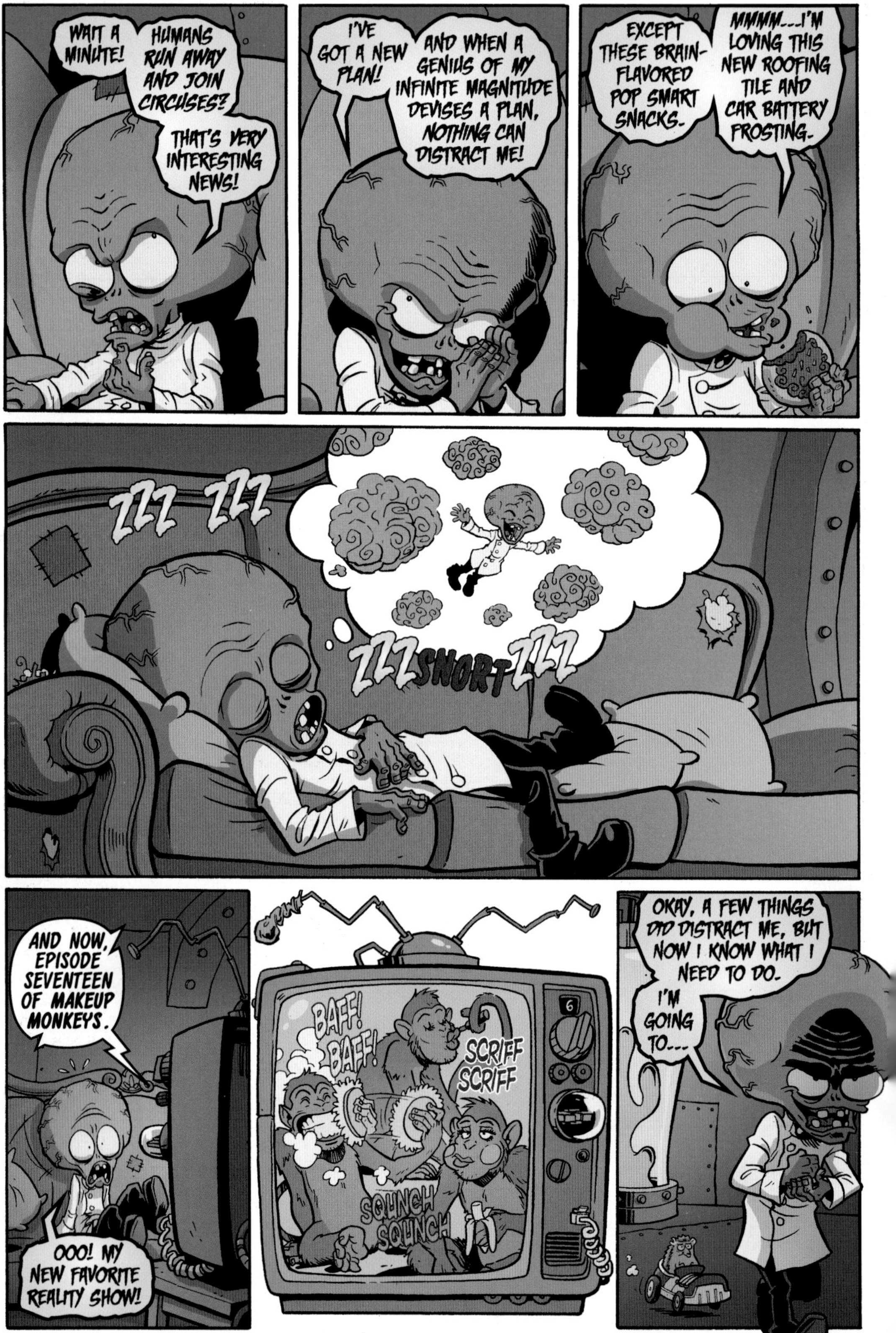

WAIT A MINUTE!
HUMANS RUN AWAY AND JOIN CIRCUSES?
THAT'S VERY INTERESTING NEWS!
I'VE GOT A NEW PLAN!
AND WHEN A GENIUS OF MY INFINITE MAGNITUDE DEVISES A PLAN, NOTHING CAN DISTRACT ME!
EXCEPT THESE BRAIN-FLAVORED POP SMART SNACKS.
MMMM...I'M LOVING THIS NEW ROOFING TILE AND CAR BATTERY FROSTING.
ZZZ ZZZ
ZZZ SNORT ZZZ
AND NOW, EPISODE SEVENTEEN OF MAKEUP MONKEYS.
OOO! MY NEW FAVORITE REALITY SHOW!
BAFF! BAFF!
SCRIFF SCRIFF
SQUNCH SQUNCH
6
OKAY, A FEW THINGS DID DISTRACT ME, BUT NOW I KNOW WHAT I NEED TO DO.
I'M GOING TO...

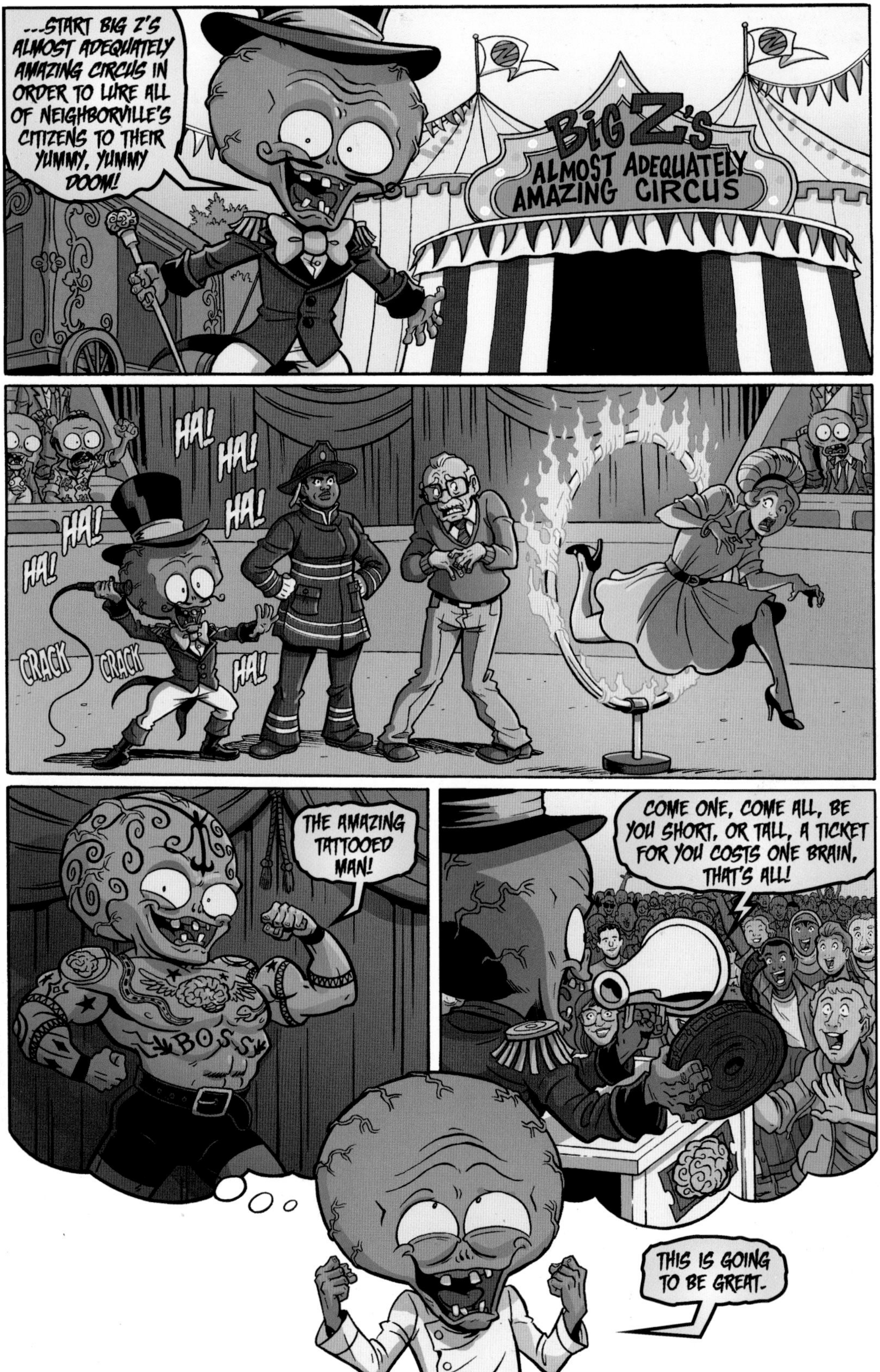
...START BIG Z'S ALMOST ADEQUATELY AMAZING CIRCUS IN ORDER TO LURE ALL OF NEIGHBORVILLE'S CITIZENS TO THEIR YUMMY, YUMMY DOOM!
BIG Z's ALMOST ADEQUATELY AMAZING CIRCUS
HA! HA! HA! HA! HA! HA!
CRACK CRACK
THE AMAZING TATTOOED MAN!
BOSS
COME ONE, COME ALL, BE YOU SHORT, OR TALL, A TICKET FOR YOU COSTS ONE BRAIN, THAT'S ALL!
THIS IS GOING TO BE GREAT.

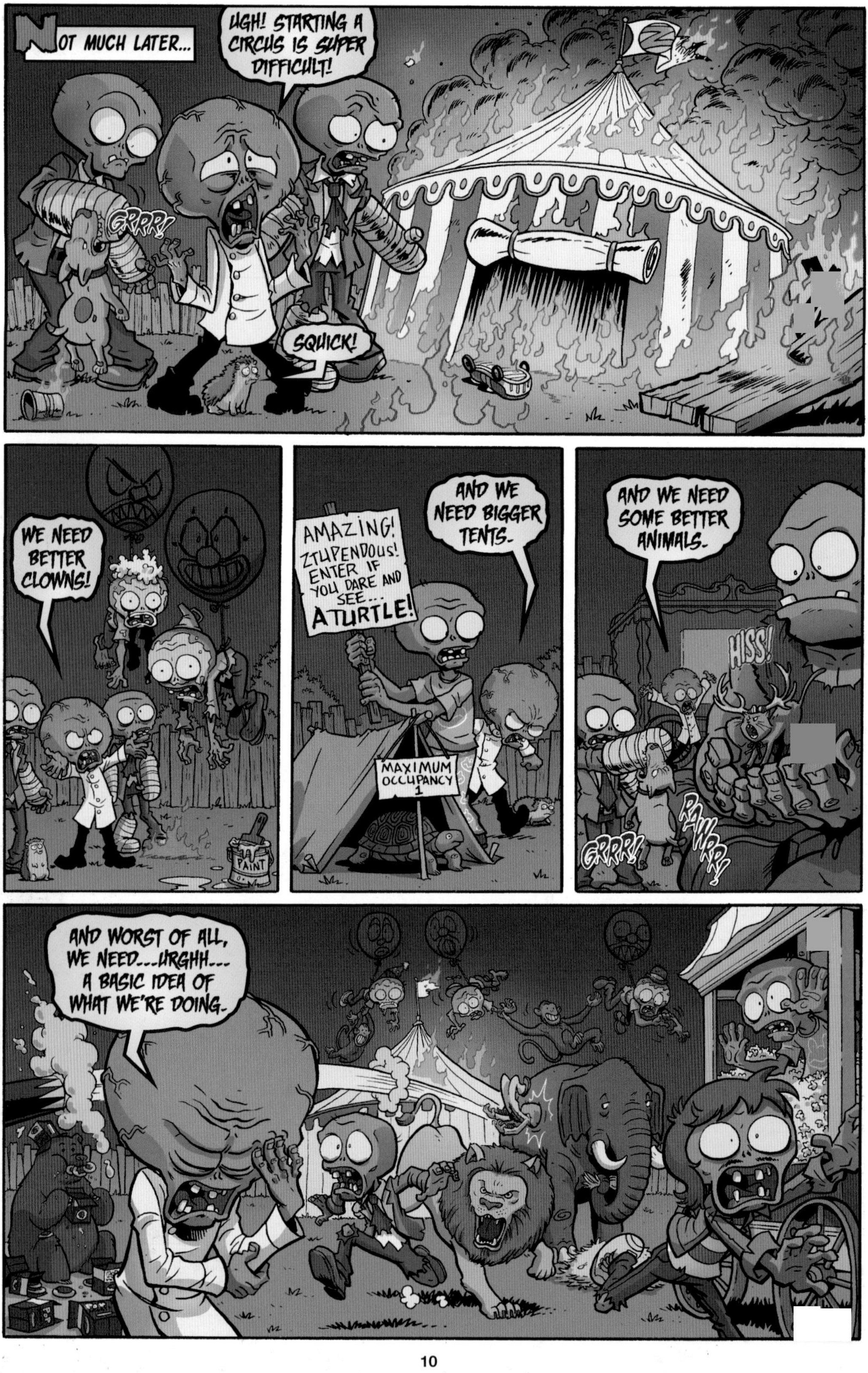
NOT MUCH LATER...
UGH! STARTING A CIRCUS IS SUPER DIFFICULT!
GRRR!
SQUICK!
WE NEED BETTER CLOWNS!
PAINT
AMAZING! ZTUPENDOUS! ENTER IF YOU DARE AND SEE... A TURTLE!
AND WE NEED BIGGER TENTS.
MAXIMUM OCCUPANCY 1
AND WE NEED SOME BETTER ANIMALS.
HISS!
RAWRR!
GRRR!
AND WORST OF ALL, WE NEED...URGHH... A BASIC IDEA OF WHAT WE'RE DOING.

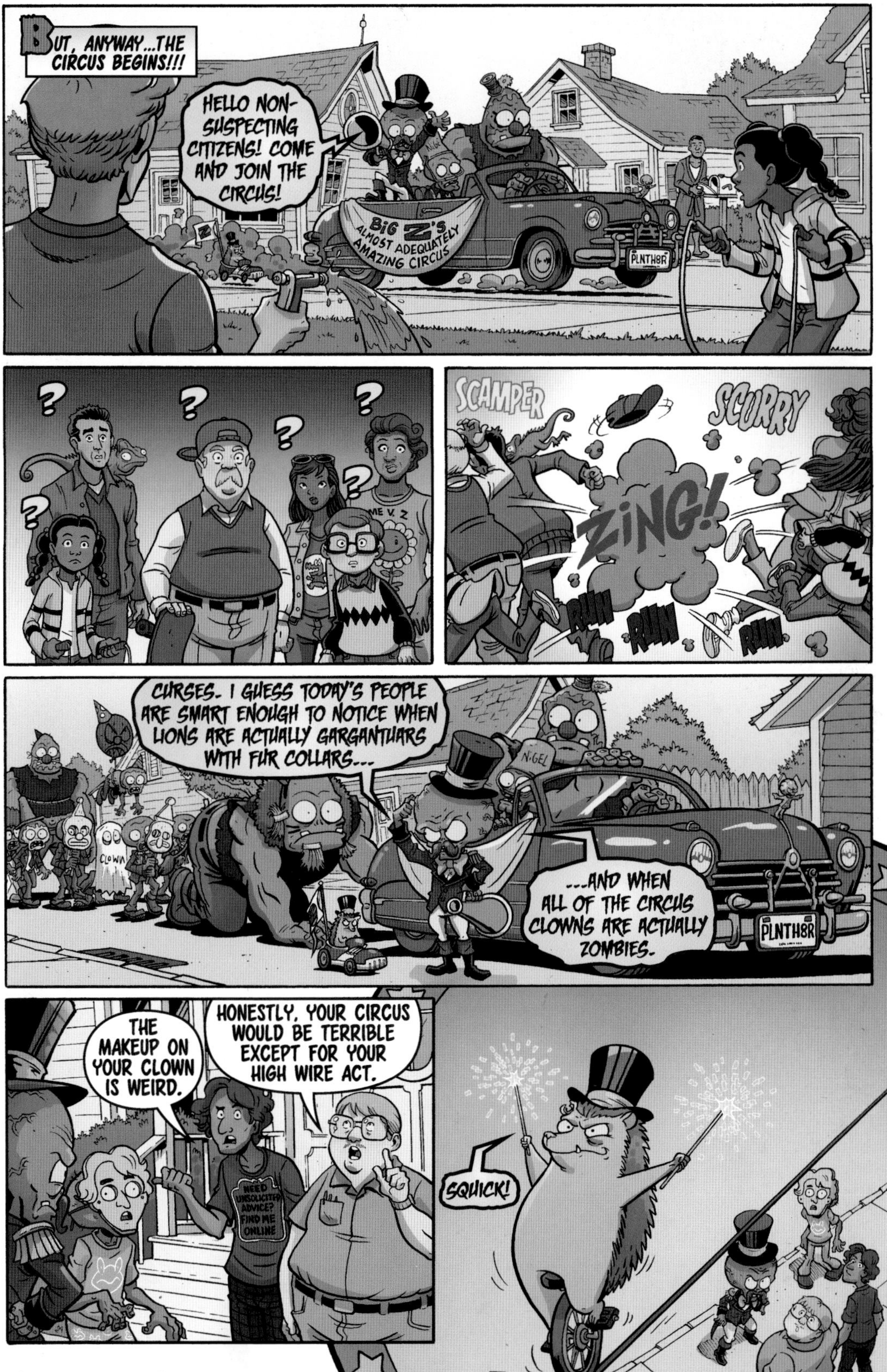
BUT, ANYWAY...THE CIRCUS BEGINS!!!
HELLO NON-SUSPECTING CITIZENS! COME AND JOIN THE CIRCUS!
BIG Z'S ALMOST ADEQUATELY AMAZING CIRCUS
PLNTH8R
SCAMPER
SCURRY
ZING!
RUN
RUN
RUN
CURSES. I GUESS TODAY'S PEOPLE ARE SMART ENOUGH TO NOTICE WHEN LIONS ARE ACTUALLY GARGANTUARS WITH FUR COLLARS...
NIGEL
CLOWN
...AND WHEN ALL OF THE CIRCUS CLOWNS ARE ACTUALLY ZOMBIES.
PLNTH8R
THE MAKEUP ON YOUR CLOWN IS WEIRD.
HONESTLY, YOUR CIRCUS WOULD BE TERRIBLE EXCEPT FOR YOUR HIGH WIRE ACT.
NEED UNSOLICITED ADVICE? FIND ME ONLINE
SQUICK!

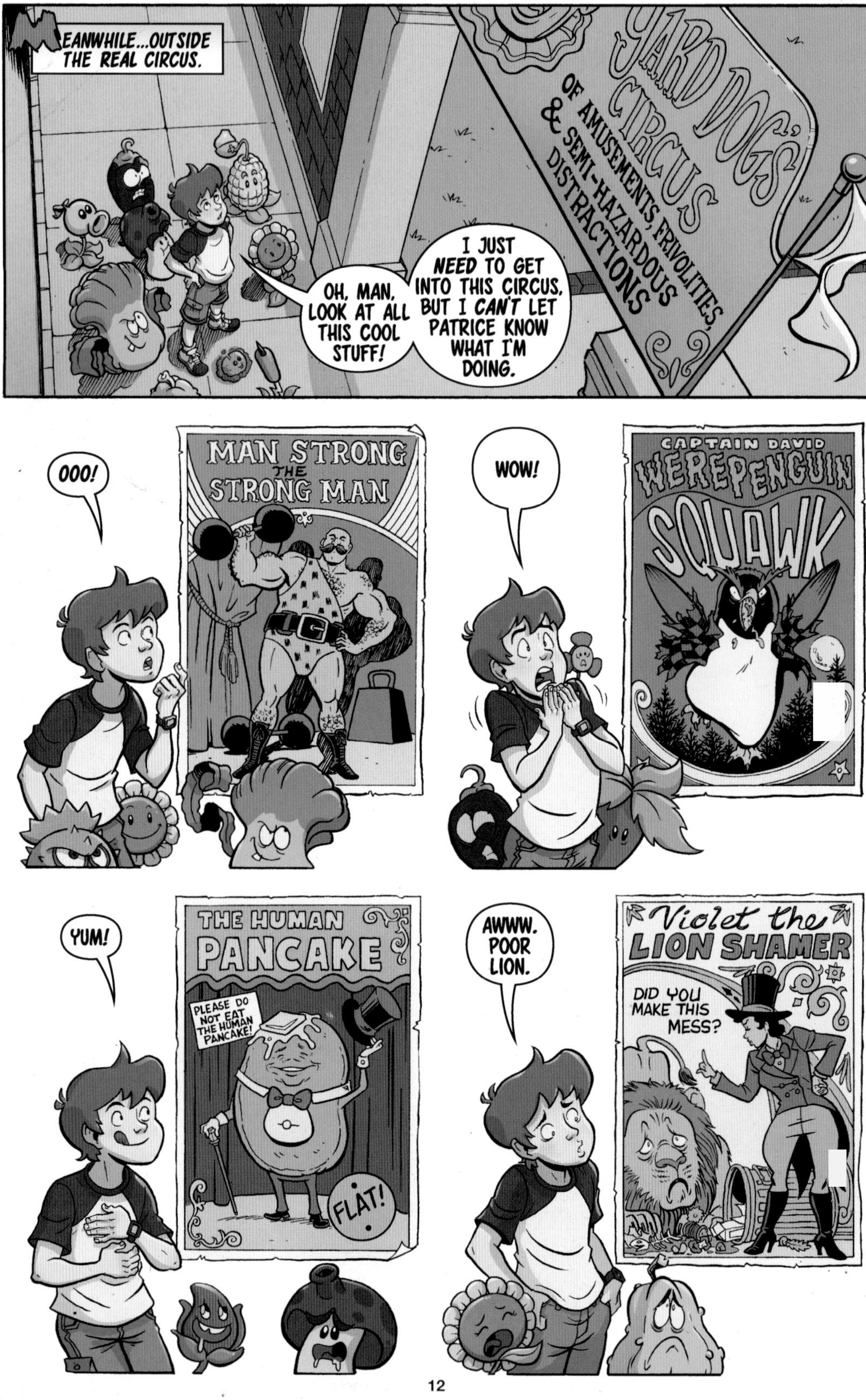
MEANWHILE...OUTSIDE THE REAL CIRCUS.
YARD DOG'S CIRCUS OF AMUSEMENTS, FRIVOLITIES, & SEMI-HAZARDOUS DISTRACTIONS
OH, MAN, LOOK AT ALL THIS COOL STUFF!
I JUST NEED TO GET INTO THIS CIRCUS, BUT I CAN'T LET PATRICE KNOW WHAT I'M DOING.
OOO!
MAN STRONG THE STRONG MAN
WOW!
CAPTAIN DAVID WEREPENGUIN SQUAWK
YUM!
THE HUMAN PANCAKE
PLEASE DO NOT EAT THE HUMAN PANCAKE!
FLAT!
AWWW. POOR LION.
Violet the LION SHAMER
DID YOU MAKE THIS MESS?

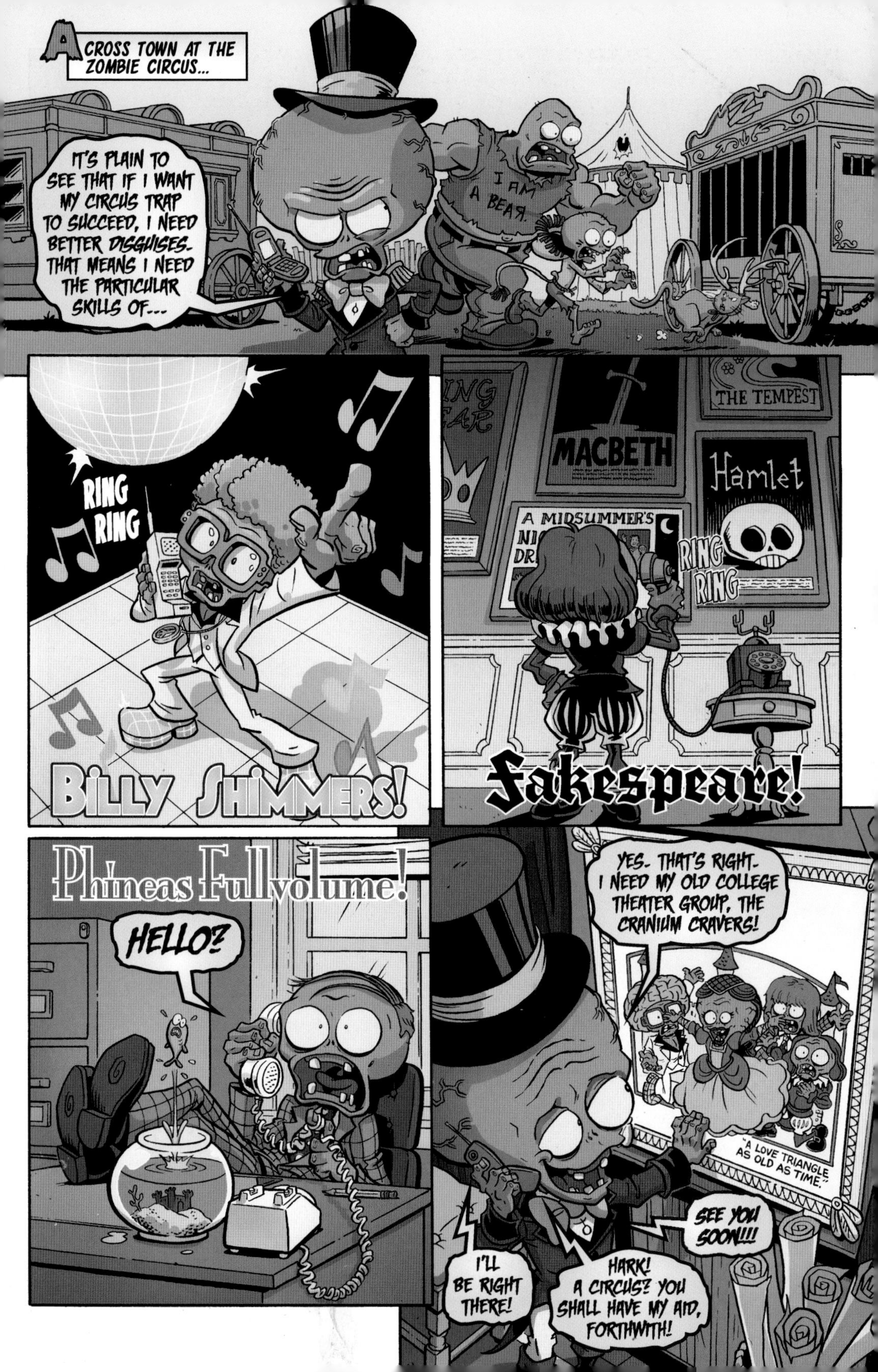
ACROSS TOWN AT THE ZOMBIE CIRCUS...
IT'S PLAIN TO SEE THAT IF I WANT MY CIRCUS TRAP TO SUCCEED, I NEED BETTER DISGUISES. THAT MEANS I NEED THE PARTICULAR SKILLS OF...
I AM A BEAR
RING RING
BILLY SHIMMERS!
THE TEMPEST
MACBETH
Hamlet
A MIDSUMMER'S
RING RING
Fakespeare!
Phineas Fullvolume!
HELLO?
YES. THAT'S RIGHT. I NEED MY OLD COLLEGE THEATER GROUP, THE CRANIUM CRAVERS!
"A LOVE TRIANGLE AS OLD AS TIME."
SEE YOU SOON!!!
I'LL BE RIGHT THERE!
HARK! A CIRCUS? YOU SHALL HAVE MY AID, FORTHWITH!

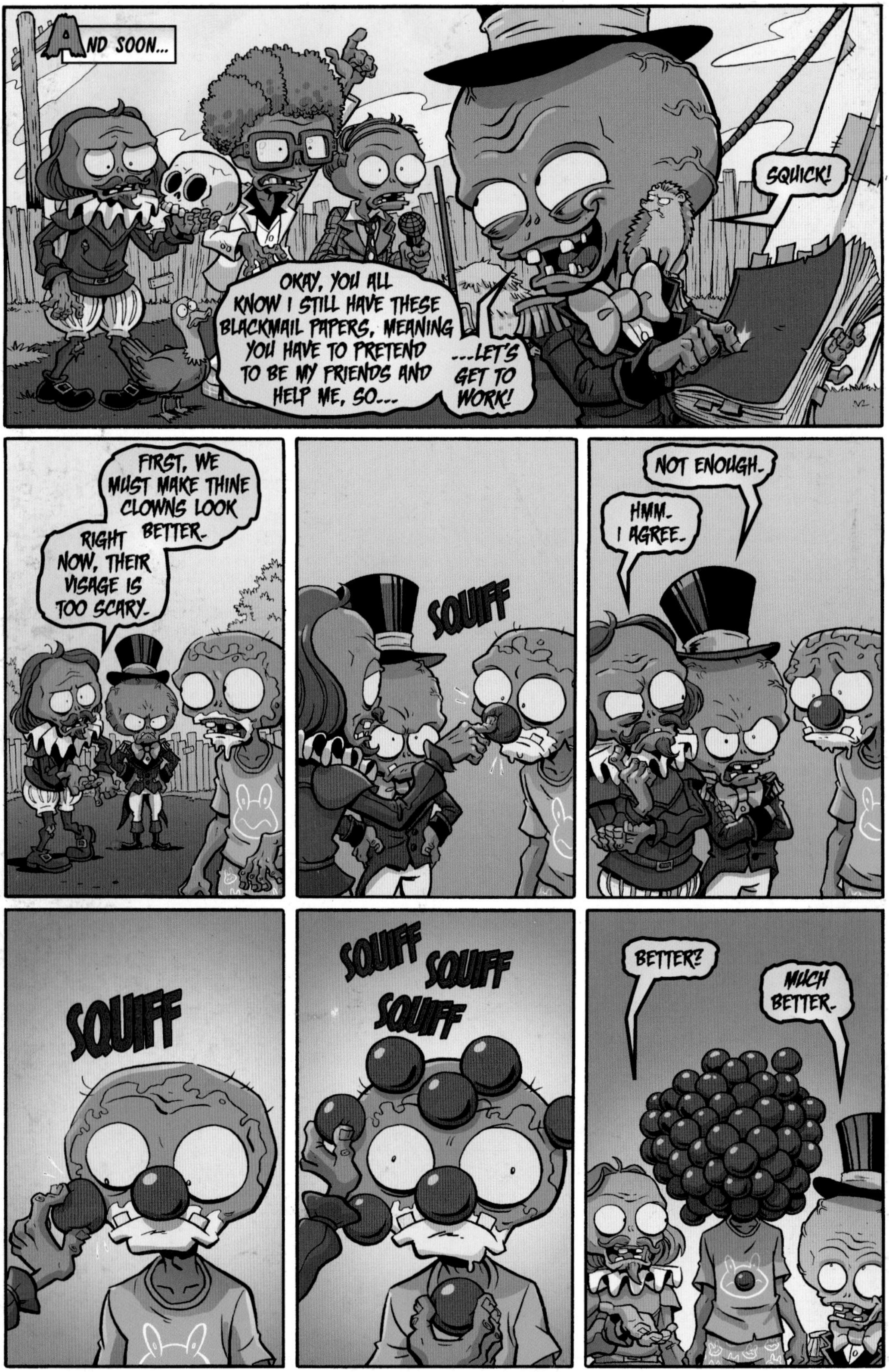
AND SOON...
OKAY, YOU ALL KNOW I STILL HAVE THESE BLACKMAIL PAPERS, MEANING YOU HAVE TO PRETEND TO BE MY FRIENDS AND HELP ME, SO...
...LET'S GET TO WORK!
SQUICK!
FIRST, WE MUST MAKE THINE CLOWNS LOOK BETTER.
RIGHT NOW, THEIR VISAGE IS TOO SCARY.
SQUIFF
HMM. I AGREE.
NOT ENOUGH.
SQUIFF
SQUIFF
SQUIFF
SQUIFF
BETTER?
MUCH BETTER.

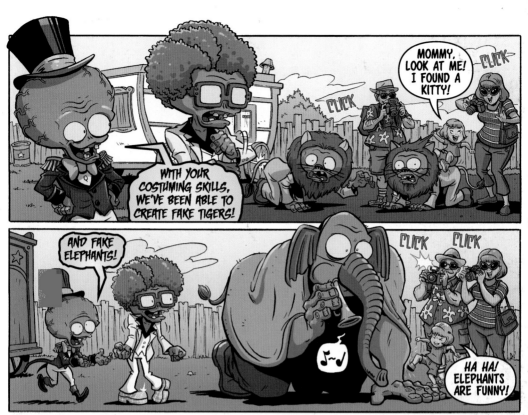

MOMMY, LOOK AT ME! I FOUND A KITTY!

CLICK CLICK

WITH YOUR COSTUMING SKILLS, WE'VE BEEN ABLE TO CREATE FAKE TIGERS!

AND FAKE ELEPHANTS!

CLICK CLICK

HA HA! ELEPHANTS ARE FUNNY!

NOW WE NEED SOME FAKE SEALS.

OKAY EVERYONE! WE BASICALLY NEED SOMEONE TO DRESS IN THESE AND THEN DO NOTHING BUT LAY AROUND AND OCCASIONALLY GRUNT.

ANY VOLUNTEERS?

BRAINS? BRAINSS. BRAINSSS? BRAINS? BRAINSS.

JOIN THE CIRCUS!

IT'S WORKING! IT'S WORKING! LOOK AT ALL THESE SNACKS, UH, I MEAN PEOPLE, WHO WANT TO JOIN MY CIRCUS!

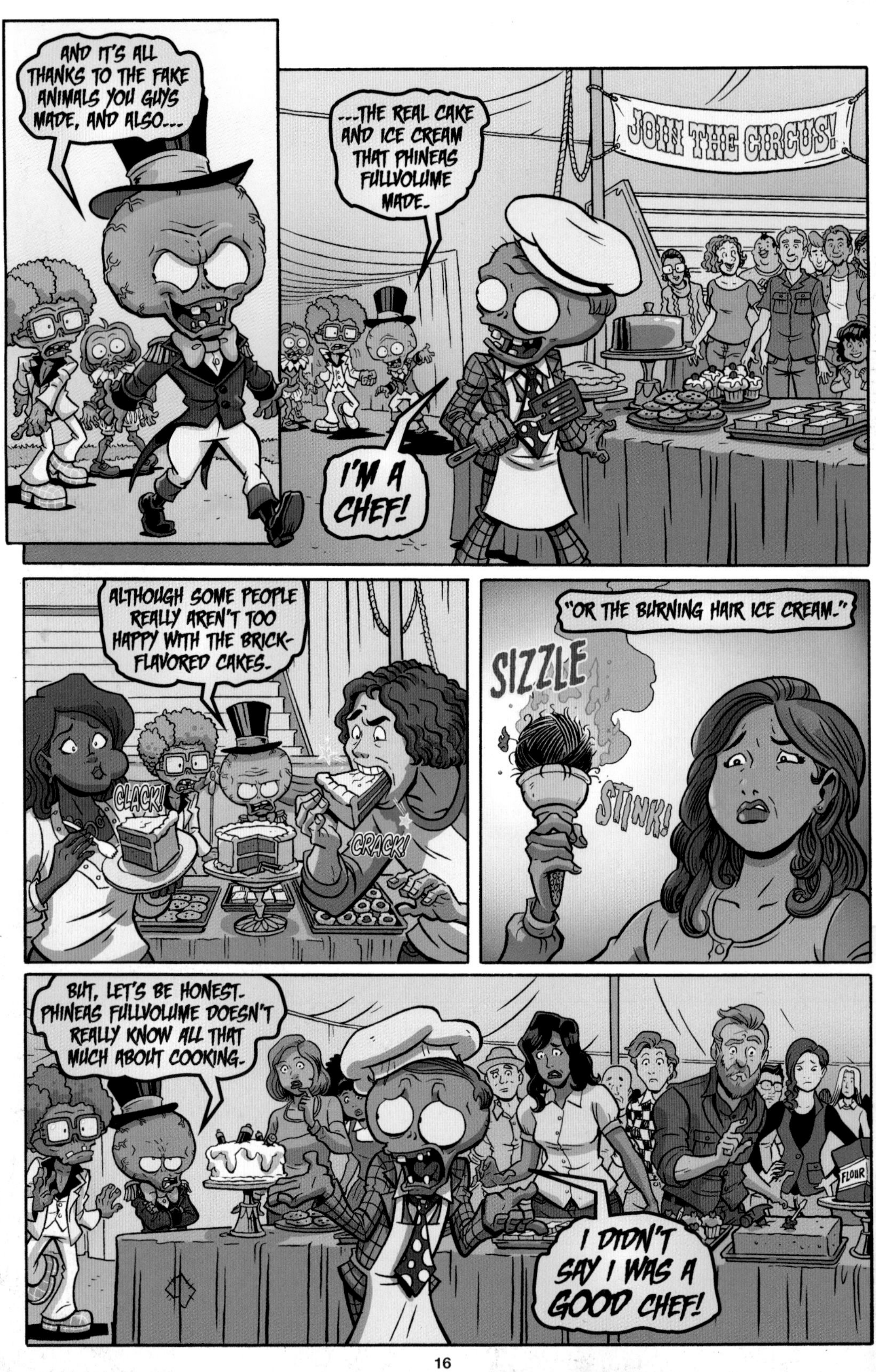
AND IT'S ALL THANKS TO THE FAKE ANIMALS YOU GUYS MADE, AND ALSO...
JOIN THE CIRCUS!
...THE REAL CAKE AND ICE CREAM THAT PHINEAS FULLVOLUME MADE.
I'M A CHEF!
ALTHOUGH SOME PEOPLE REALLY AREN'T TOO HAPPY WITH THE BRICK-FLAVORED CAKES.
CLACK!
CRACK!
"OR THE BURNING HAIR ICE CREAM."
SIZZLE
STINK!
BUT, LET'S BE HONEST. PHINEAS FULLVOLUME DOESN'T REALLY KNOW ALL THAT MUCH ABOUT COOKING.
FLOUR
I DIDN'T SAY I WAS A GOOD CHEF!

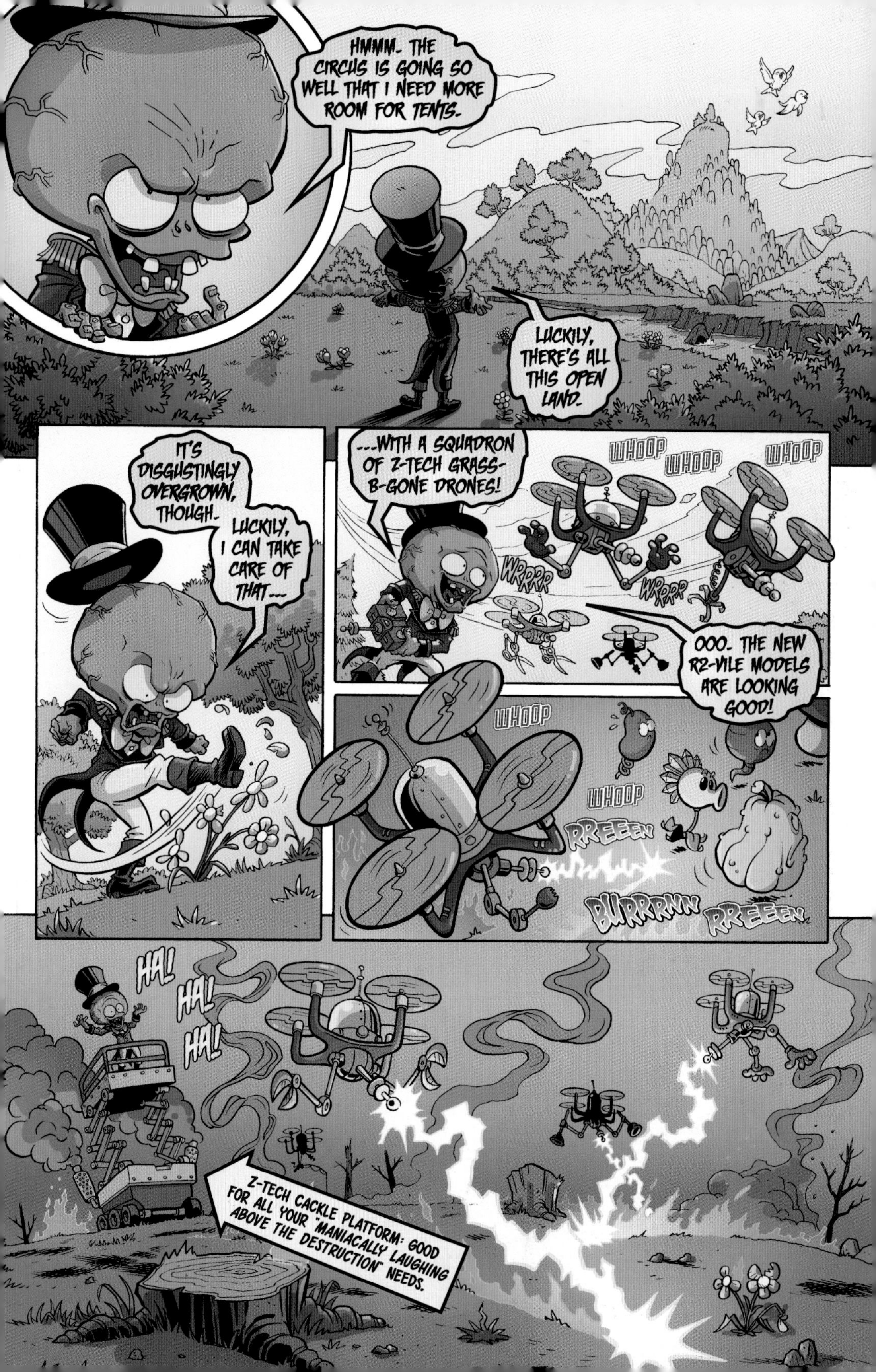
HMMM. THE CIRCUS IS GOING SO WELL THAT I NEED MORE ROOM FOR TENTS.
LUCKILY, THERE'S ALL THIS OPEN LAND.
IT'S DISGUSTINGLY OVERGROWN, THOUGH.
LUCKILY, I CAN TAKE CARE OF THAT...
...WITH A SQUADRON OF Z-TECH GRASS-B-GONE DRONES!
WHOOP
WHOOP
WHOOP
WRRRR
WRRRR
OOO. THE NEW R2-VILE MODELS ARE LOOKING GOOD!
WHOOP
WHOOP
RREEEN
BURRRNN
RREEEN
HA!
HA!
HA!
Z-TECH CACKLE PLATFORM: GOOD FOR ALL YOUR "MANIACALLY LAUGHING ABOVE THE DESTRUCTION" NEEDS.

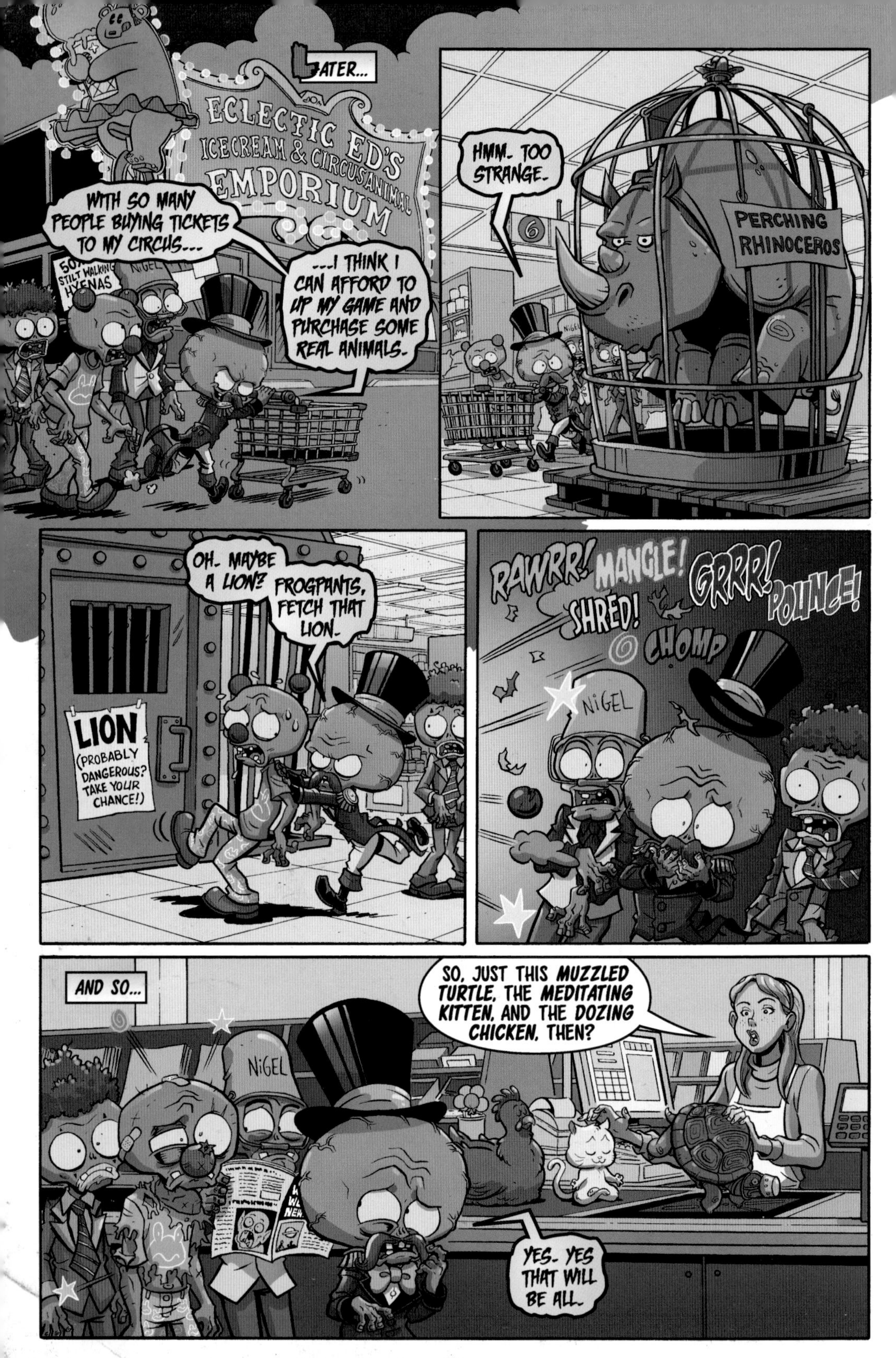
LATER...
ECLECTIC ED'S
ICECREAM & CIRCUSANIMAL
EMPORIUM
50%
STILT WALKING
HYENAS
NIGEL
WITH SO MANY PEOPLE BUYING TICKETS TO MY CIRCUS...
...I THINK I CAN AFFORD TO UP MY GAME AND PURCHASE SOME REAL ANIMALS.
HMM. TOO STRANGE.
6
PERCHING RHINOCEROS
OH. MAYBE A LION?
FROGPANTS, FETCH THAT LION.
LION
(PROBABLY DANGEROUS? TAKE YOUR CHANCE!)
RAWRR! MANGLE! GRRR! POUNCE!
SHRED! CHOMP
NIGEL
AND SO...
SO, JUST THIS MUZZLED TURTLE, THE MEDITATING KITTEN, AND THE DOZING CHICKEN, THEN?
NIGEL
YES. YES THAT WILL BE ALL.

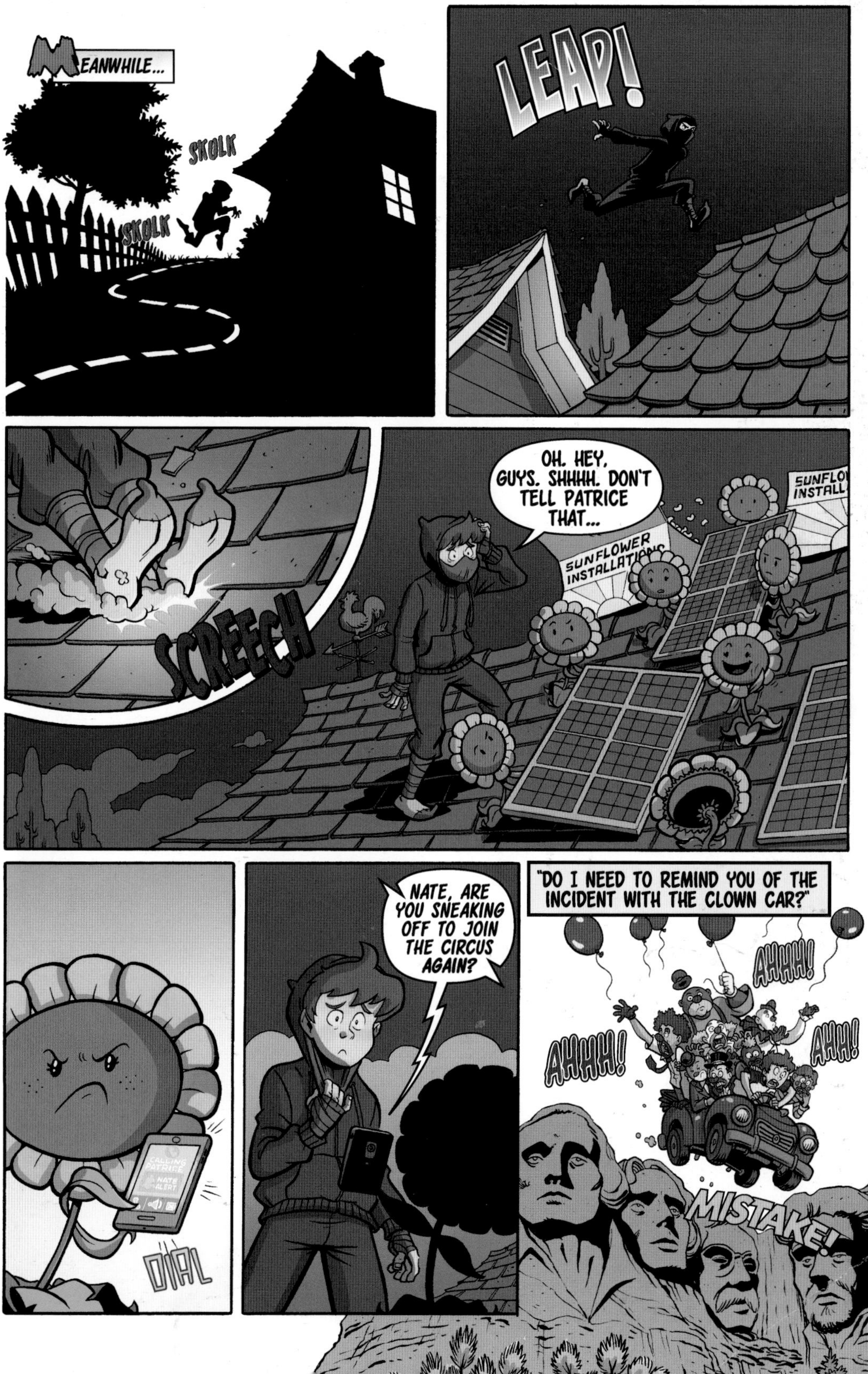
MEANWHILE...
SKOLK
SKOLK
LEAP!
SCREECH
OH. HEY, GUYS. SHHHH. DON'T TELL PATRICE THAT...
SUNFLOWER INSTALLATIONS
NATE, ARE YOU SNEAKING OFF TO JOIN THE CIRCUS AGAIN?
CALLING PATRICE
NATE ALERT
DIAL
"DO I NEED TO REMIND YOU OF THE INCIDENT WITH THE CLOWN CAR?"
AHHH!
AHHH!
AHH!
MISTAKE!

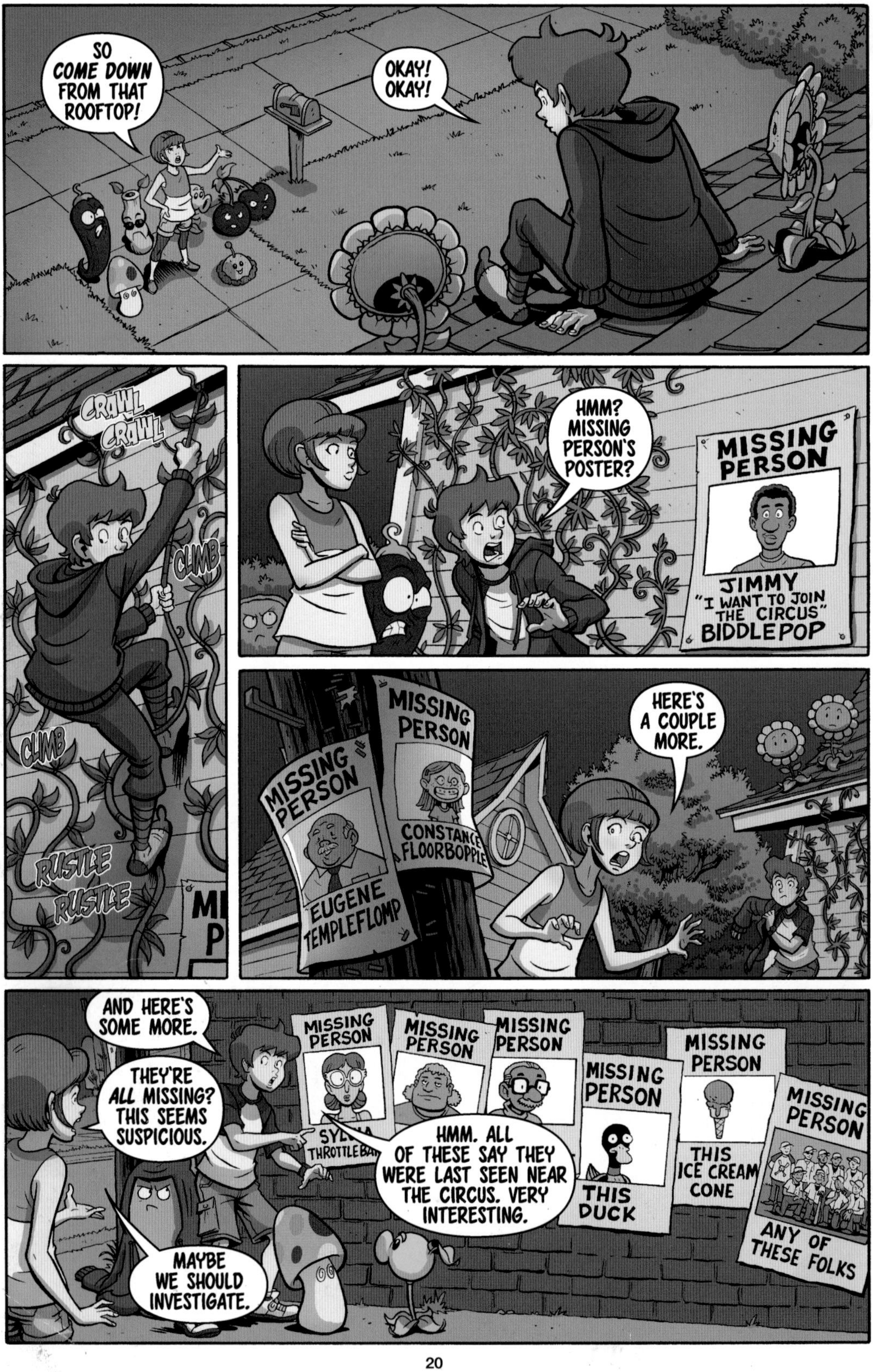
SO COME DOWN FROM THAT ROOFTOP!
OKAY! OKAY!
CRAWL
CRAWL
CLIMB
CLIMB
RUSTLE
RUSTLE
HMM? MISSING PERSON'S POSTER?
MISSING PERSON
JIMMY "I WANT TO JOIN THE CIRCUS" BIDDLEPOP
MISSING PERSON
EUGENE TEMPLEFLOMP
MISSING PERSON
CONSTANCE FLOORBOPPLE
HERE'S A COUPLE MORE.
AND HERE'S SOME MORE.
THEY'RE ALL MISSING? THIS SEEMS SUSPICIOUS.
MISSING PERSON
MISSING PERSON
MISSING PERSON
MISSING PERSON
THIS DUCK
MISSING PERSON
THIS ICE CREAM CONE
MISSING PERSON
ANY OF THESE FOLKS
HMM. ALL OF THESE SAY THEY WERE LAST SEEN NEAR THE CIRCUS. VERY INTERESTING.
MAYBE WE SHOULD INVESTIGATE.

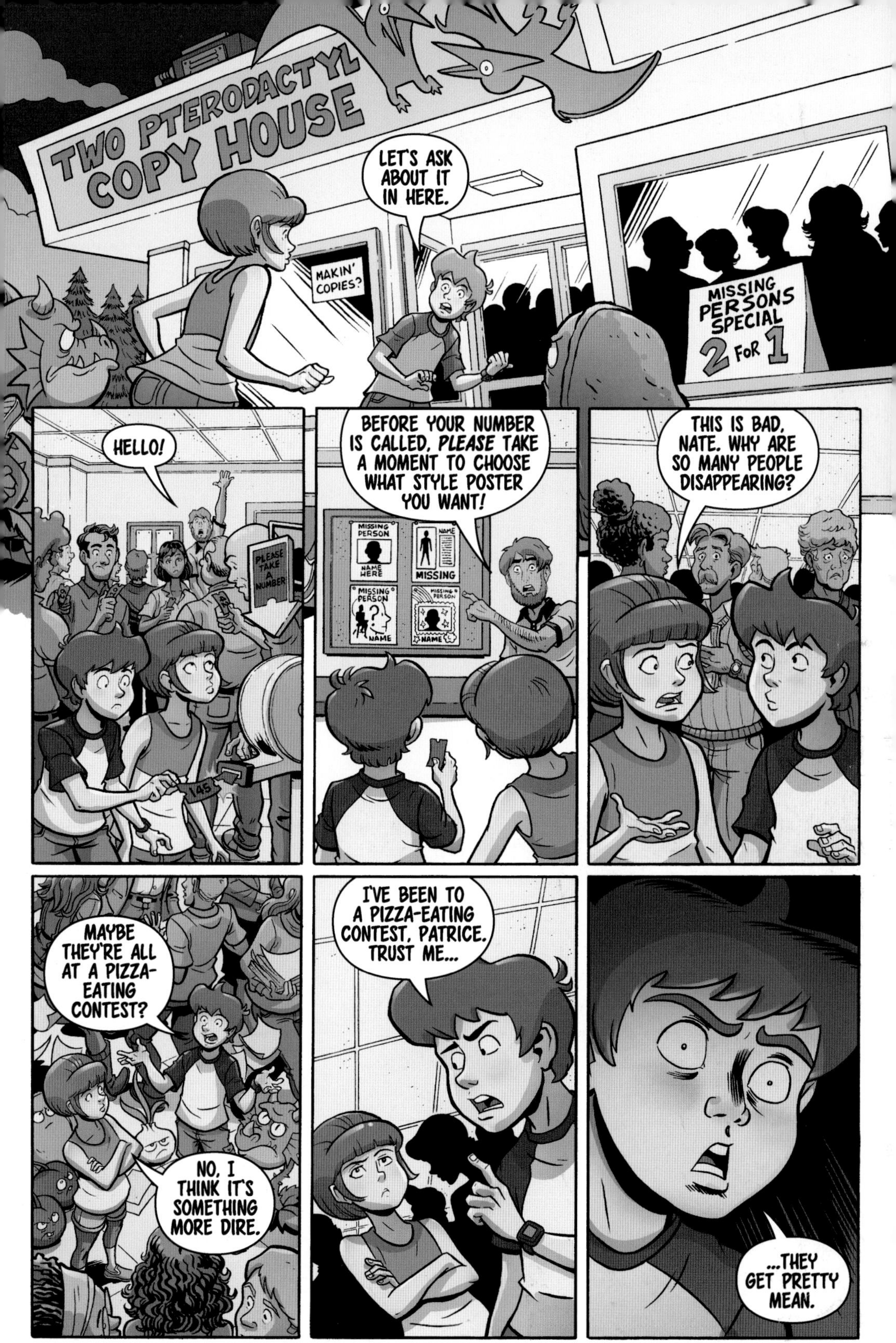
TWO PTERODACTYL COPY HOUSE
LET'S ASK ABOUT IT IN HERE.
MAKIN' COPIES?
MISSING PERSONS SPECIAL 2 FOR 1
HELLO!
PLEASE TAKE A NUMBER
145
BEFORE YOUR NUMBER IS CALLED, PLEASE TAKE A MOMENT TO CHOOSE WHAT STYLE POSTER YOU WANT!
MISSING PERSON NAME HERE
NAME MISSING
MISSING PERSON ? NAME
MISSING PERSON NAME
THIS IS BAD, NATE. WHY ARE SO MANY PEOPLE DISAPPEARING?
MAYBE THEY'RE ALL AT A PIZZA-EATING CONTEST?
NO, I THINK IT'S SOMETHING MORE DIRE.
I'VE BEEN TO A PIZZA-EATING CONTEST, PATRICE. TRUST ME...
...THEY GET PRETTY MEAN.

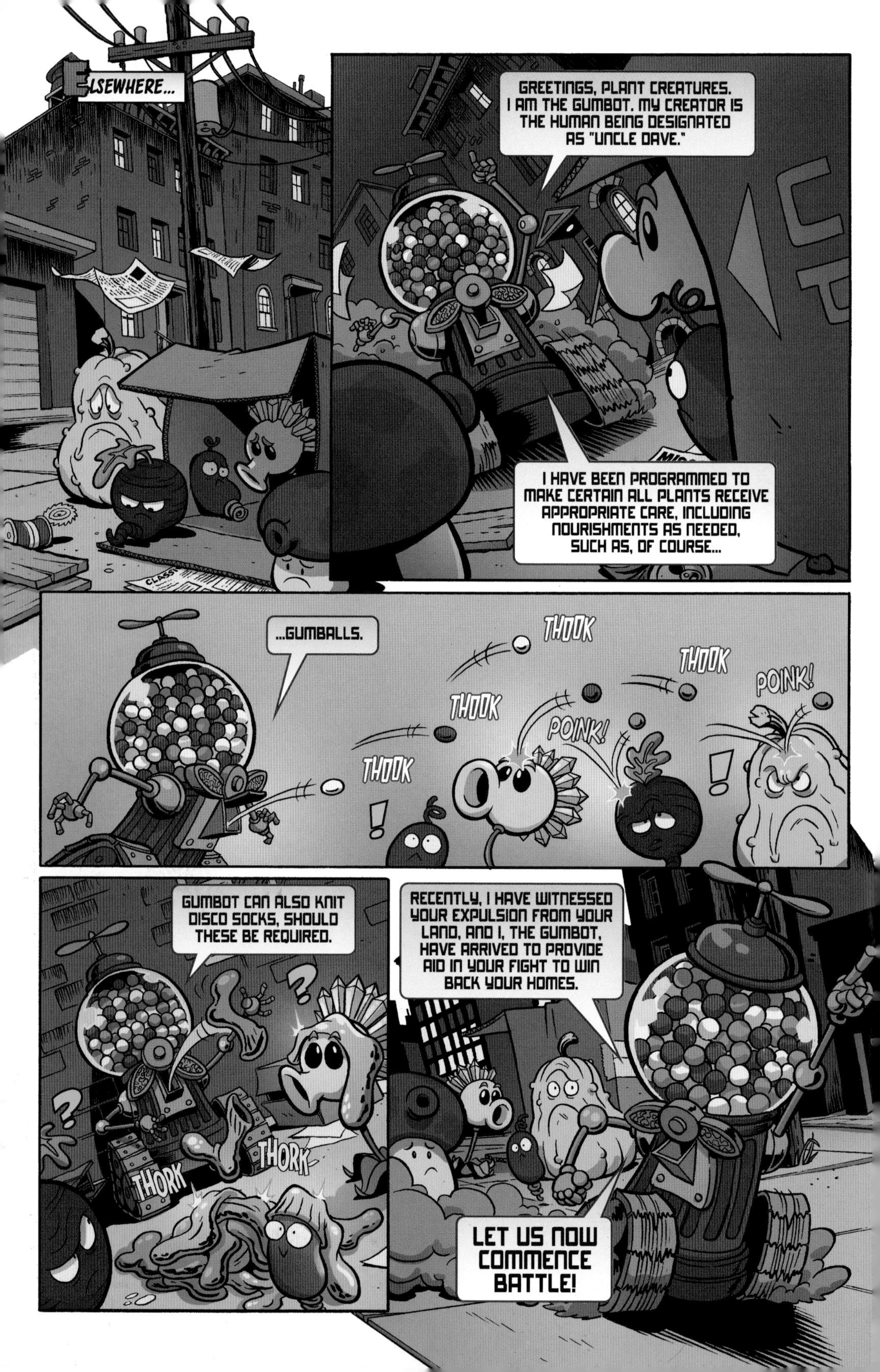
ELSEWHERE...
GREETINGS, PLANT CREATURES. I AM THE GUMBOT. MY CREATOR IS THE HUMAN BEING DESIGNATED AS "UNCLE DAVE."
I HAVE BEEN PROGRAMMED TO MAKE CERTAIN ALL PLANTS RECEIVE APPROPRIATE CARE, INCLUDING NOURISHMENTS AS NEEDED, SUCH AS, OF COURSE...
...GUMBALLS.
THOOK
THOOK
THOOK
THOOK
POINK!
POINK!
GUMBOT CAN ALSO KNIT DISCO SOCKS, SHOULD THESE BE REQUIRED.
THORK
THORK
RECENTLY, I HAVE WITNESSED YOUR EXPULSION FROM YOUR LAND, AND I, THE GUMBOT, HAVE ARRIVED TO PROVIDE AID IN YOUR FIGHT TO WIN BACK YOUR HOMES.
LET US NOW COMMENCE BATTLE!

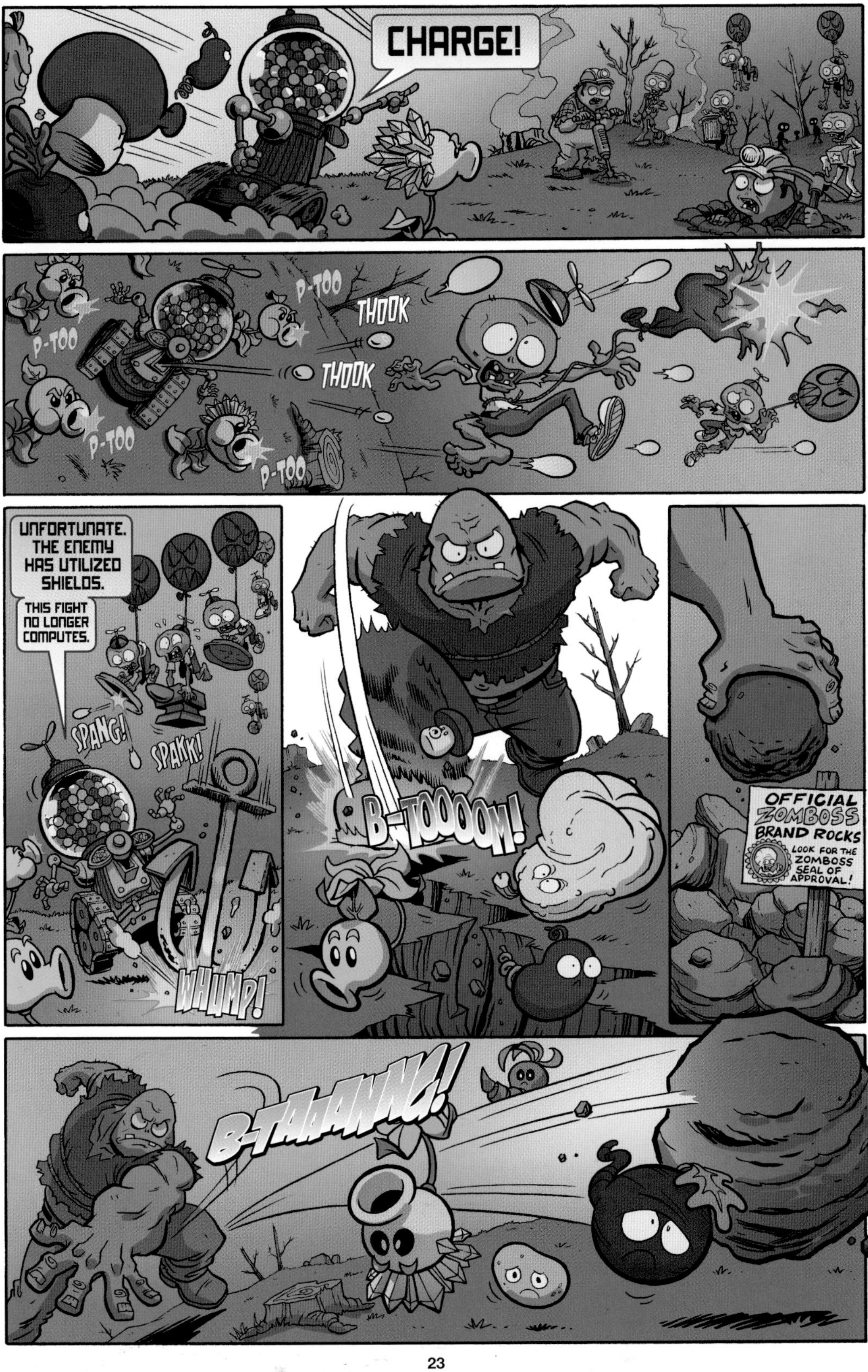
CHARGE!
P-TOO
P-TOO
THOOK
THOOK
P-TOO
P-TOO
UNFORTUNATE. THE ENEMY HAS UTILIZED SHIELDS.
THIS FIGHT NO LONGER COMPUTES.
SPANG!
SPAKK!
WHUMP!
B-TOOOOM!
OFFICIAL ZOMBOSS BRAND ROCKS
LOOK FOR THE ZOMBOSS SEAL OF APPROVAL!
B-TAAANNG!

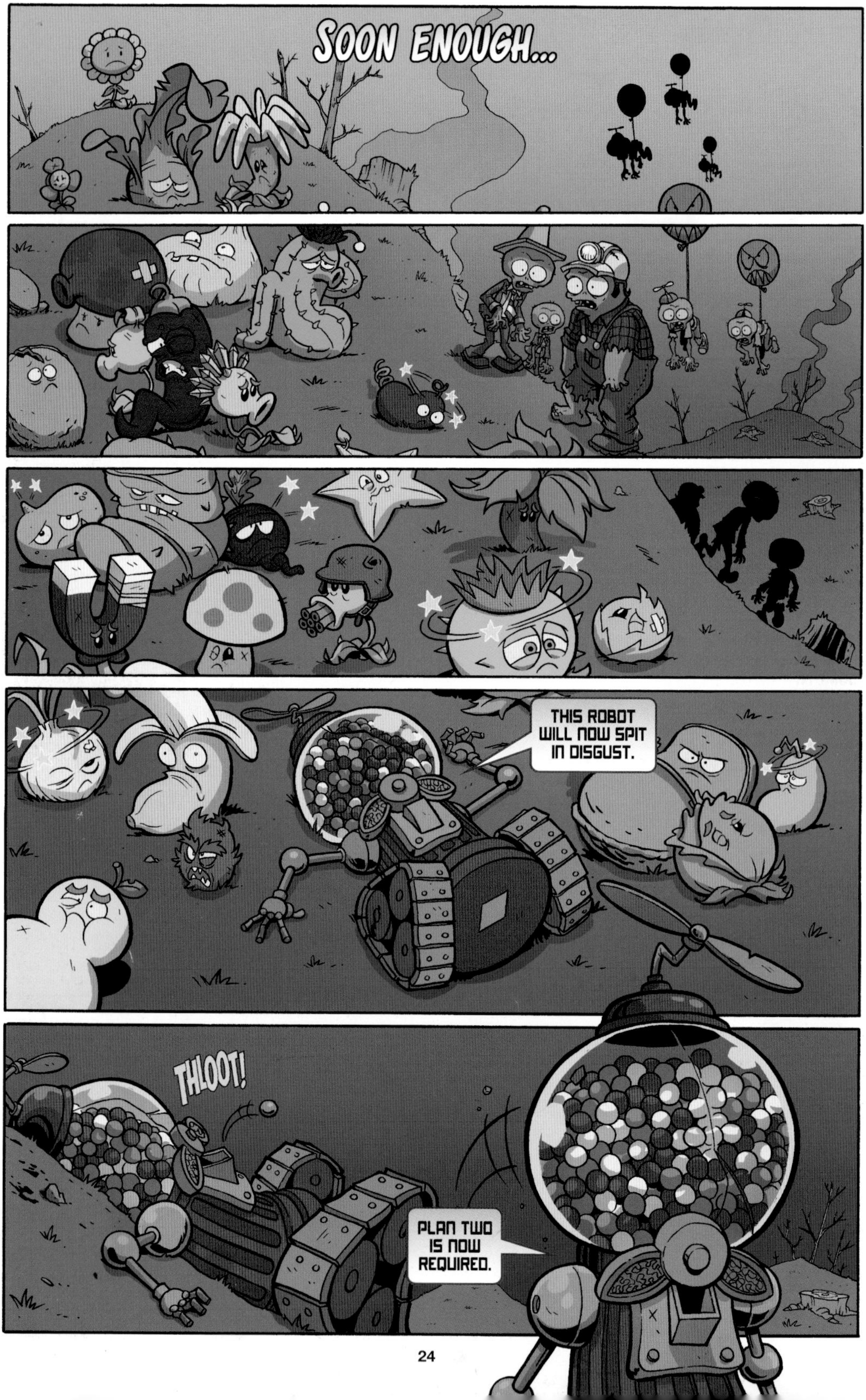
SOON ENOUGH...
THIS ROBOT WILL NOW SPIT IN DISGUST.
THLOOT!
PLAN TWO IS NOW REQUIRED.

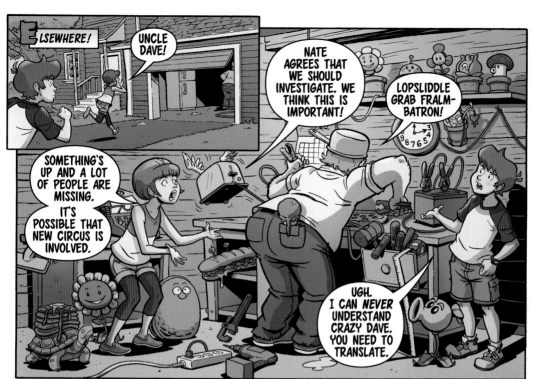

ELSEWHERE!

UNCLE DAVE!

NATE AGREES THAT WE SHOULD INVESTIGATE. WE THINK THIS IS IMPORTANT!

LOPSLIDDLE GRAB FRALM-BATRON!

SOMETHING'S UP AND A LOT OF PEOPLE ARE MISSING.

IT'S POSSIBLE THAT NEW CIRCUS IS INVOLVED.

UGH. I CAN *NEVER* UNDERSTAND CRAZY DAVE. YOU NEED TO TRANSLATE.

UNCLE DAVE SAYS THAT *HE'S* BEEN DOING SOMETHING VERY IMPORTANT, TOO.

CREME BRULE BRIDDLE-POP!

HE SAYS HE'S BEEN WORKING ON GLOVES.

GRAK GRAK AARGH SPLANK.

GLOVES THAT HAVE TONGUES.

SHRABBLE!

YEAH. HE'S BEEN EXPERIMENTING WITH GLOVES THAT HAVE TONGUES.

CORNDOG FLUME HELM!

HE FINDS THIS VERY IMPORTANT.

BLAAT!

SPLATTTT!

OOOOO-KAY. GREAT.

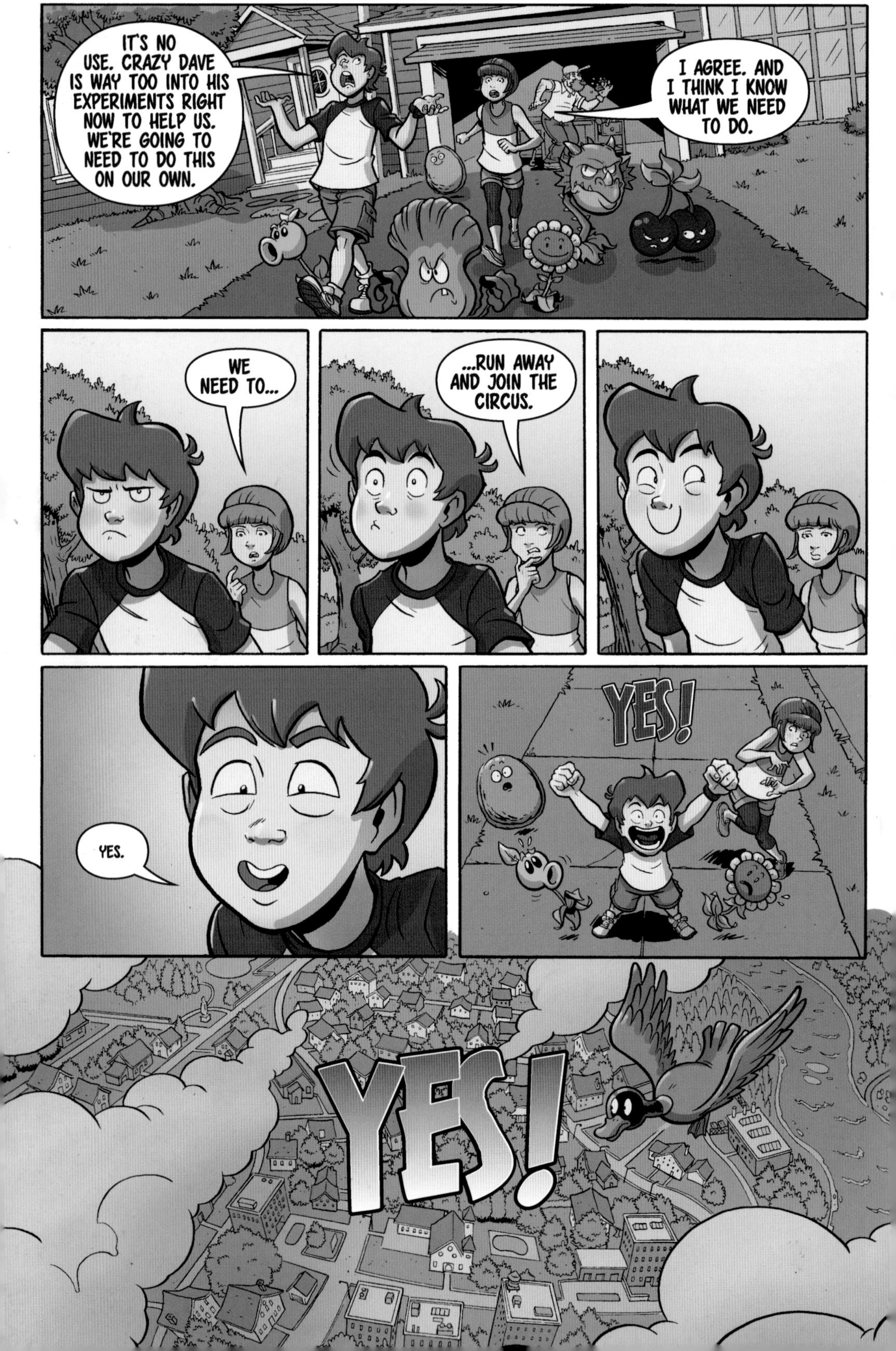
IT'S NO USE. CRAZY DAVE IS WAY TOO INTO HIS EXPERIMENTS RIGHT NOW TO HELP US. WE'RE GOING TO NEED TO DO THIS ON OUR OWN.
I AGREE. AND I THINK I KNOW WHAT WE NEED TO DO.
WE NEED TO...
...RUN AWAY AND JOIN THE CIRCUS.
YES.
YES!
YES!

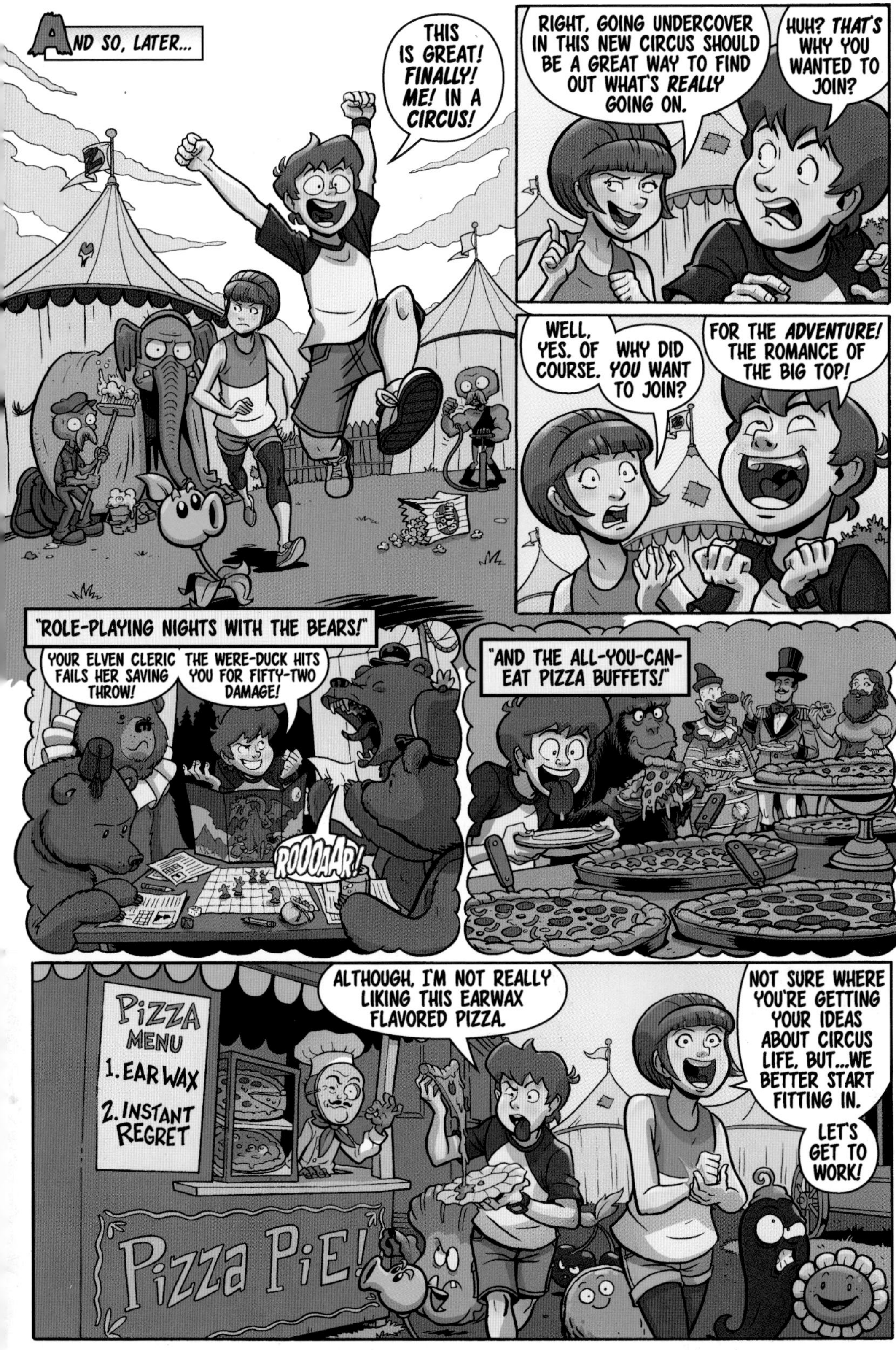
AND SO, LATER...
THIS IS GREAT! FINALLY! ME! IN A CIRCUS!
RIGHT, GOING UNDERCOVER IN THIS NEW CIRCUS SHOULD BE A GREAT WAY TO FIND OUT WHAT'S REALLY GOING ON.
HUH? THAT'S WHY YOU WANTED TO JOIN?
WELL, YES. OF COURSE.
WHY DID YOU WANT TO JOIN?
FOR THE ADVENTURE! THE ROMANCE OF THE BIG TOP!
"ROLE-PLAYING NIGHTS WITH THE BEARS!"
YOUR ELVEN CLERIC FAILS HER SAVING THROW!
THE WERE-DUCK HITS YOU FOR FIFTY-TWO DAMAGE!
ROOOAAAR!
"AND THE ALL-YOU-CAN-EAT PIZZA BUFFETS!"
PIZZA MENU
1. EAR WAX
2. INSTANT REGRET
PIZZA PIE!
ALTHOUGH, I'M NOT REALLY LIKING THIS EARWAX FLAVORED PIZZA.
NOT SURE WHERE YOU'RE GETTING YOUR IDEAS ABOUT CIRCUS LIFE, BUT...WE BETTER START FITTING IN.
LET'S GET TO WORK!

CIRCUS JOBS!

Giving the elephant his back rubs!

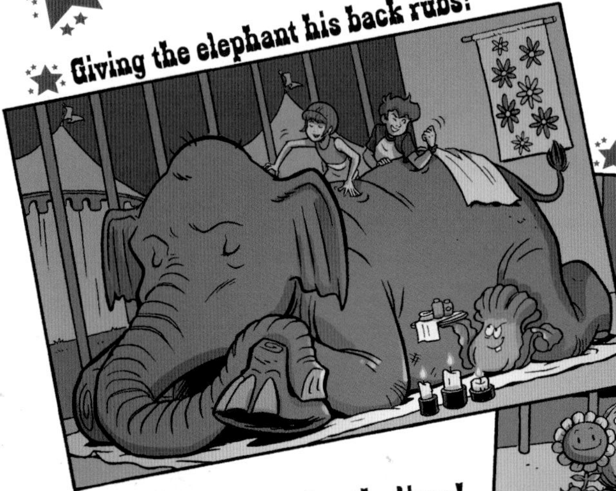

Reading bedtime stories to the bears!

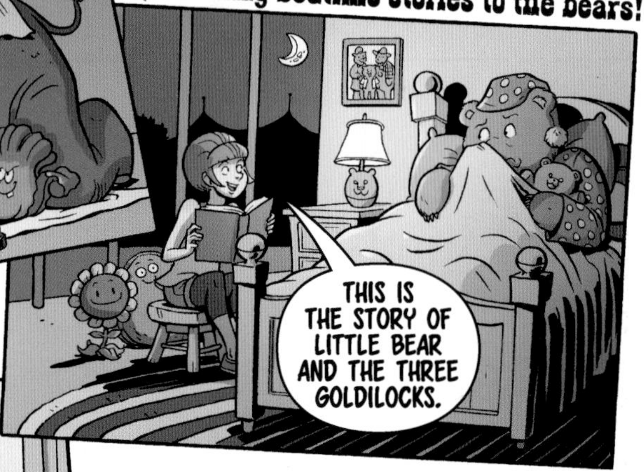
THIS IS THE STORY OF LITTLE BEAR AND THE THREE GOLDILOCKS.

Cleaning up after the lions!

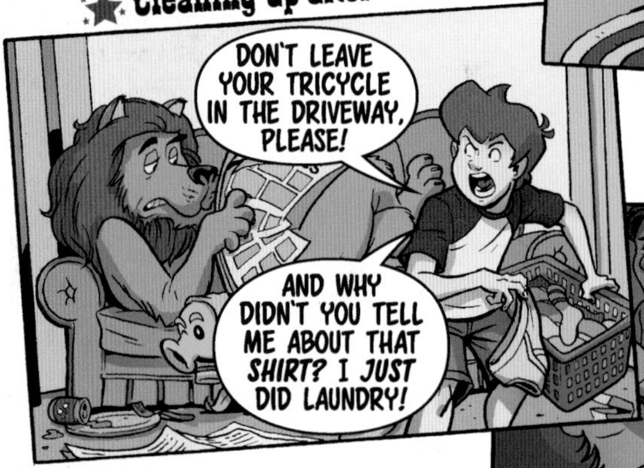
DON'T LEAVE YOUR TRICYCLE IN THE DRIVEWAY, PLEASE!
AND WHY DIDN'T YOU TELL ME ABOUT THAT *SHIRT?* I *JUST* DID LAUNDRY!

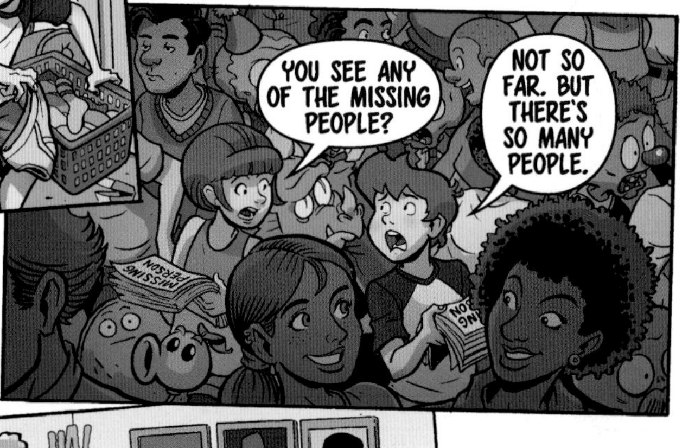
YOU SEE ANY OF THE MISSING PEOPLE?
NOT SO FAR. BUT THERE'S SO MANY PEOPLE.

Hairstyling the laughing hyena!

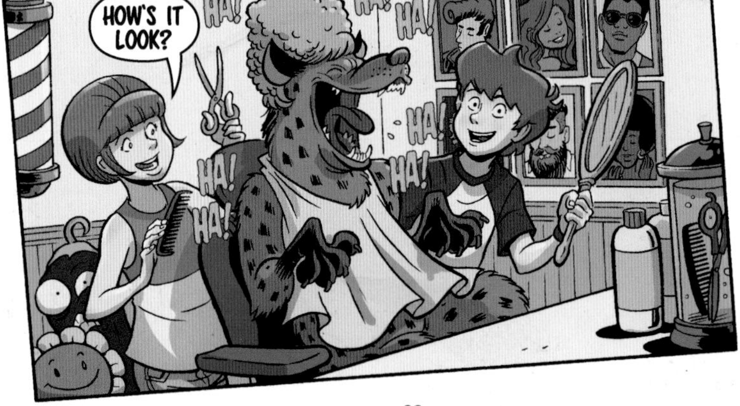
HOW'S IT LOOK?
HA!
HA!
HA!
HA!
HA!
HA!
HA!
HA!

THE SEARCH CONTINUES...

HMM.

PIZZA INGREDIENTS

AND...

MISSING THIS UNFLOWER

NOPE. WRONG PLANT.

I DON'T THINK THAT'S HER.

MISSING A CATTAIL

NOPE. WRONG.

THE NOSE IS DIFFERENT.

MISSING COLETTE MAYFLEET

HMMM. CLOSE BUT...NO.

MISSING BENEDICT ROOT

WHERE YOU OFF TO NOW? WE HAVEN'T FOUND ANYONE, YET!

I HAVE TO TAKE THESE BANANA PIZZAS TO THE CHIMPANZEES.

MISSING

IT'S FRUSTRATING, BECAUSE I WANT TO KEEP SEARCHING.

THERE HAS TO BE A CLUE SOMEWHERE, SOME LITTLE HINT AS TO WHAT'S GOING ON.

RIGHT. IF ONLY WE COULD UNCOVER SOME SMALL, SEEM-INGLY INSIGNIFICANT FACT THAT WOULD GIVE US SOME UNDERSTANDING...

...NO MATTER HOW SLIGHT, OF WHERE THOSE PEOPLE HAVE GONE.

AHHHH!

29

STILL NOTHING IN THE MAIL!

THIS IS SO FRUSTRATING! EVER SINCE I SAW ON THE TELEVISION THAT PEOPLE WILL RUN AWAY TO JOIN A CIRCUS...

...I'VE WORKED HARD TO BUILD THIS CIRCUS AS A MEANS OF LURING PEOPLE HERE SO THAT I CAN EAT THEIR BRAINS.

AND NOW I'VE GATHERED OVER A HUNDRED OF NEIGHBORVILLE'S CITIZENS, BUT WE CAN'T DEVOUR THEM YET...

...BECAUSE MR. STUBBINS INSISTS THAT EVERYBODY WAITS ON A LATE SHIPMENT OF BRAIN-B-CUE SAUCE!

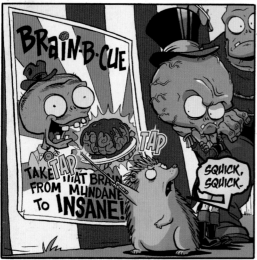

BRAIN·B·CUE

TAKE THAT BRAIN FROM MUNDANE TO INSANE!

TAP TAP TAP

SQUICK, SQUICK.

HUH. I THINK THIS MIGHT BE... A CLUE.

YEP.

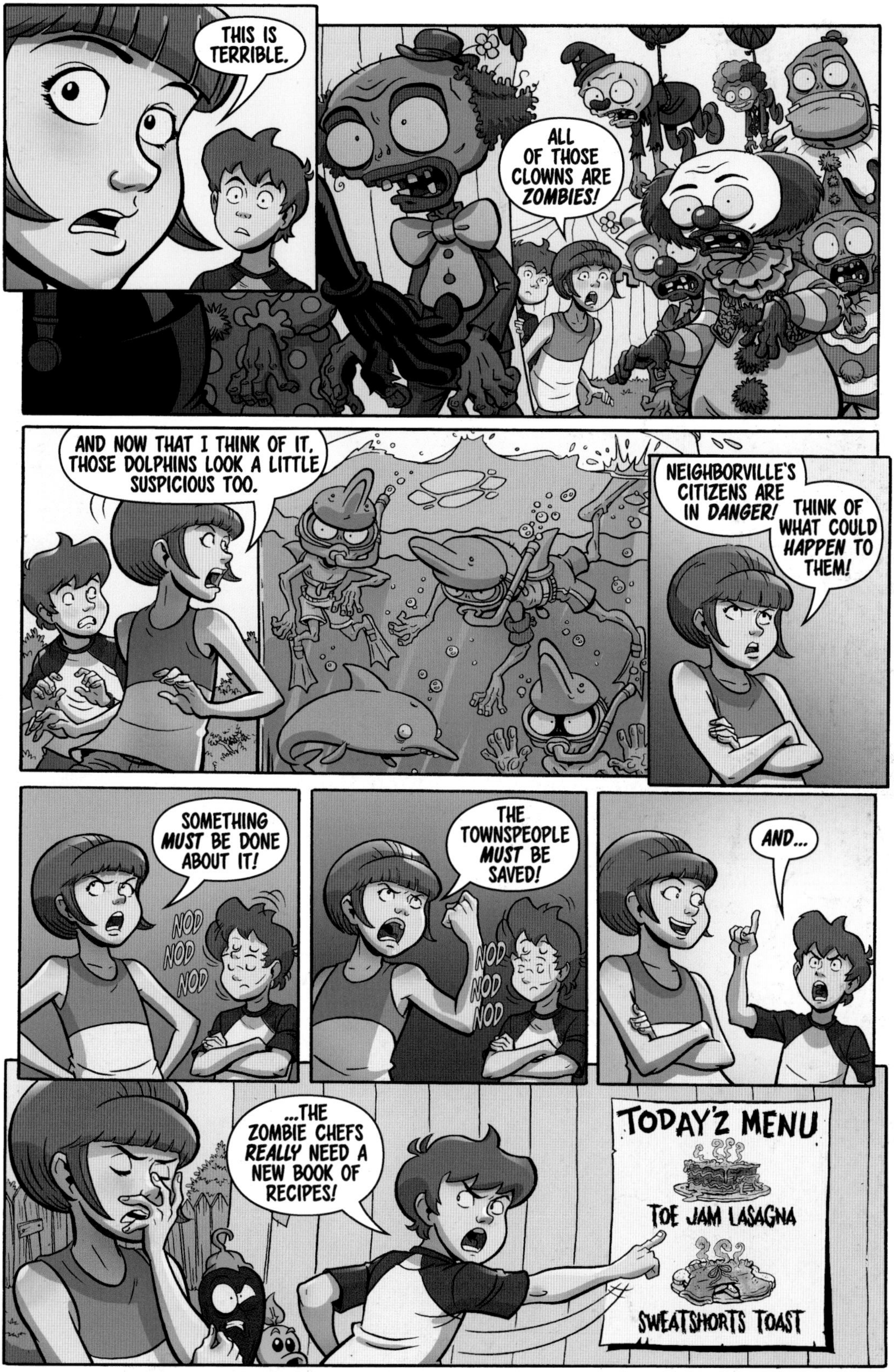
THIS IS TERRIBLE.
ALL OF THOSE CLOWNS ARE ZOMBIES!
AND NOW THAT I THINK OF IT, THOSE DOLPHINS LOOK A LITTLE SUSPICIOUS TOO.
NEIGHBORVILLE'S CITIZENS ARE IN DANGER!
THINK OF WHAT COULD HAPPEN TO THEM!
SOMETHING MUST BE DONE ABOUT IT!
NOD NOD NOD
THE TOWNSPEOPLE MUST BE SAVED!
NOD NOD NOD
AND...
...THE ZOMBIE CHEFS REALLY NEED A NEW BOOK OF RECIPES!
TODAY'Z MENU
TOE JAM LASAGNA
SWEATSHORTS TOAST

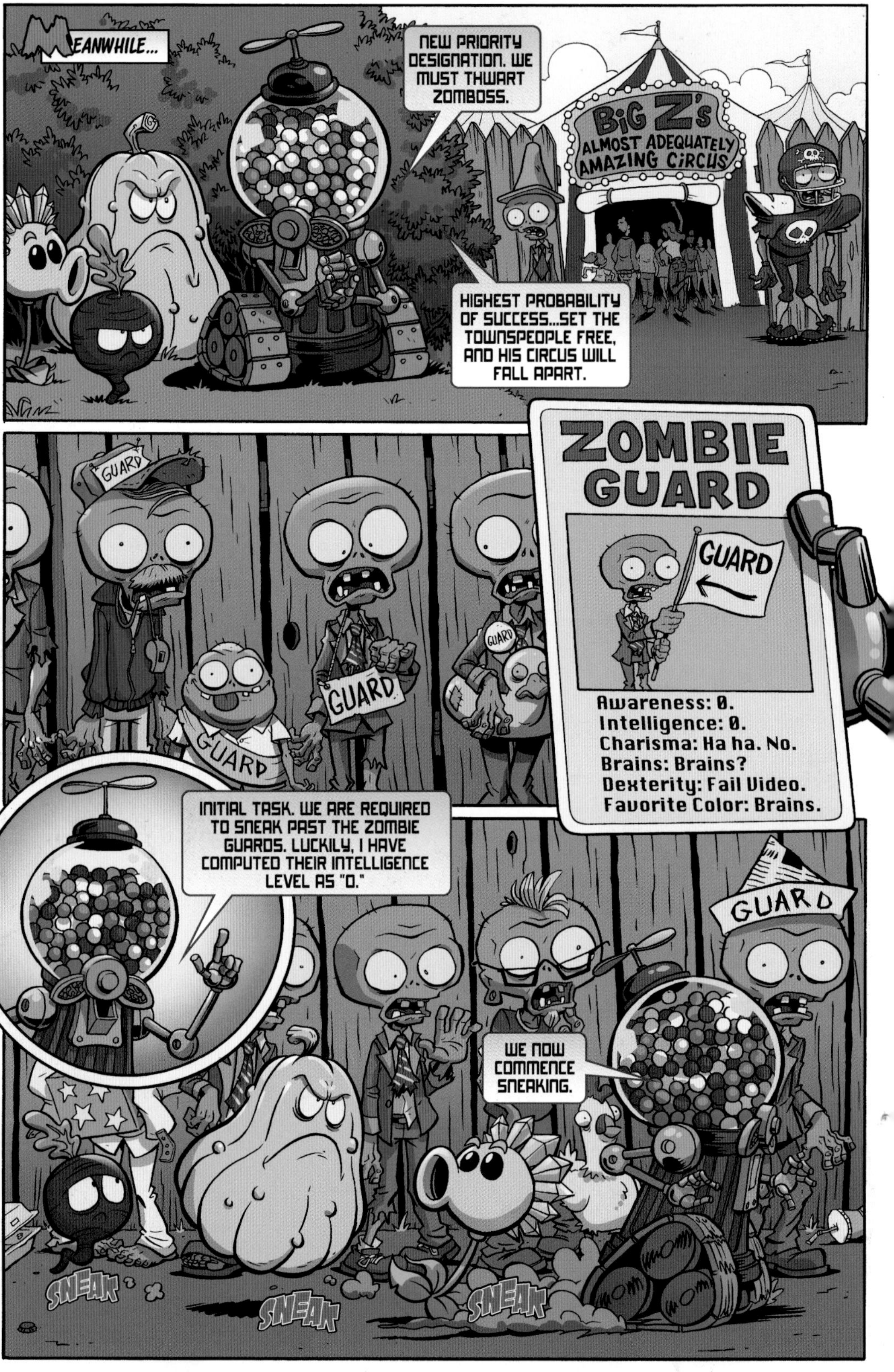
MEANWHILE...
NEW PRIORITY DESIGNATION. WE MUST THWART ZOMBOSS.
BIG Z'S ALMOST ADEQUATELY AMAZING CIRCUS
HIGHEST PROBABILITY OF SUCCESS...SET THE TOWNSPEOPLE FREE, AND HIS CIRCUS WILL FALL APART.
GUARD
GUARD
GUARD
GUARD
ZOMBIE GUARD
GUARD
Awareness: 0.
Intelligence: 0.
Charisma: Ha ha. No.
Brains: Brains?
Dexterity: Fail Video.
Favorite Color: Brains.
INITIAL TASK. WE ARE REQUIRED TO SNEAK PAST THE ZOMBIE GUARDS. LUCKILY, I HAVE COMPUTED THEIR INTELLIGENCE LEVEL AS "0."
GUARD
WE NOW COMMENCE SNEAKING.
SNEAK
SNEAK
SNEAK

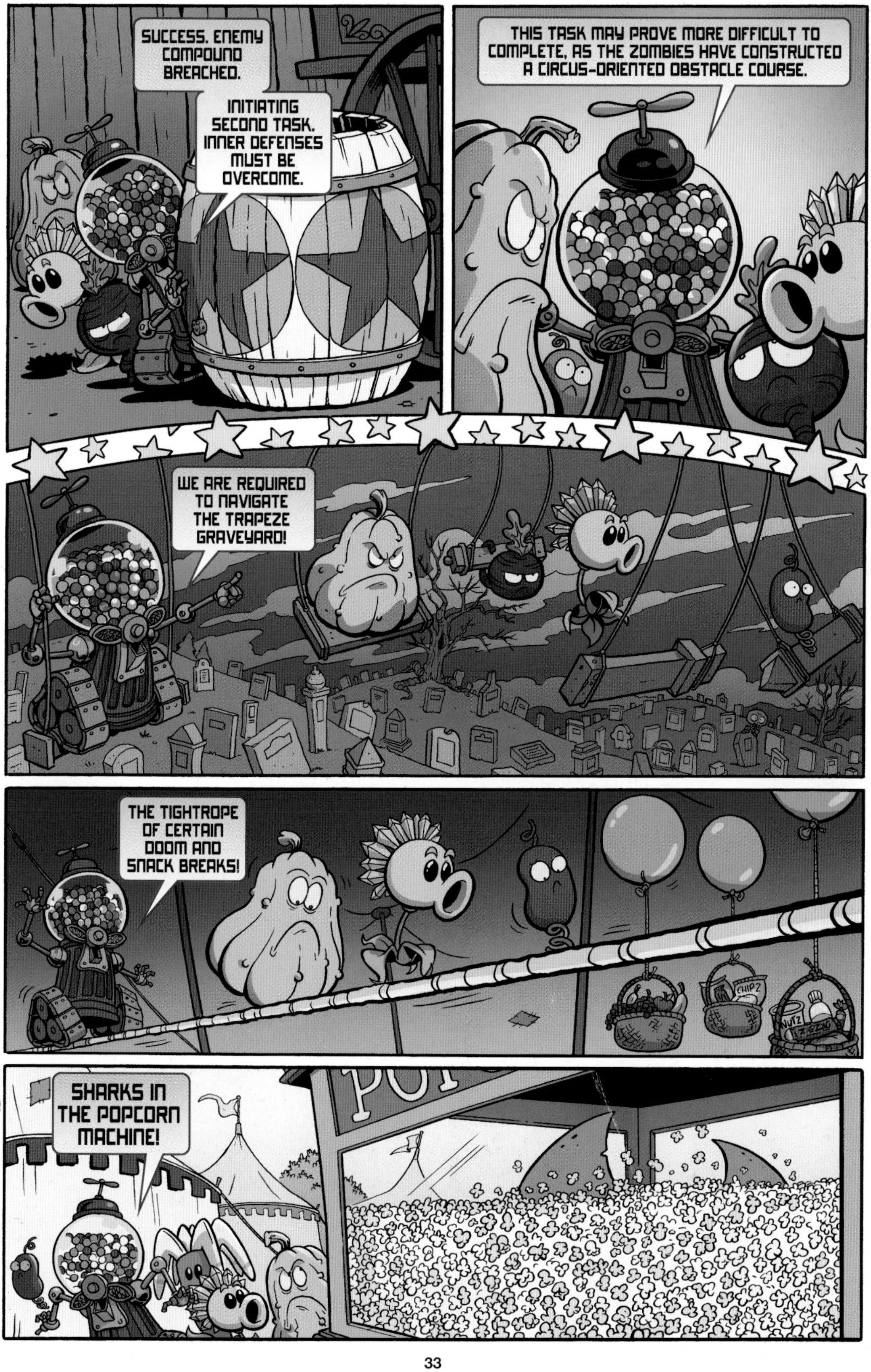

SUCCESS. ENEMY COMPOUND BREACHED.
INITIATING SECOND TASK. INNER DEFENSES MUST BE OVERCOME.
THIS TASK MAY PROVE MORE DIFFICULT TO COMPLETE, AS THE ZOMBIES HAVE CONSTRUCTED A CIRCUS-ORIENTED OBSTACLE COURSE.
WE ARE REQUIRED TO NAVIGATE THE TRAPEZE GRAVEYARD!
THE TIGHTROPE OF CERTAIN DOOM AND SNACK BREAKS!
CHIPZ
NUTZ
SHARKS IN THE POPCORN MACHINE!

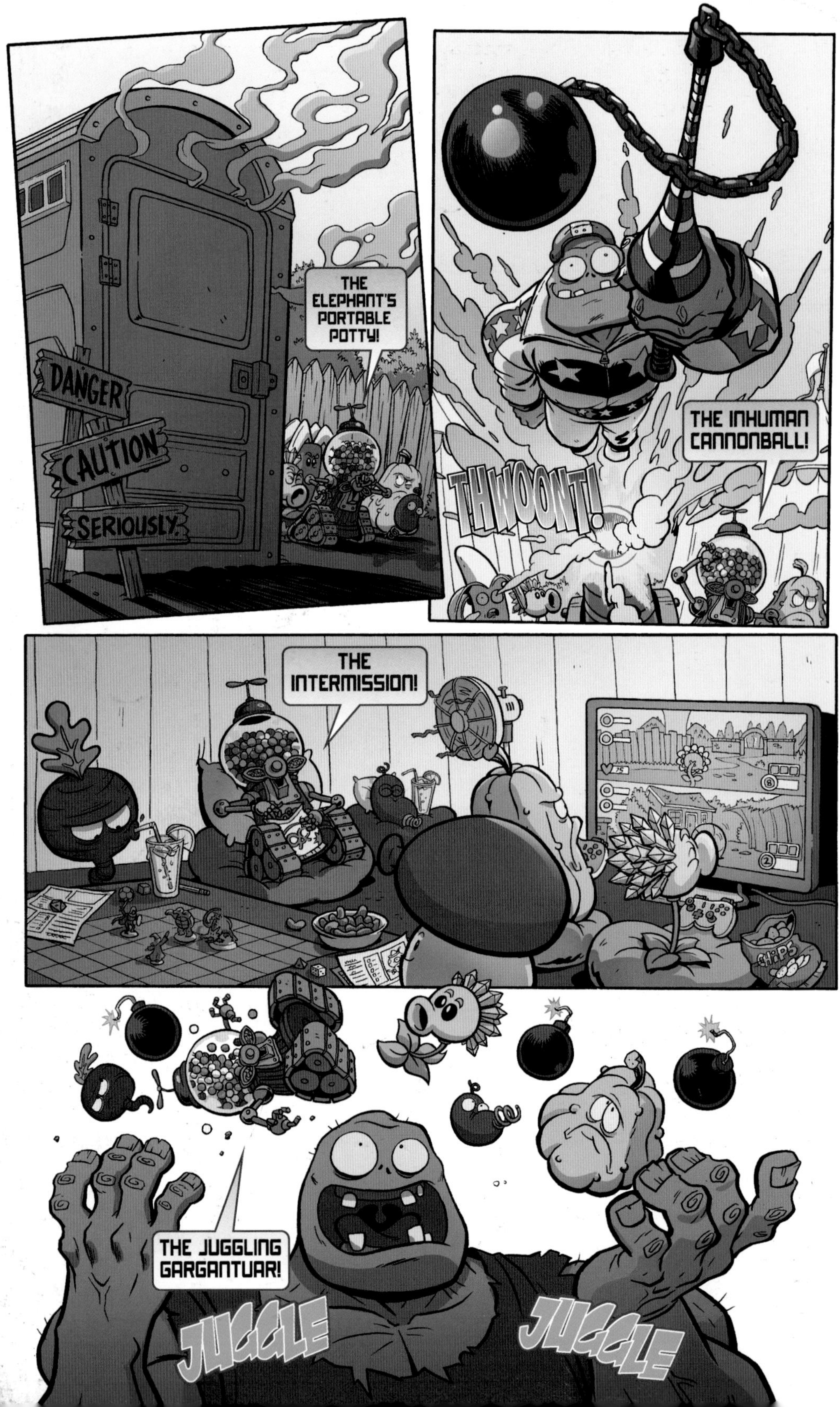
DANGER
CAUTION
SERIOUSLY.
THE ELEPHANT'S PORTABLE POTTY!
THE INHUMAN CANNONBALL!
THWOONT!
THE INTERMISSION!
CHIPS
THE JUGGLING GARGANTUAR!
JUGGLE
JUGGLE

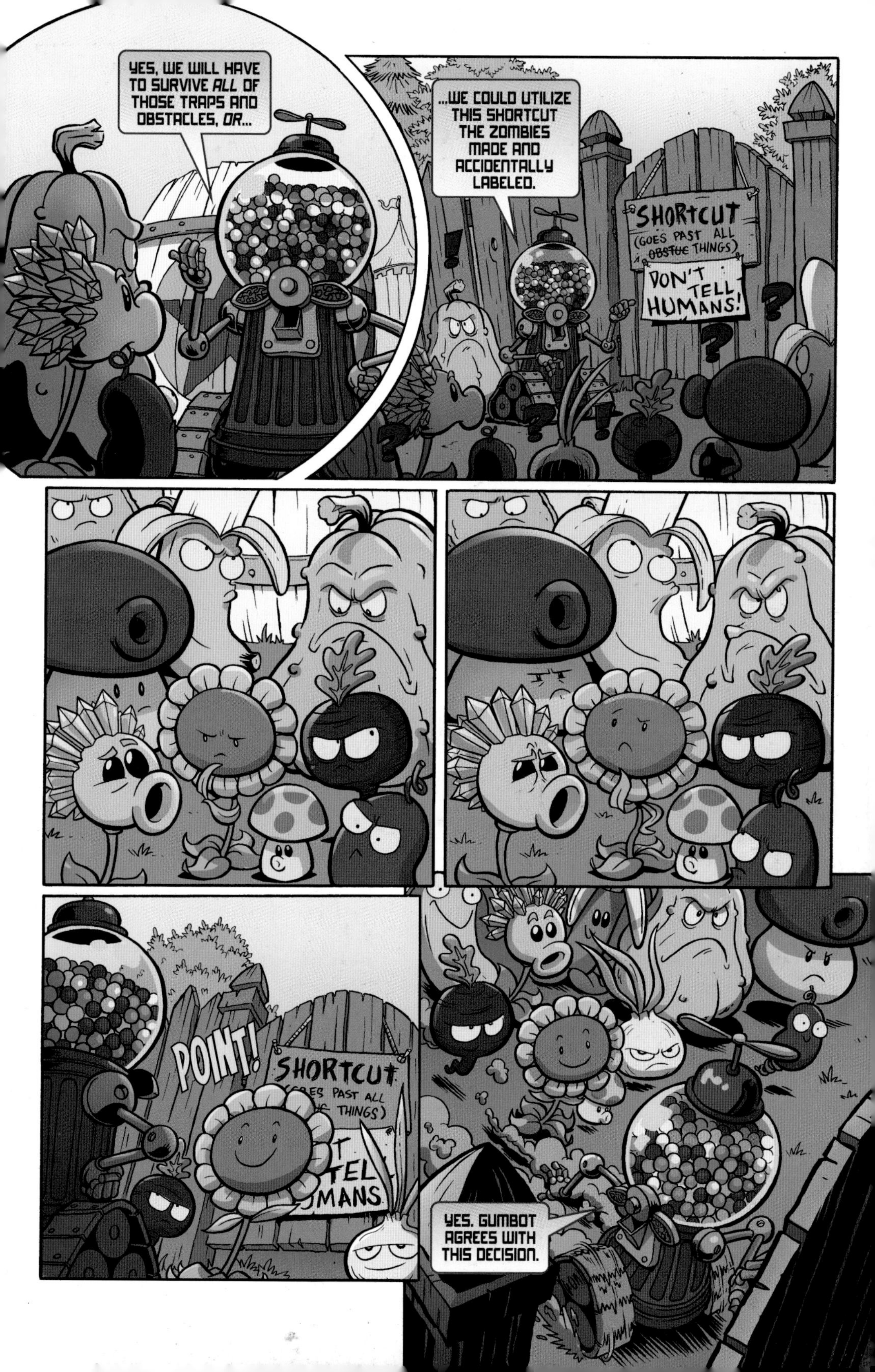
YES, WE WILL HAVE TO SURVIVE ALL OF THOSE TRAPS AND OBSTACLES, OR...
...WE COULD UTILIZE THIS SHORTCUT THE ZOMBIES MADE AND ACCIDENTALLY LABELED.
SHORTCUT (GOES PAST ALL OBSTUE THINGS)
DON'T TELL HUMANS!
POINT!
YES. GUMBOT AGREES WITH THIS DECISION.

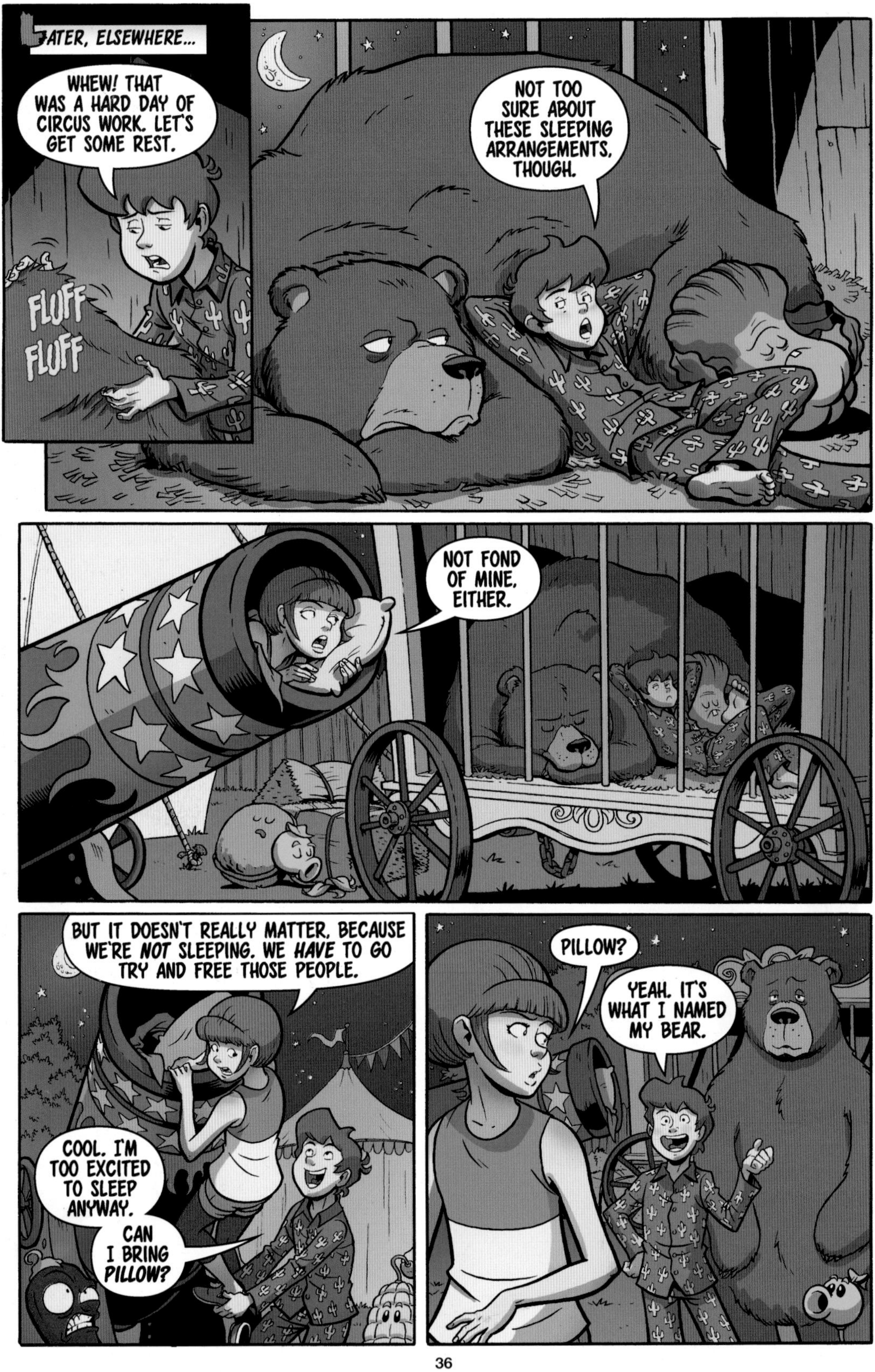
LATER, ELSEWHERE...
WHEW! THAT WAS A HARD DAY OF CIRCUS WORK. LET'S GET SOME REST.
FLUFF
FLUFF
NOT TOO SURE ABOUT THESE SLEEPING ARRANGEMENTS, THOUGH.
NOT FOND OF MINE, EITHER.
BUT IT DOESN'T REALLY MATTER, BECAUSE WE'RE *NOT* SLEEPING. WE *HAVE* TO GO TRY AND FREE THOSE PEOPLE.
COOL. I'M TOO EXCITED TO SLEEP ANYWAY.
CAN I BRING *PILLOW?*
PILLOW?
YEAH. IT'S WHAT I NAMED MY BEAR.

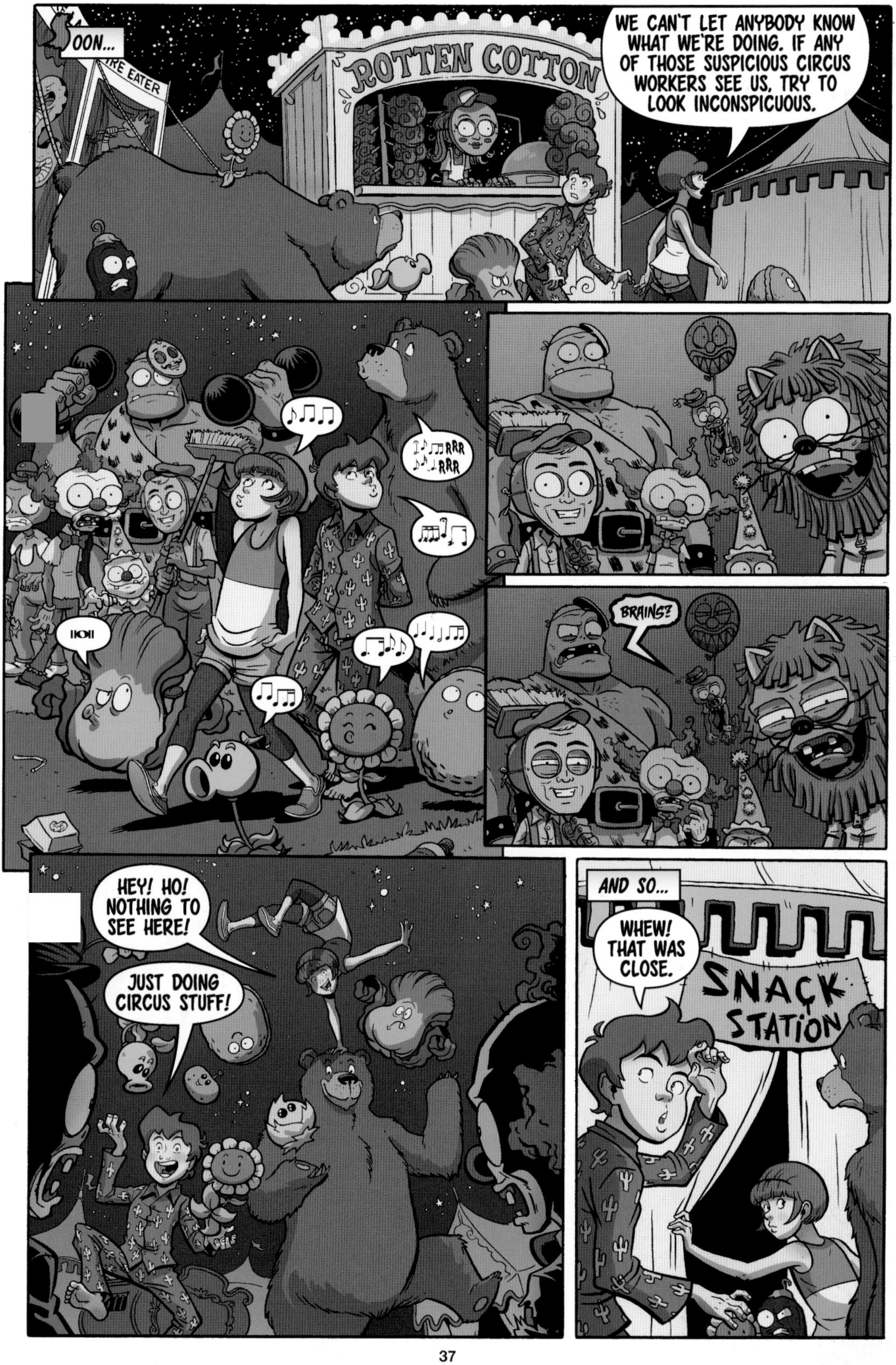
OON...
RE EATER
ROTTEN COTTON
WE CAN'T LET ANYBODY KNOW WHAT WE'RE DOING. IF ANY OF THOSE SUSPICIOUS CIRCUS WORKERS SEE US, TRY TO LOOK INCONSPICUOUS.
BRAINS?
HEY! HO! NOTHING TO SEE HERE!
JUST DOING CIRCUS STUFF!
AND SO...
WHEW! THAT WAS CLOSE.
SNACK STATION

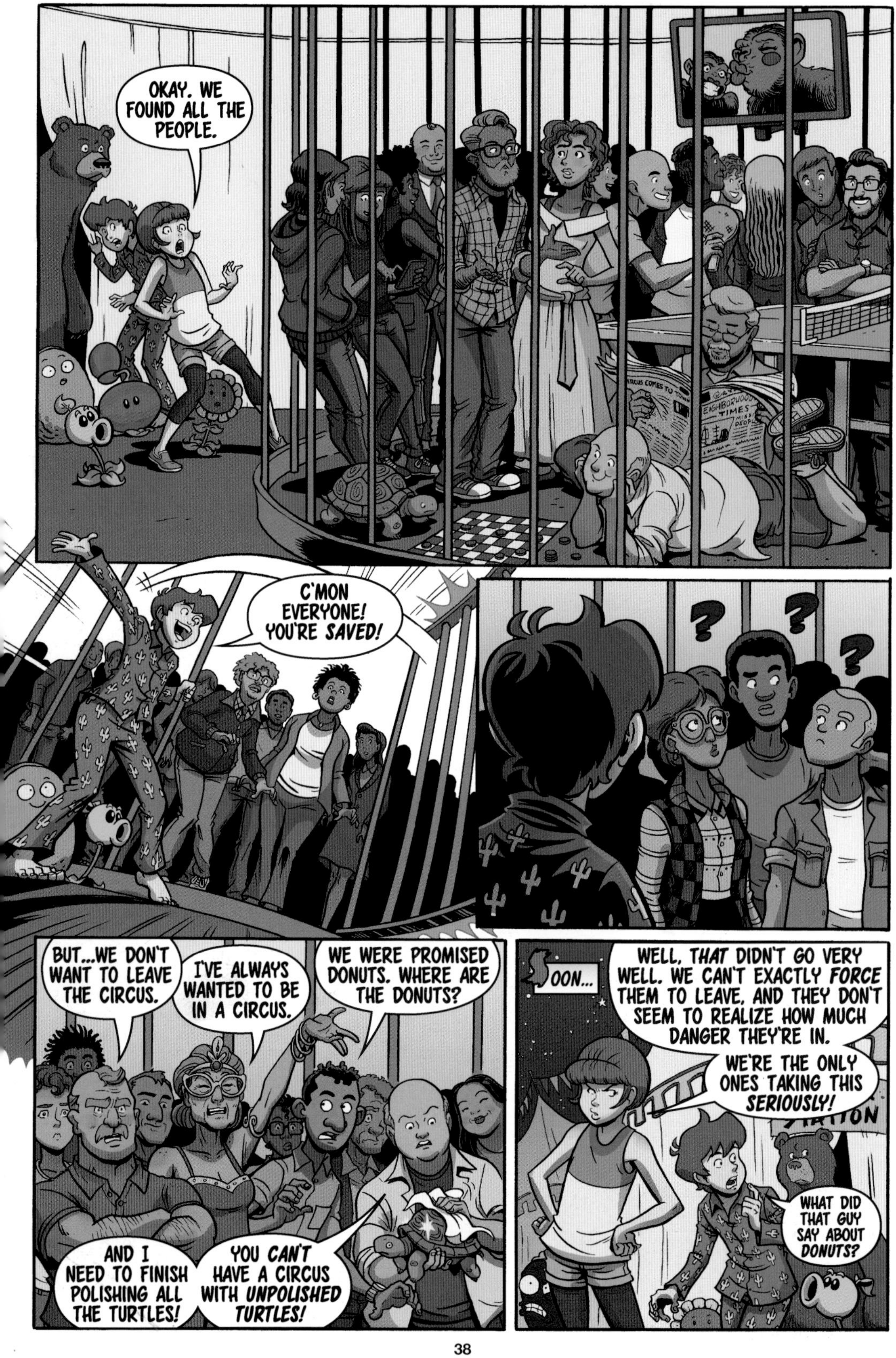
OKAY. WE FOUND ALL THE PEOPLE.
C'MON EVERYONE! YOU'RE *SAVED!*
BUT...WE DON'T WANT TO LEAVE THE CIRCUS.
I'VE ALWAYS WANTED TO BE IN A CIRCUS.
WE WERE PROMISED DONUTS. WHERE ARE THE DONUTS?
AND I NEED TO FINISH POLISHING ALL THE TURTLES!
YOU *CAN'T* HAVE A CIRCUS WITH *UNPOLISHED TURTLES!*
SOON...
WELL, *THAT* DIDN'T GO VERY WELL. WE CAN'T EXACTLY *FORCE* THEM TO LEAVE, AND THEY DON'T SEEM TO REALIZE HOW MUCH DANGER THEY'RE IN.
WE'RE THE ONLY ONES TAKING THIS *SERIOUSLY!*
WHAT DID THAT GUY SAY ABOUT *DONUTS?*

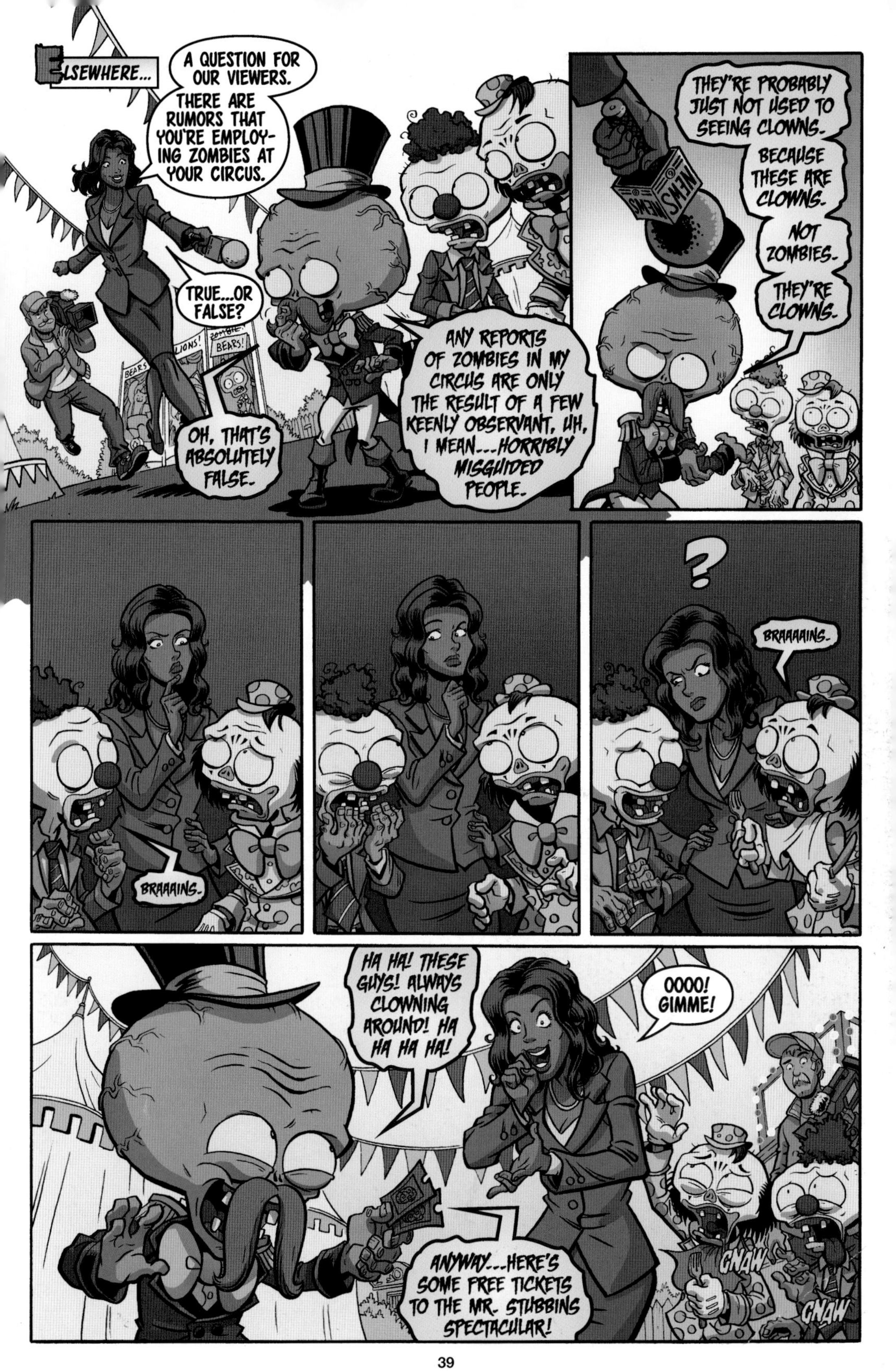
ELSEWHERE...
A QUESTION FOR OUR VIEWERS.
THERE ARE RUMORS THAT YOU'RE EMPLOYING ZOMBIES AT YOUR CIRCUS.
TRUE...OR FALSE?
LIONS!
BEARS!
OH, THAT'S ABSOLUTELY FALSE.
ANY REPORTS OF ZOMBIES IN MY CIRCUS ARE ONLY THE RESULT OF A FEW KEENLY OBSERVANT, UH, I MEAN...HORRIBLY MISGUIDED PEOPLE.
NEWS
THEY'RE PROBABLY JUST NOT USED TO SEEING CLOWNS.
BECAUSE THESE ARE CLOWNS.
NOT ZOMBIES.
THEY'RE CLOWNS.
BRAAAINS.
?
BRAAAAINS.
HA HA! THESE GUYS! ALWAYS CLOWNING AROUND! HA HA HA HA!
OOOO! GIMME!
ANYWAY...HERE'S SOME FREE TICKETS TO THE MR. STUBBINS SPECTACULAR!
GNAW
GNAW

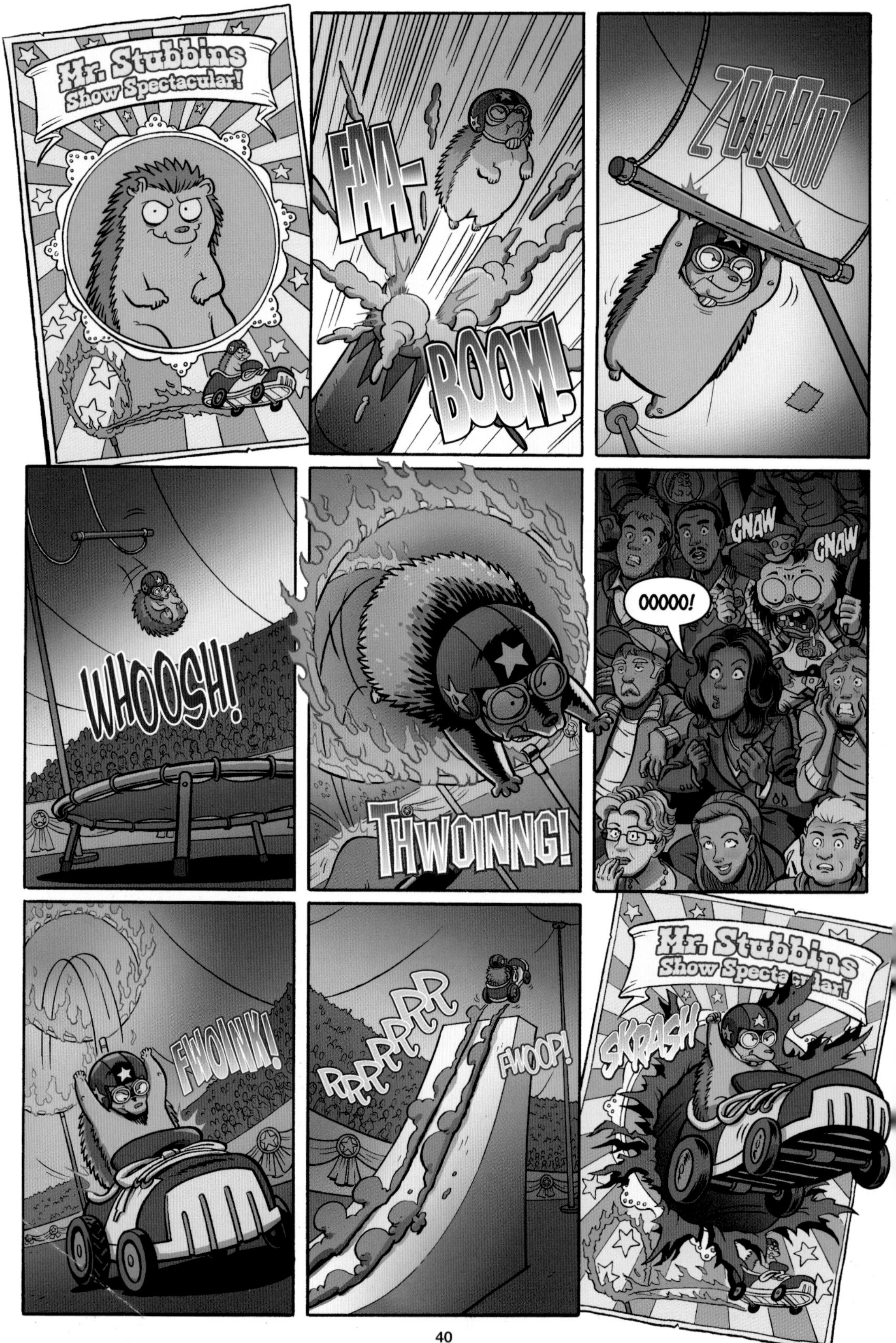
Mr. Stubbins Show Spectacular!
FAA-
BOOM!
ZOOOM
WHOOSH!
THWOINNG!
GNAW
GNAW
OOOOO!
FWOINK!
RRRRRRRR
FWOOP!
Mr. Stubbins Show Spectacular!
SKRASH

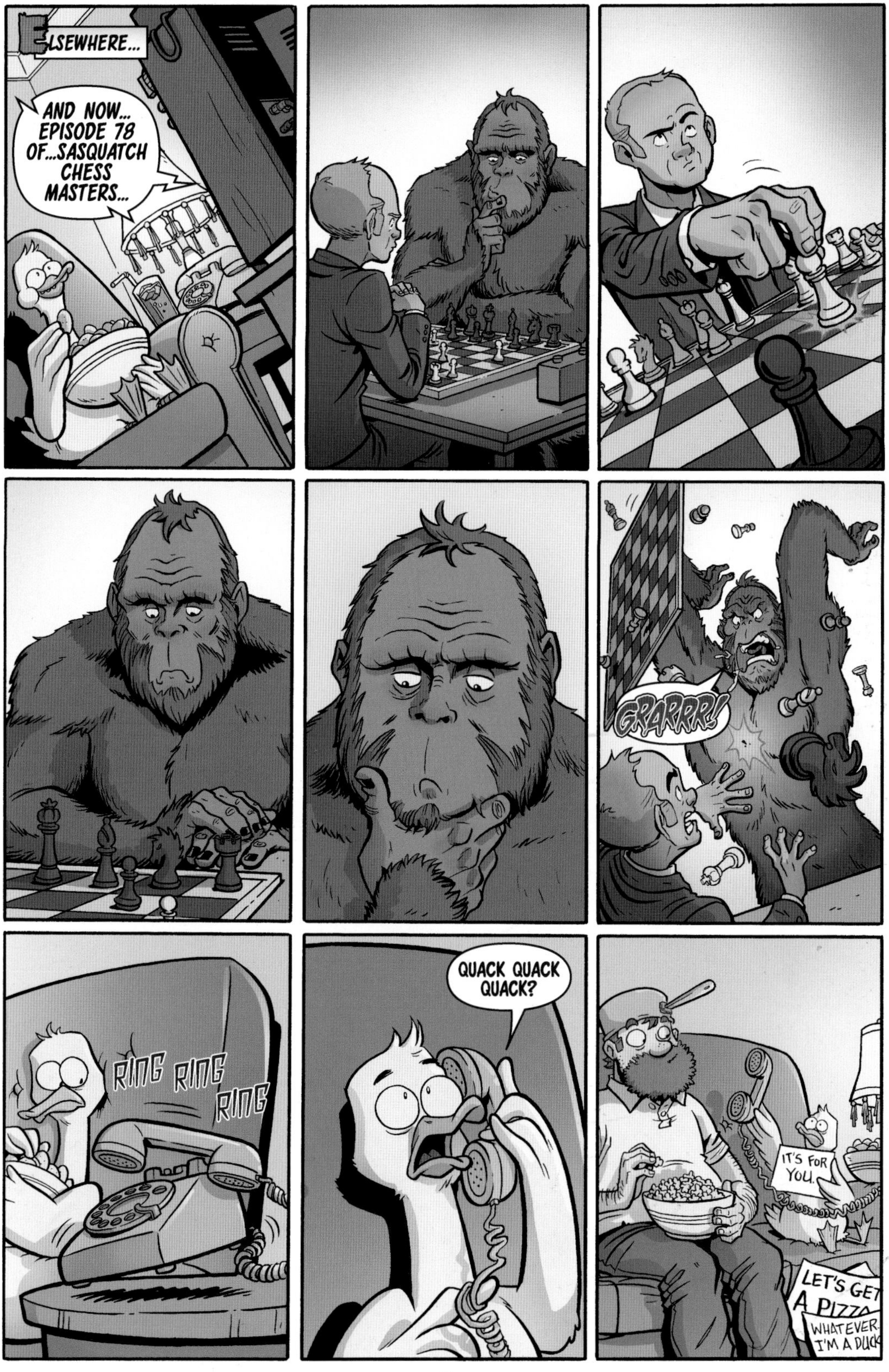
ELSEWHERE...
AND NOW... EPISODE 78 OF...SASQUATCH CHESS MASTERS...
GRARRR!
RING RING RING
QUACK QUACK QUACK?
IT'S FOR YOU.
LET'S GET A PIZZA
WHATEVER. I'M A DUCK

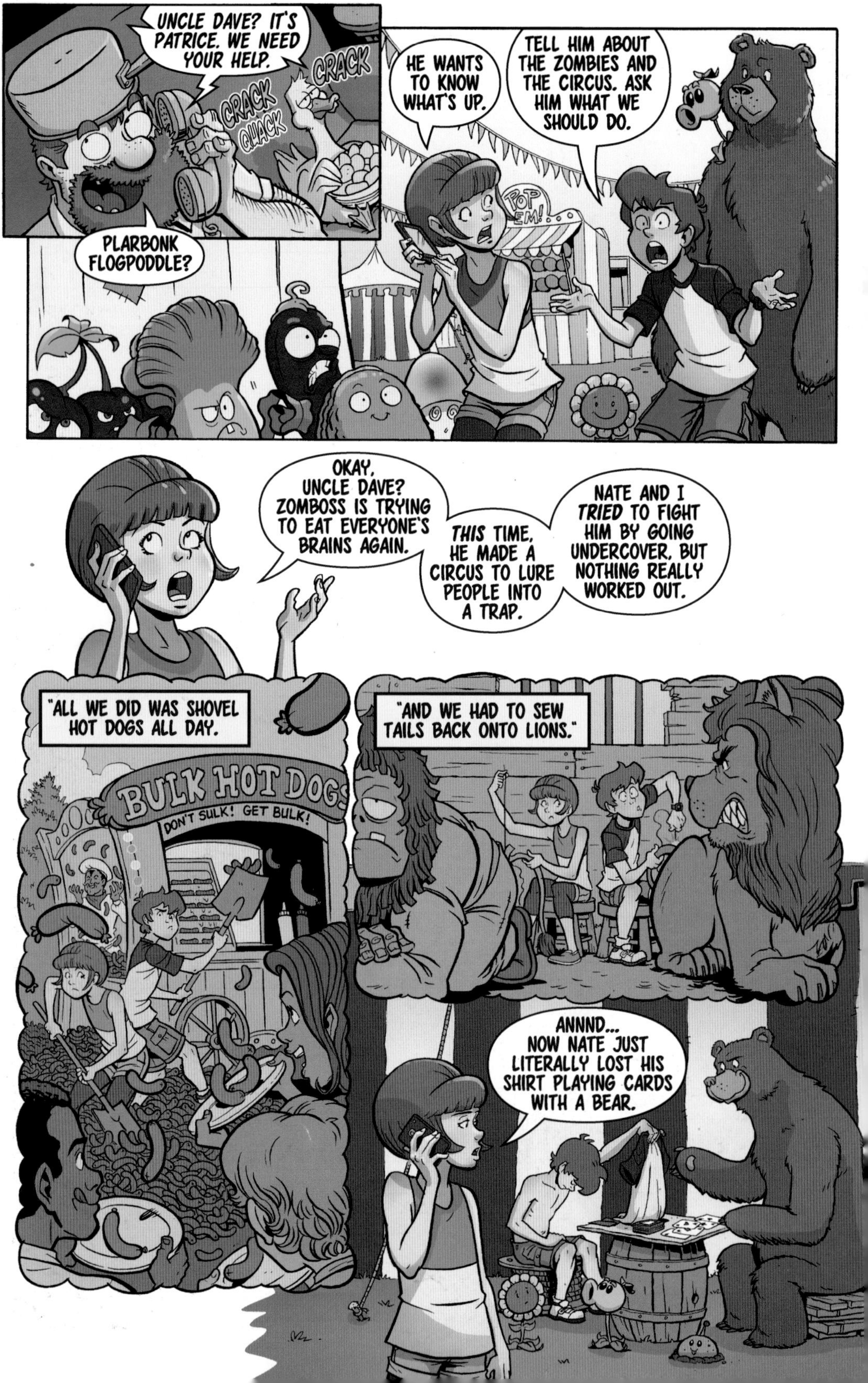
UNCLE DAVE? IT'S PATRICE. WE NEED YOUR HELP.
CRACK
CRACK
QUACK
PLARBONK FLOGPODDLE?
HE WANTS TO KNOW WHAT'S UP.
TELL HIM ABOUT THE ZOMBIES AND THE CIRCUS. ASK HIM WHAT WE SHOULD DO.
POP 'EM!
OKAY, UNCLE DAVE? ZOMBOSS IS TRYING TO EAT EVERYONE'S BRAINS AGAIN.
THIS TIME, HE MADE A CIRCUS TO LURE PEOPLE INTO A TRAP.
NATE AND I TRIED TO FIGHT HIM BY GOING UNDERCOVER, BUT NOTHING REALLY WORKED OUT.
"ALL WE DID WAS SHOVEL HOT DOGS ALL DAY.
BULK HOT DOGS
DON'T SULK! GET BULK!
"AND WE HAD TO SEW TAILS BACK ONTO LIONS."
ANNND... NOW NATE JUST LITERALLY LOST HIS SHIRT PLAYING CARDS WITH A BEAR.

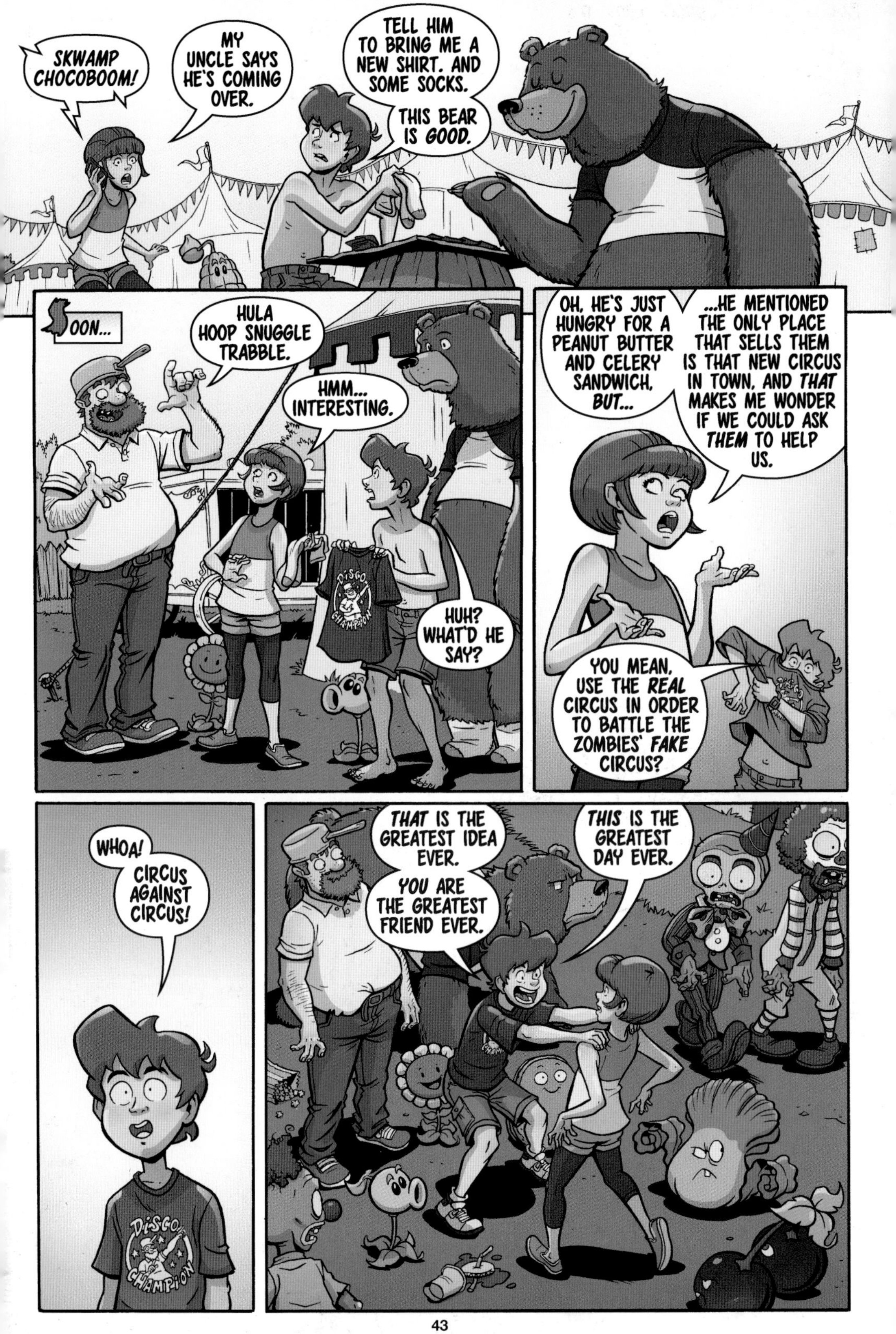
SKWAMP CHOCOBOOM!
MY UNCLE SAYS HE'S COMING OVER.
TELL HIM TO BRING ME A NEW SHIRT. AND SOME SOCKS.
THIS BEAR IS GOOD.
SOON...
HULA HOOP SNUGGLE TRABBLE.
HMM... INTERESTING.
HUH? WHAT'D HE SAY?
OH, HE'S JUST HUNGRY FOR A PEANUT BUTTER AND CELERY SANDWICH, BUT...
...HE MENTIONED THE ONLY PLACE THAT SELLS THEM IS THAT NEW CIRCUS IN TOWN, AND THAT MAKES ME WONDER IF WE COULD ASK THEM TO HELP US.
YOU MEAN, USE THE REAL CIRCUS IN ORDER TO BATTLE THE ZOMBIES' FAKE CIRCUS?
WHOA!
CIRCUS AGAINST CIRCUS!
THAT IS THE GREATEST IDEA EVER.
YOU ARE THE GREATEST FRIEND EVER.
THIS IS THE GREATEST DAY EVER.
DISCO CHAMPION

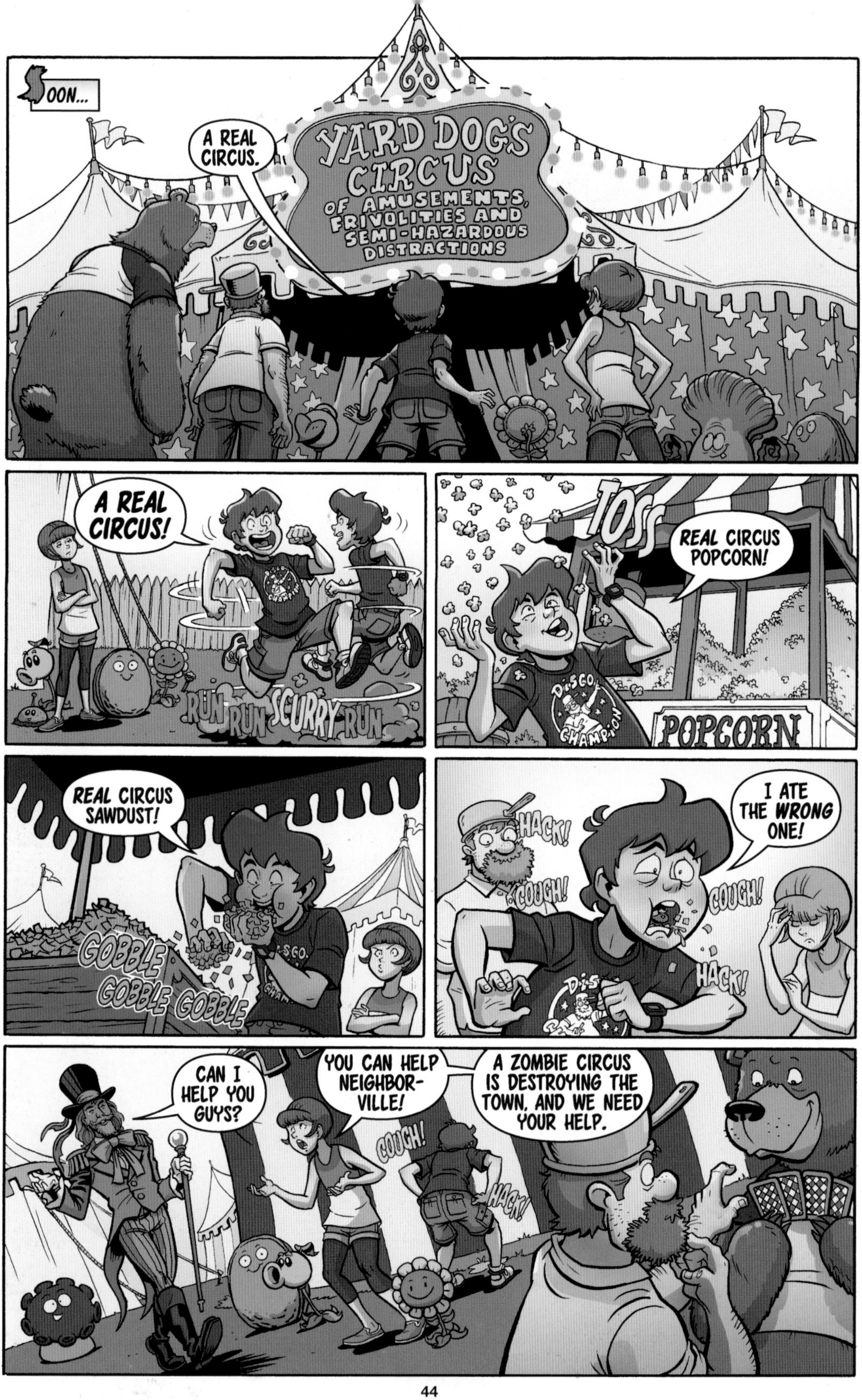
SOON...
A REAL CIRCUS.
YARD DOG'S CIRCUS OF AMUSEMENTS, FRIVOLITIES AND SEMI-HAZARDOUS DISTRACTIONS
A REAL CIRCUS!
RUN RUN SCURRY RUN
TOSS
REAL CIRCUS POPCORN!
POPCORN
REAL CIRCUS SAWDUST!
GOBBLE GOBBLE GOBBLE GOBBLE
HACK!
COUGH!
I ATE THE WRONG ONE!
COUGH!
HACK!
CAN I HELP YOU GUYS?
YOU CAN HELP NEIGHBOR-VILLE!
A ZOMBIE CIRCUS IS DESTROYING THE TOWN, AND WE NEED YOUR HELP.
COUGH!
HACK!

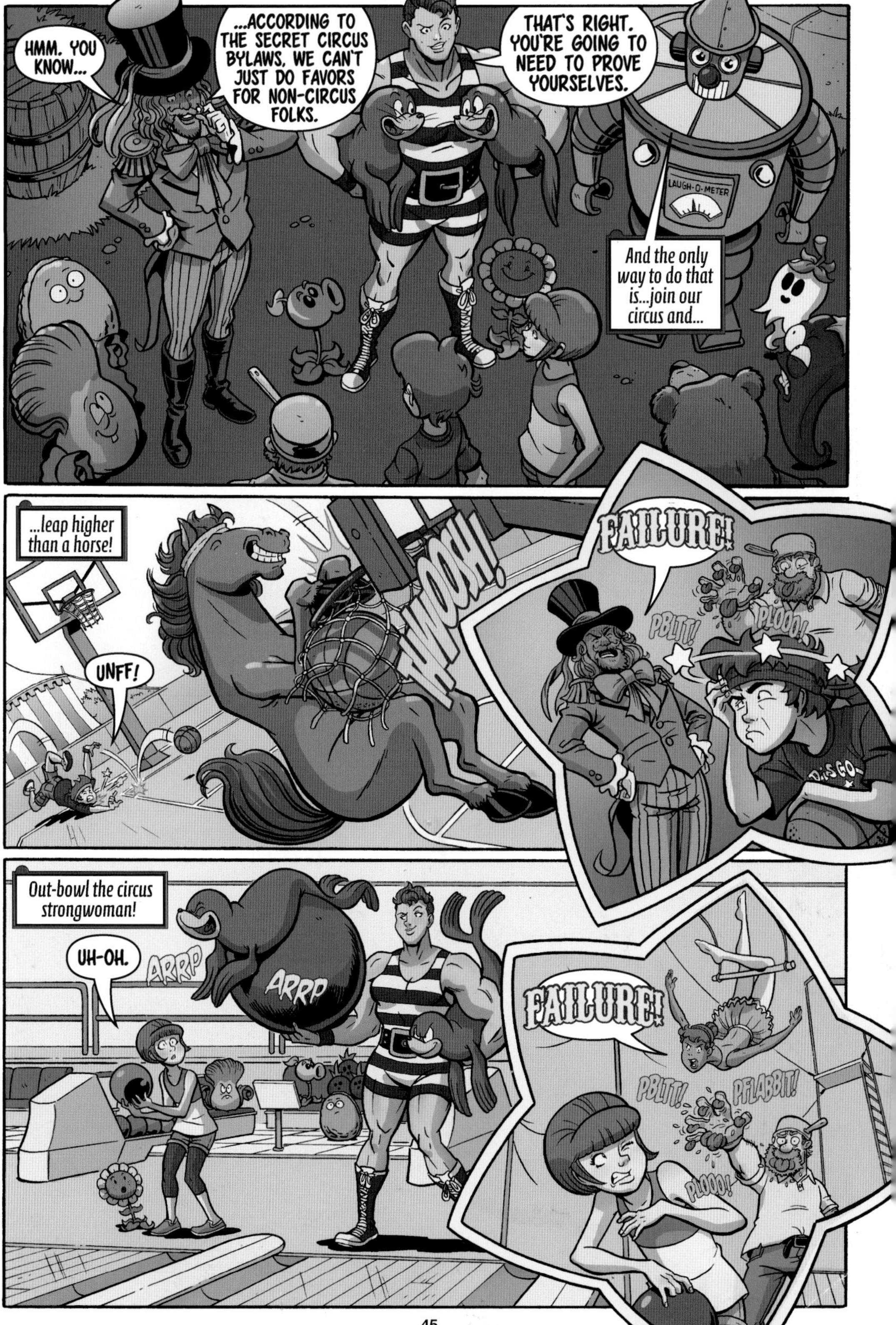
HMM. YOU KNOW...
...ACCORDING TO THE SECRET CIRCUS BYLAWS, WE CAN'T JUST DO FAVORS FOR NON-CIRCUS FOLKS.
THAT'S RIGHT. YOU'RE GOING TO NEED TO PROVE YOURSELVES.
LAUGH-O-METER
And the only way to do that is...join our circus and...
...leap higher than a horse!
UNFF!
THWOOSH!
FAILURE!
PBLTT!
PLOOO!
DISCO
Out-bowl the circus strongwoman!
UH-OH.
ARRP
ARRP
FAILURE!
PBLTT!
PFLABBIT!
PLOOO!

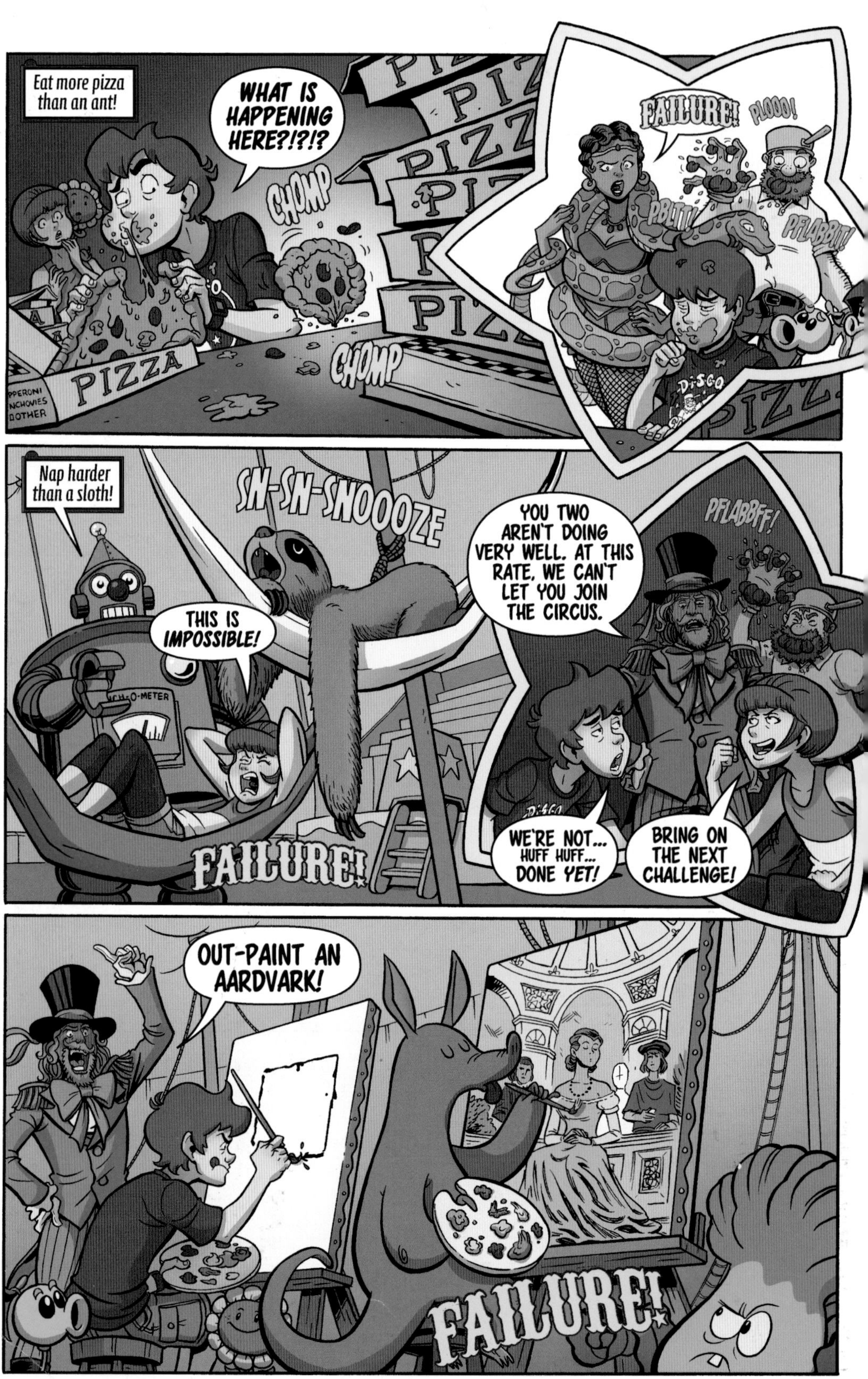

Eat more pizza than an ant!
WHAT IS HAPPENING HERE?!?!?
CHOMP
PIZZA
PPERONI
NCHOVIES
OTHER
CHOMP
FAILURE!
PLOOO!
PBLTT!
PFLABBIT!
DISCO
Nap harder than a sloth!
SN-SN-SNOOOZE
THIS IS IMPOSSIBLE!
FAILURE!
YOU TWO AREN'T DOING VERY WELL. AT THIS RATE, WE CAN'T LET YOU JOIN THE CIRCUS.
PFLABBFF!
WE'RE NOT... HUFF HUFF... DONE YET!
BRING ON THE NEXT CHALLENGE!
OUT-PAINT AN AARDVARK!
FAILURE!

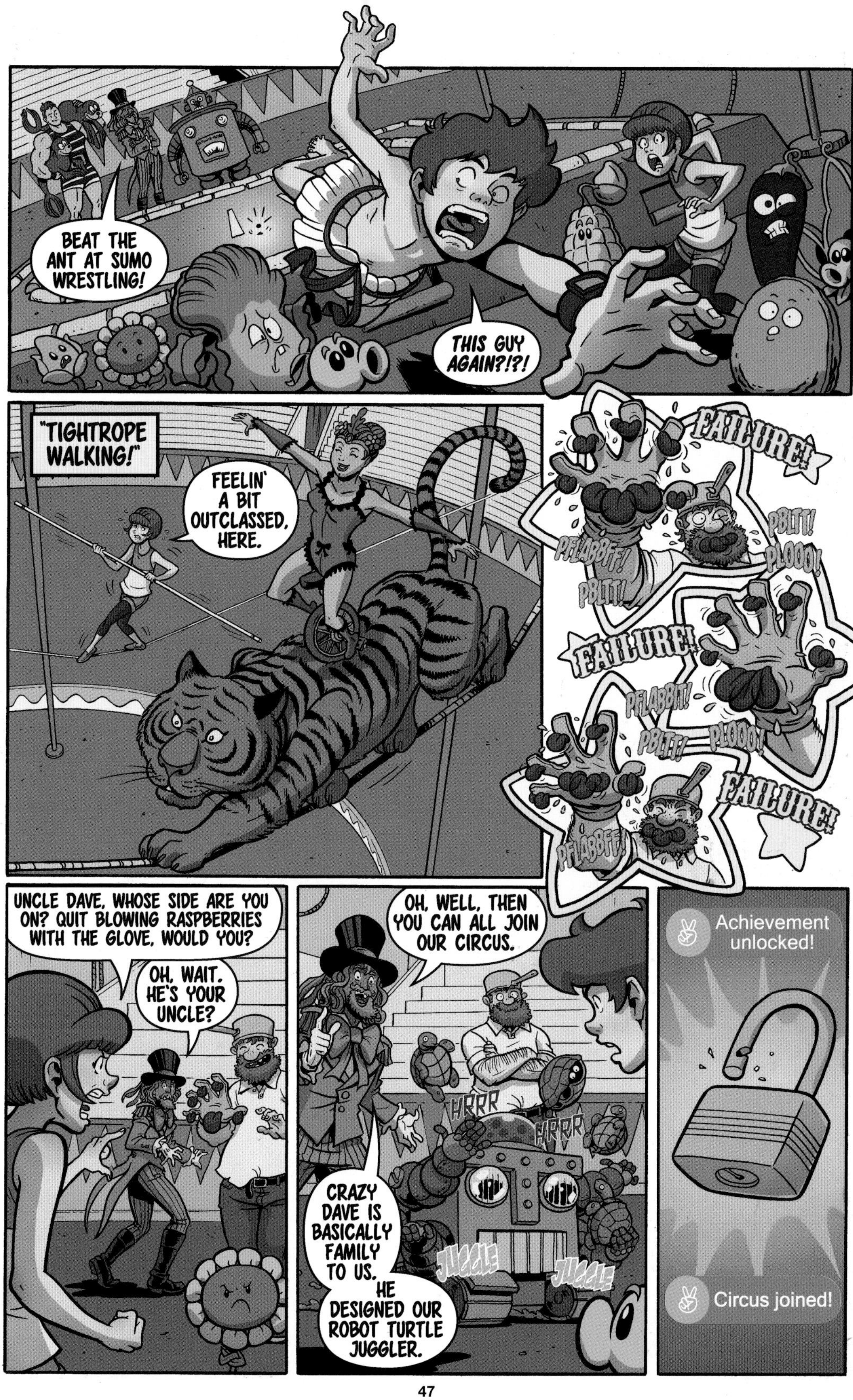
BEAT THE ANT AT SUMO WRESTLING!
THIS GUY AGAIN?!?!
"TIGHTROPE WALKING!"
FEELIN' A BIT OUTCLASSED, HERE.
FAILURE!
PBLTT!
PLOOO!
PFLABBFT!
PBLTT!
FAILURE!
PFLABBIT!
PBLTT!
PLOOO!
FAILURE!
PFLABBFT!
UNCLE DAVE, WHOSE SIDE ARE YOU ON? QUIT BLOWING RASPBERRIES WITH THE GLOVE, WOULD YOU?
OH, WAIT. HE'S YOUR UNCLE?
OH, WELL, THEN YOU CAN ALL JOIN OUR CIRCUS.
HRRR
HRRR
CRAZY DAVE IS BASICALLY FAMILY TO US.
HE DESIGNED OUR ROBOT TURTLE JUGGLER.
JUGGLE
JUGGLE
Achievement unlocked!
Circus joined!

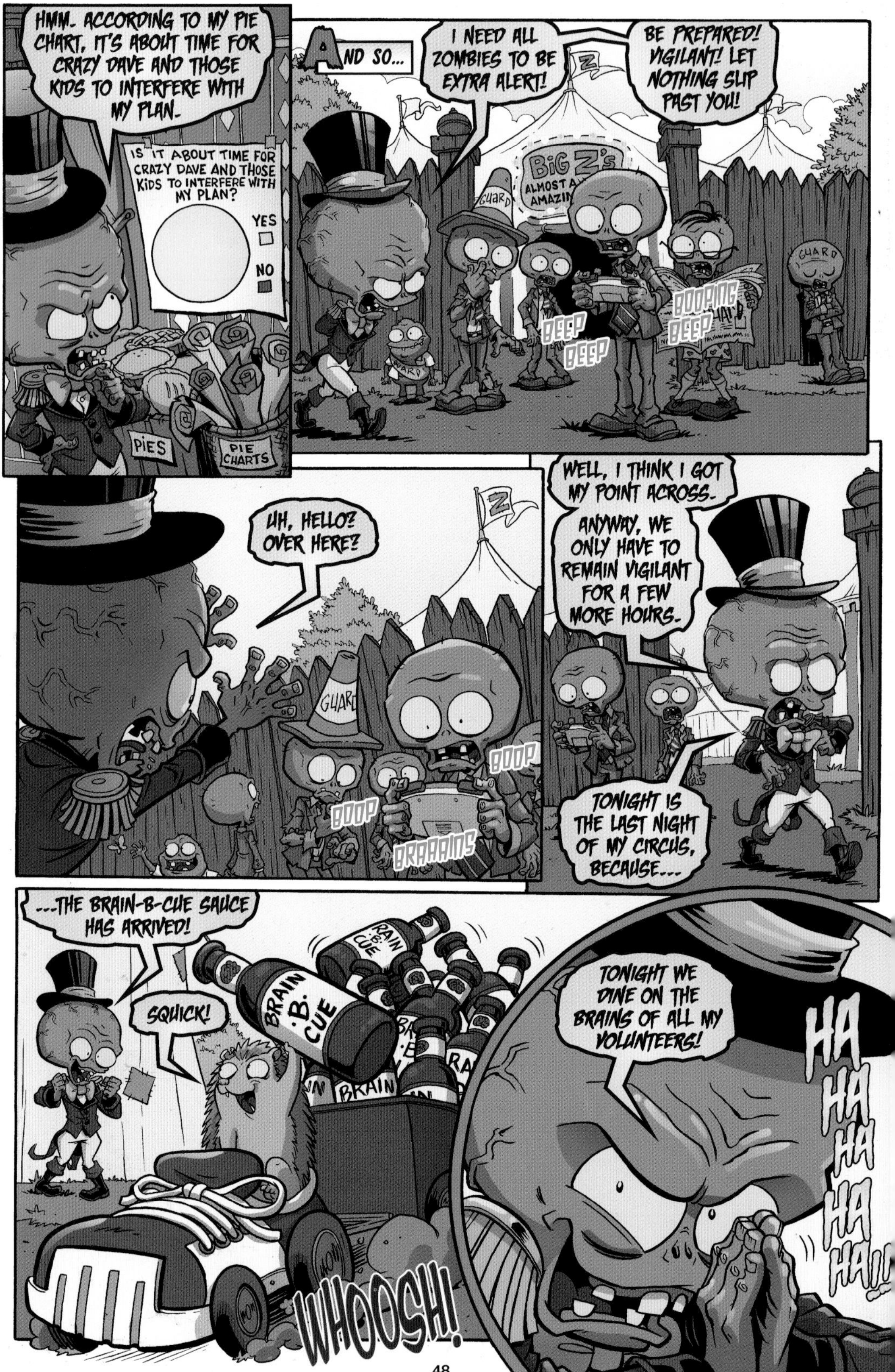
HMM. ACCORDING TO MY PIE CHART, IT'S ABOUT TIME FOR CRAZY DAVE AND THOSE KIDS TO INTERFERE WITH MY PLAN.
IS IT ABOUT TIME FOR CRAZY DAVE AND THOSE KIDS TO INTERFERE WITH MY PLAN?
YES
NO
PIES
PIE CHARTS
AND SO...
I NEED ALL ZOMBIES TO BE EXTRA ALERT!
BE PREPARED! VIGILANT! LET NOTHING SLIP PAST YOU!
BIG Z'S
GUARD
BEEP
BEEP
BOOPING
BEEP
GUARD
UH, HELLO? OVER HERE?
GUARD
BOOP
BOOP
BRAAAINS
WELL, I THINK I GOT MY POINT ACROSS.
ANYWAY, WE ONLY HAVE TO REMAIN VIGILANT FOR A FEW MORE HOURS.
TONIGHT IS THE LAST NIGHT OF MY CIRCUS, BECAUSE...
...THE BRAIN-B-CUE SAUCE HAS ARRIVED!
SQUICK!
BRAIN B CUE
BRAIN
TONIGHT WE DINE ON THE BRAINS OF ALL MY VOLUNTEERS!
HA HA HA HA HA!!
WHOOSH!

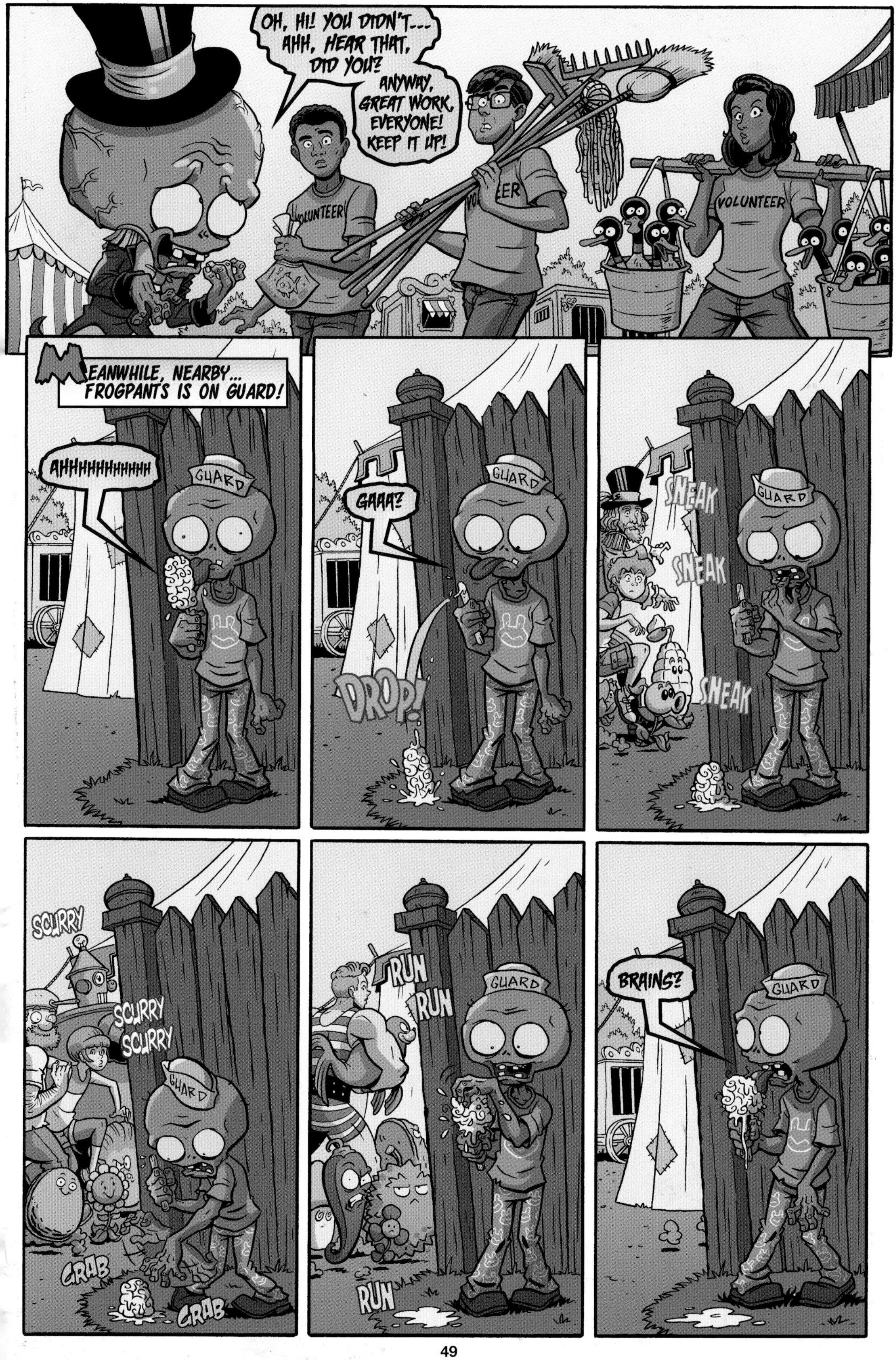
OH, HI! YOU DIDN'T... AHH, HEAR THAT, DID YOU?
ANYWAY, GREAT WORK, EVERYONE! KEEP IT UP!
VOLUNTEER
VOLUNTEER
VOLUNTEER
MEANWHILE, NEARBY... FROGPANTS IS ON GUARD!
AHHHHHHHHHHH
GUARD
GAAA?
GUARD
DROP!
SNEAK
SNEAK
SNEAK
GUARD
SCURRY
SCURRY
SCURRY
GUARD
GRAB
GRAB
RUN
RUN
GUARD
RUN
BRAINS?
GUARD

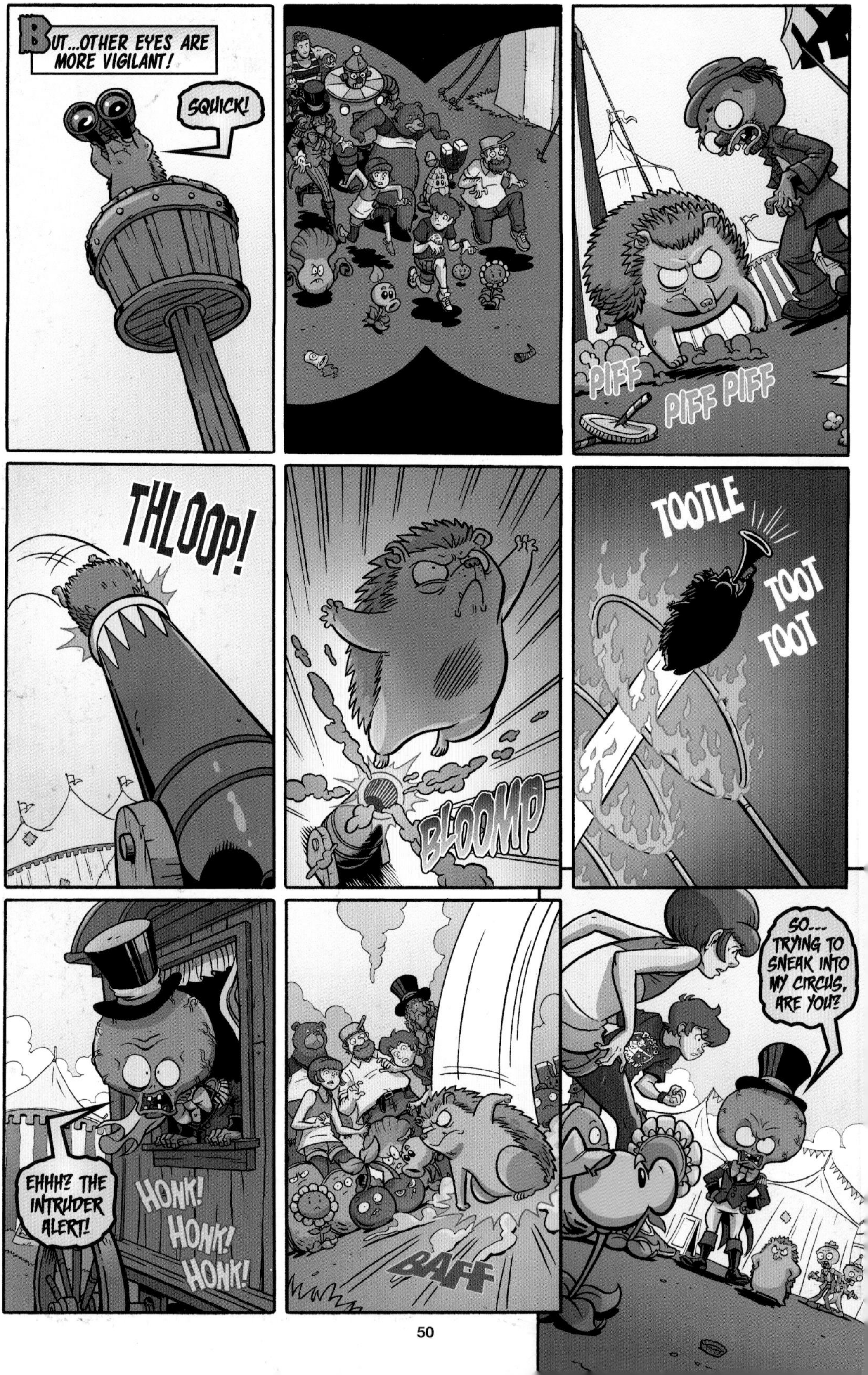
BUT...OTHER EYES ARE MORE VIGILANT!
SQUICK!
PIFF
PIFF PIFF
THLOOP!
BLOOMP
TOOTLE
TOOT
TOOT
EHHH? THE INTRUDER ALERT!
HONK!
HONK!
HONK!
BAFF
SO... TRYING TO SNEAK INTO MY CIRCUS, ARE YOU?

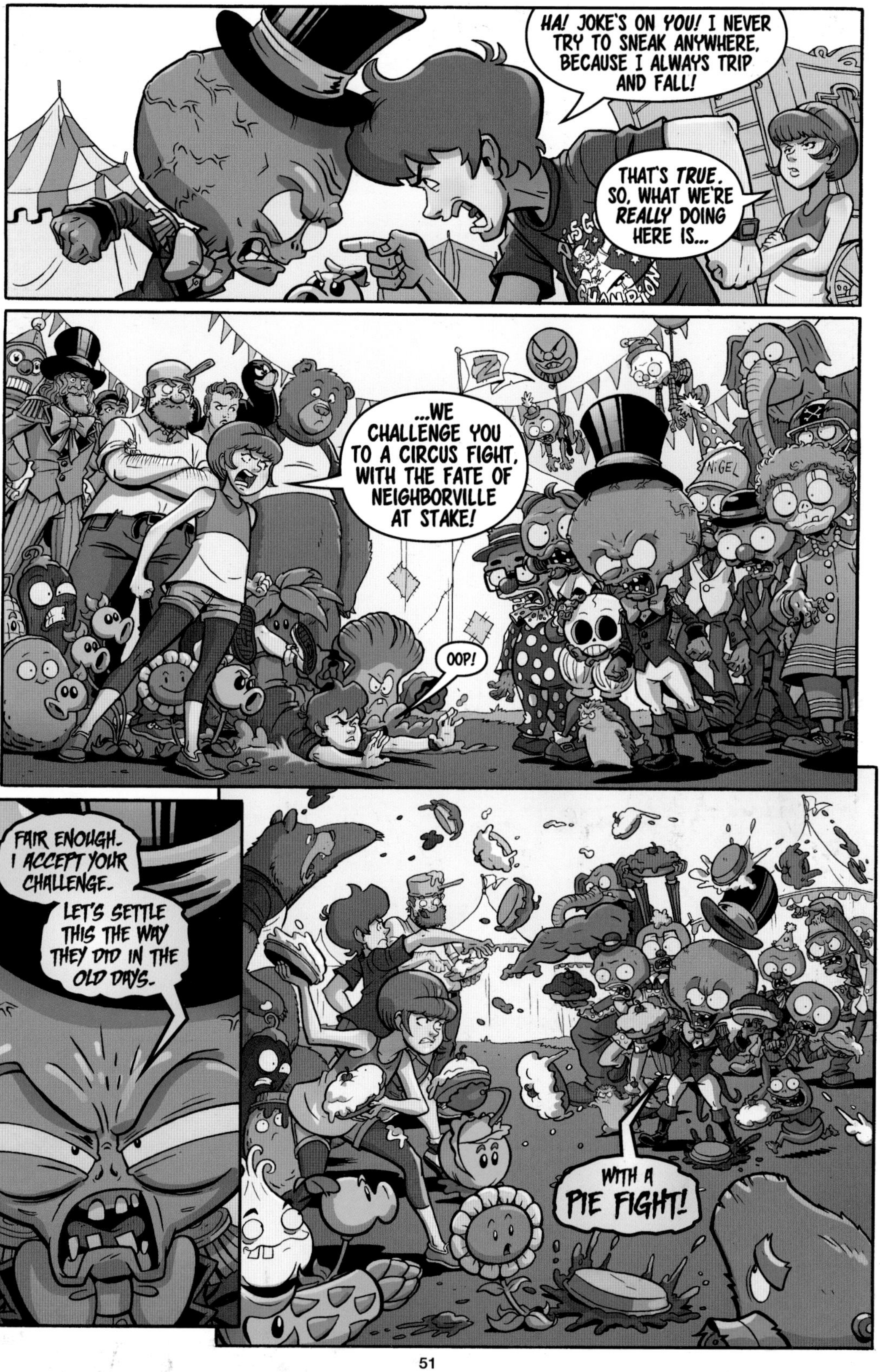
HA! JOKE'S ON YOU! I NEVER TRY TO SNEAK ANYWHERE, BECAUSE I ALWAYS TRIP AND FALL!
THAT'S TRUE. SO, WHAT WE'RE REALLY DOING HERE IS...
...WE CHALLENGE YOU TO A CIRCUS FIGHT, WITH THE FATE OF NEIGHBORVILLE AT STAKE!
OOP!
NIGEL
FAIR ENOUGH. I ACCEPT YOUR CHALLENGE.
LET'S SETTLE THIS THE WAY THEY DID IN THE OLD DAYS.
WITH A PIE FIGHT!

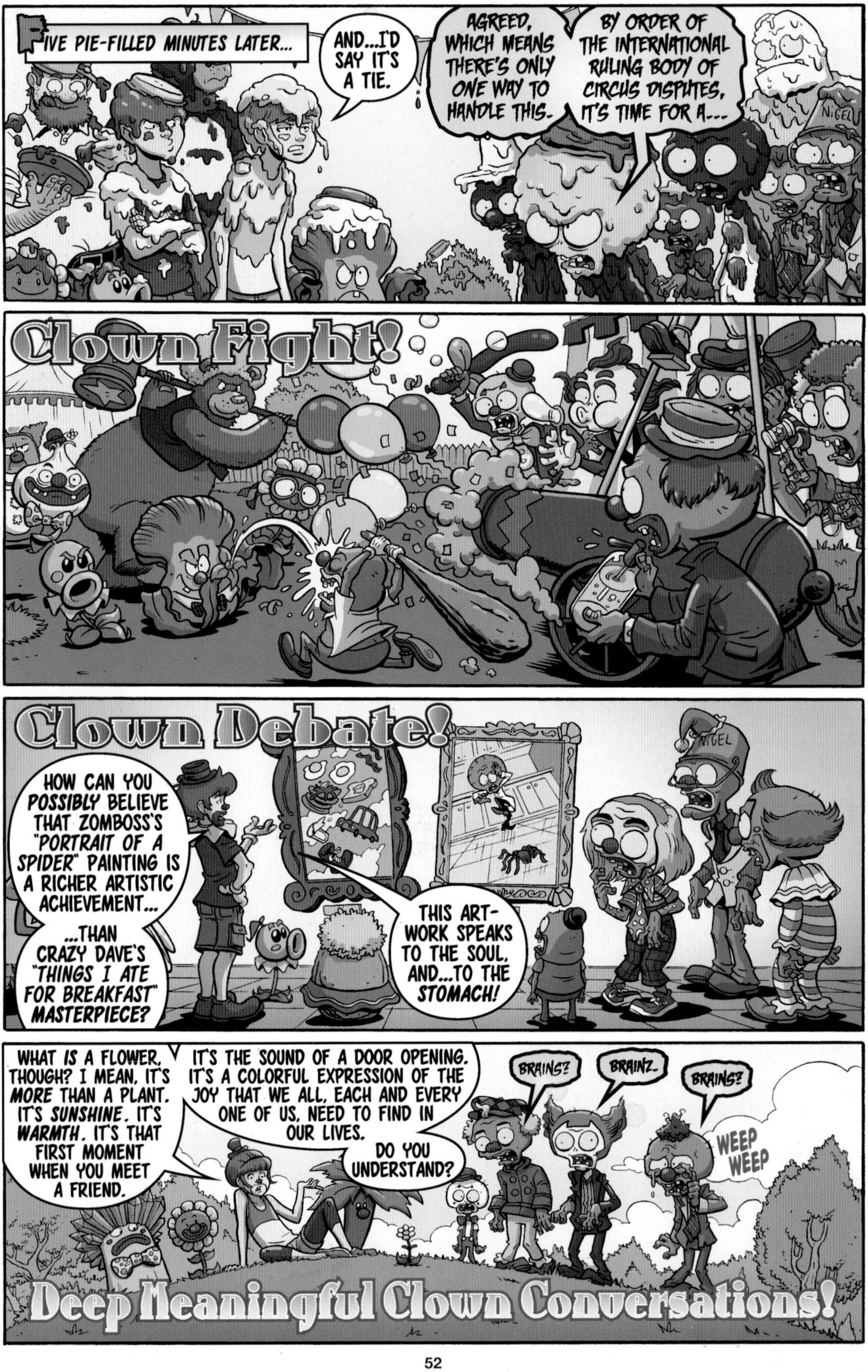
FIVE PIE-FILLED MINUTES LATER...
AND...I'D SAY IT'S A TIE.
AGREED, WHICH MEANS THERE'S ONLY ONE WAY TO HANDLE THIS.
BY ORDER OF THE INTERNATIONAL RULING BODY OF CIRCUS DISPUTES, IT'S TIME FOR A...
NIGEL
Clown Fight!
Clown Debate!
NIGEL
HOW CAN YOU POSSIBLY BELIEVE THAT ZOMBOSS'S "PORTRAIT OF A SPIDER" PAINTING IS A RICHER ARTISTIC ACHIEVEMENT...
...THAN CRAZY DAVE'S "THINGS I ATE FOR BREAKFAST" MASTERPIECE?
THIS ART-WORK SPEAKS TO THE SOUL, AND...TO THE STOMACH!
WHAT IS A FLOWER, THOUGH? I MEAN, IT'S MORE THAN A PLANT. IT'S SUNSHINE. IT'S WARMTH. IT'S THAT FIRST MOMENT WHEN YOU MEET A FRIEND.
IT'S THE SOUND OF A DOOR OPENING. IT'S A COLORFUL EXPRESSION OF THE JOY THAT WE ALL, EACH AND EVERY ONE OF US, NEED TO FIND IN OUR LIVES.
DO YOU UNDERSTAND?
BRAINS?
BRAINZ.
BRAINS?
WEEP WEEP
Deep Meaningful Clown Conversations!

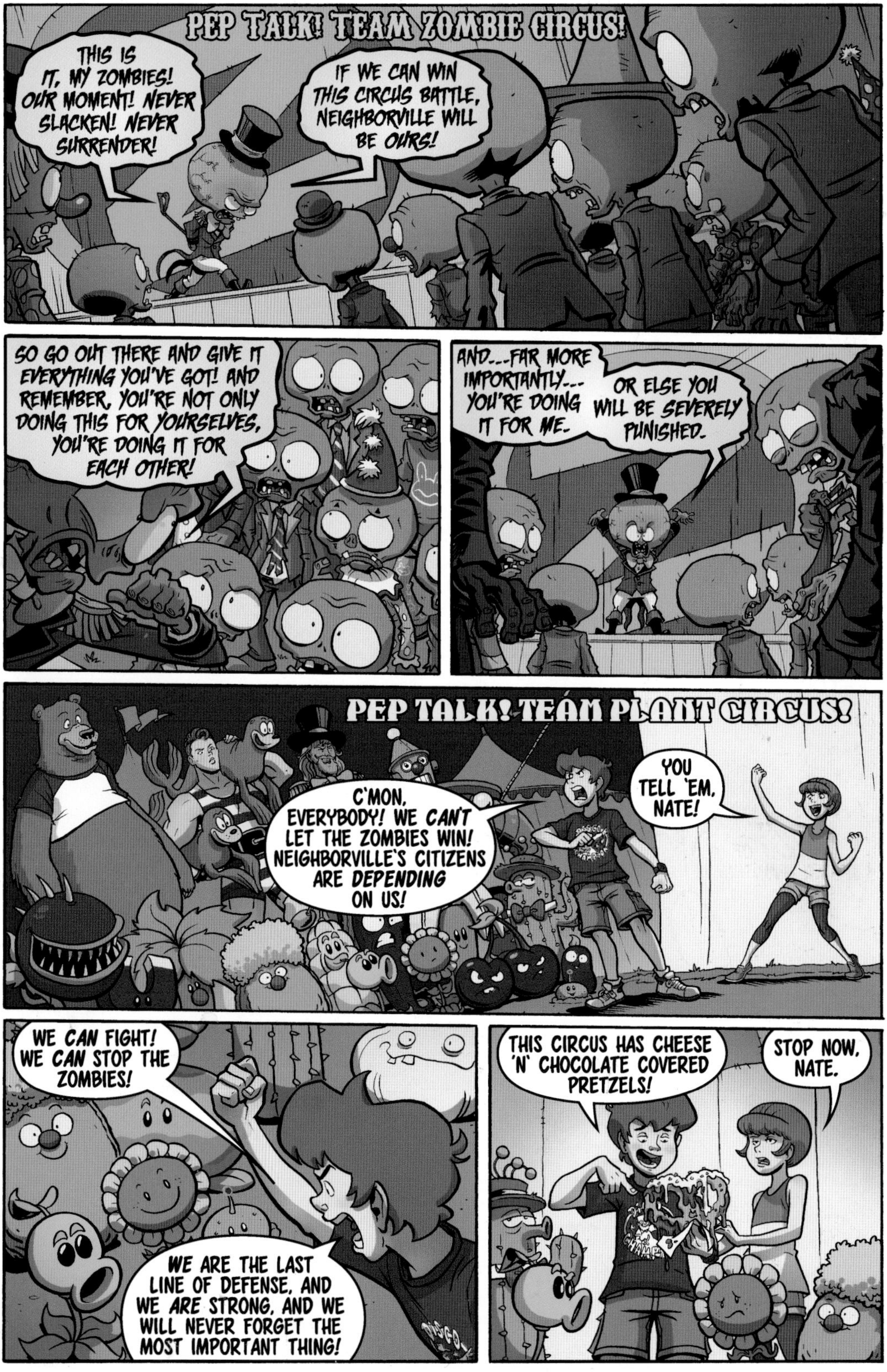

PEP TALK! TEAM ZOMBIE CIRCUS!
THIS IS IT, MY ZOMBIES! OUR MOMENT! NEVER SLACKEN! NEVER SURRENDER!
IF WE CAN WIN THIS CIRCUS BATTLE, NEIGHBORVILLE WILL BE OURS!
SO GO OUT THERE AND GIVE IT EVERYTHING YOU'VE GOT! AND REMEMBER, YOU'RE NOT ONLY DOING THIS FOR YOURSELVES, YOU'RE DOING IT FOR EACH OTHER!
AND...FAR MORE IMPORTANTLY... YOU'RE DOING IT FOR ME.
OR ELSE YOU WILL BE SEVERELY PUNISHED.
PEP TALK! TEAM PLANT CIRCUS!
C'MON, EVERYBODY! WE CAN'T LET THE ZOMBIES WIN! NEIGHBORVILLE'S CITIZENS ARE DEPENDING ON US!
YOU TELL 'EM, NATE!
WE CAN FIGHT! WE CAN STOP THE ZOMBIES!
WE ARE THE LAST LINE OF DEFENSE, AND WE ARE STRONG, AND WE WILL NEVER FORGET THE MOST IMPORTANT THING!
THIS CIRCUS HAS CHEESE 'N' CHOCOLATE COVERED PRETZELS!
STOP NOW, NATE.

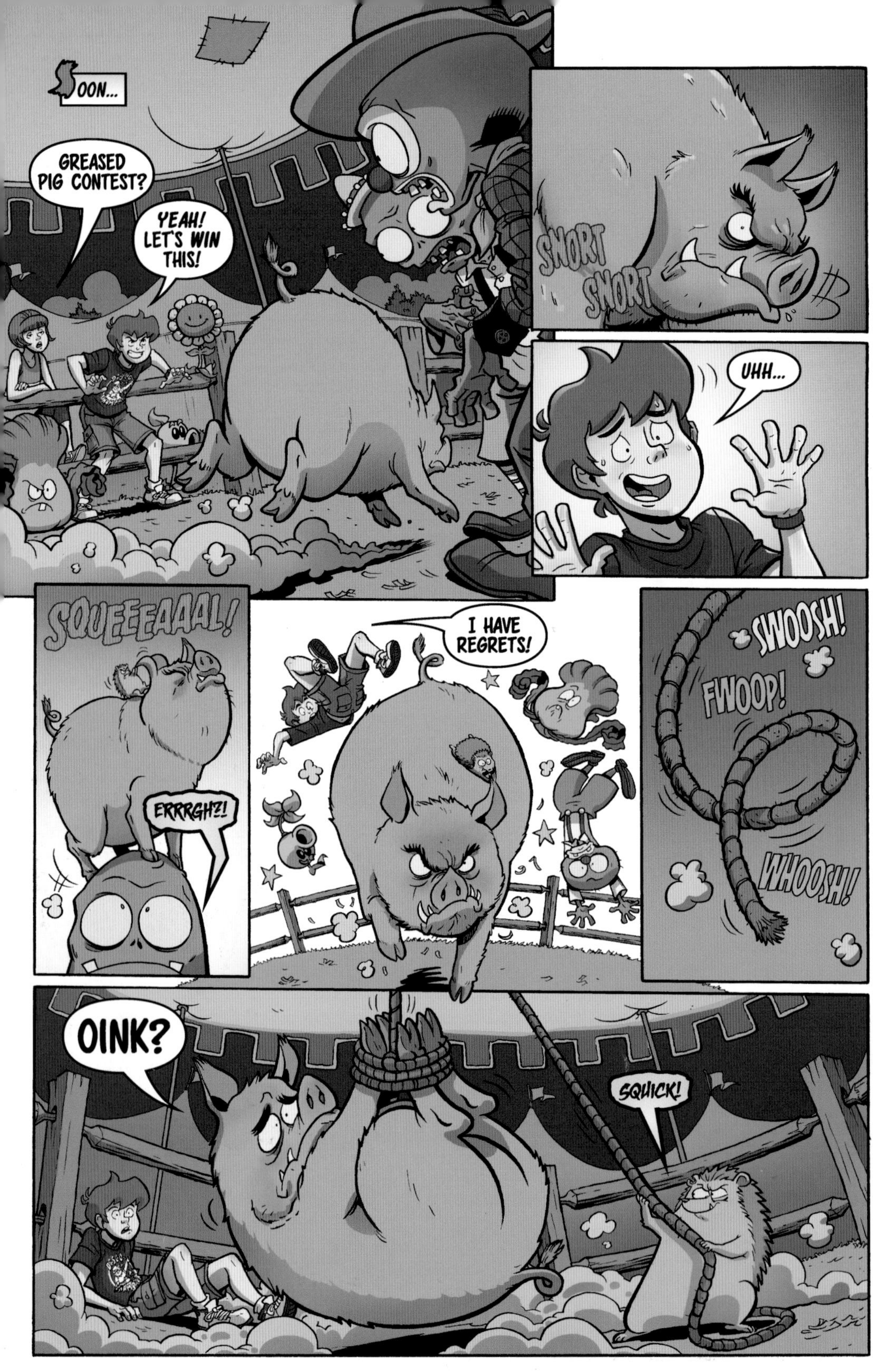
SOON...
GREASED PIG CONTEST?
YEAH! LET'S WIN THIS!
SNORT
SNORT
UHH...
SQUEEEAAAL!
ERRRGH?!
I HAVE REGRETS!
SWOOSH!
FWOOP!
WHOOSH!
OINK?
SQUICK!

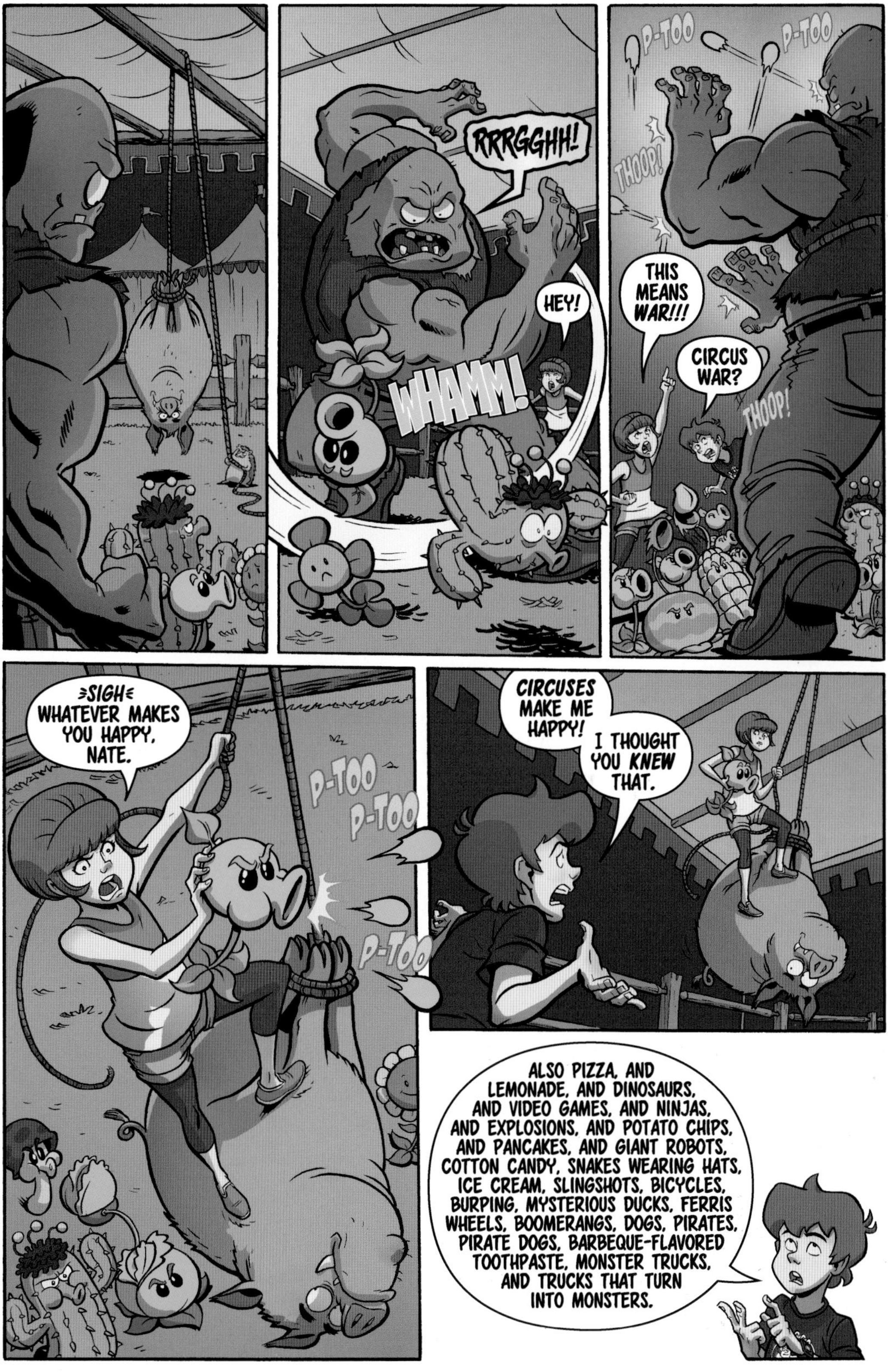
RRRGGHH!
HEY!
WHAMM!
P-TOO
P-TOO
THOOP!
THIS MEANS WAR!!!
CIRCUS WAR?
THOOP!
SIGH WHATEVER MAKES YOU HAPPY, NATE.
P-TOO
P-TOO
P-TOO
CIRCUSES MAKE ME HAPPY!
I THOUGHT YOU KNEW THAT.
ALSO PIZZA, AND LEMONADE, AND DINOSAURS, AND VIDEO GAMES, AND NINJAS, AND EXPLOSIONS, AND POTATO CHIPS, AND PANCAKES, AND GIANT ROBOTS, COTTON CANDY, SNAKES WEARING HATS, ICE CREAM, SLINGSHOTS, BICYCLES, BURPING, MYSTERIOUS DUCKS, FERRIS WHEELS, BOOMERANGS, DOGS, PIRATES, PIRATE DOGS, BARBEQUE-FLAVORED TOOTHPASTE, MONSTER TRUCKS, AND TRUCKS THAT TURN INTO MONSTERS.

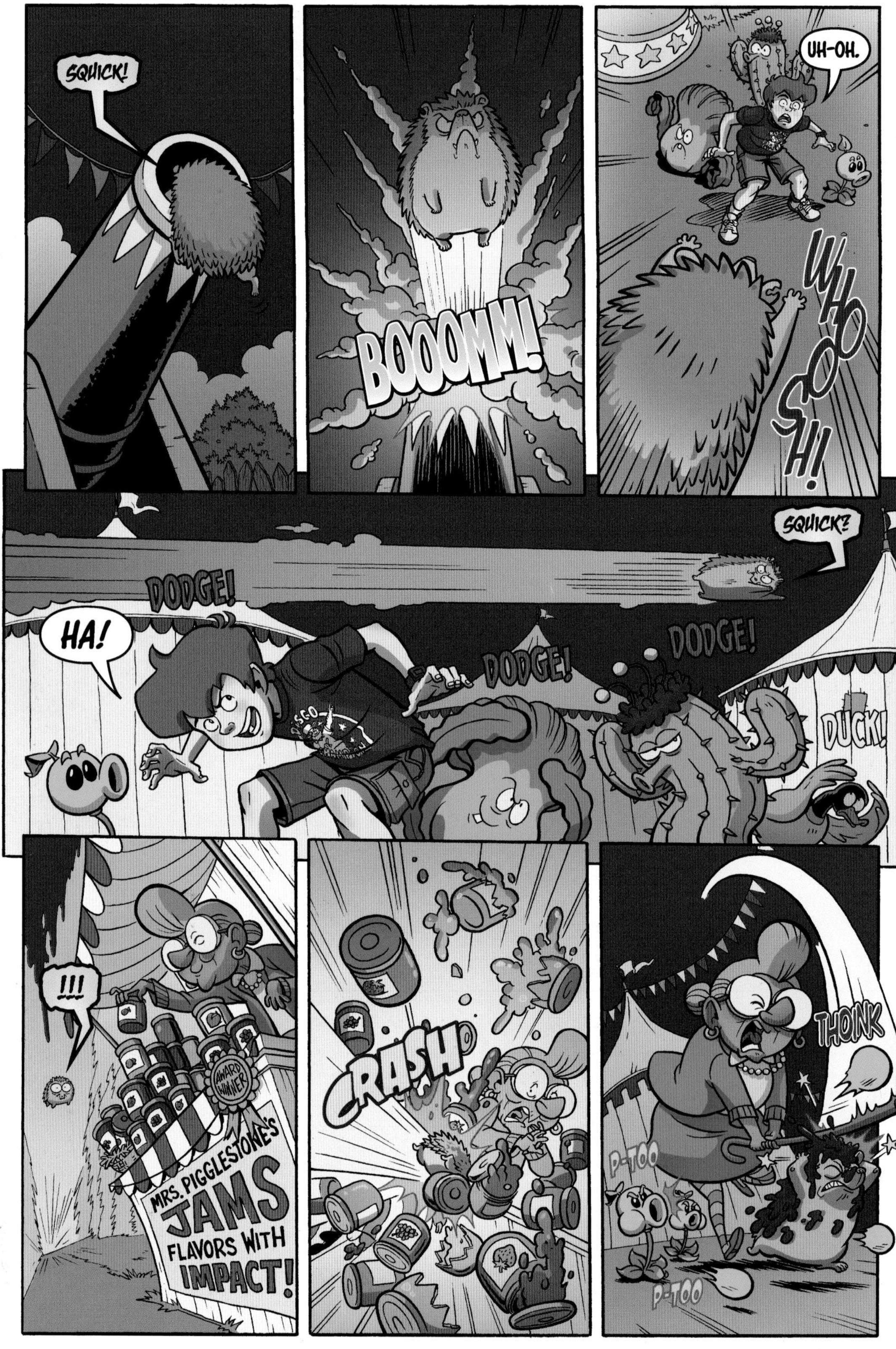
SQUICK!
BOOOMM!
UH-OH.
WHOOSH!
SQUICK?
DODGE!
HA!
DODGE!
DODGE!
DUCK!
!!!
AWARD WINNER
MRS. PIGGLESTONE'S JAMS FLAVORS WITH IMPACT!
CRASH
THONK
P-TOO
P-TOO

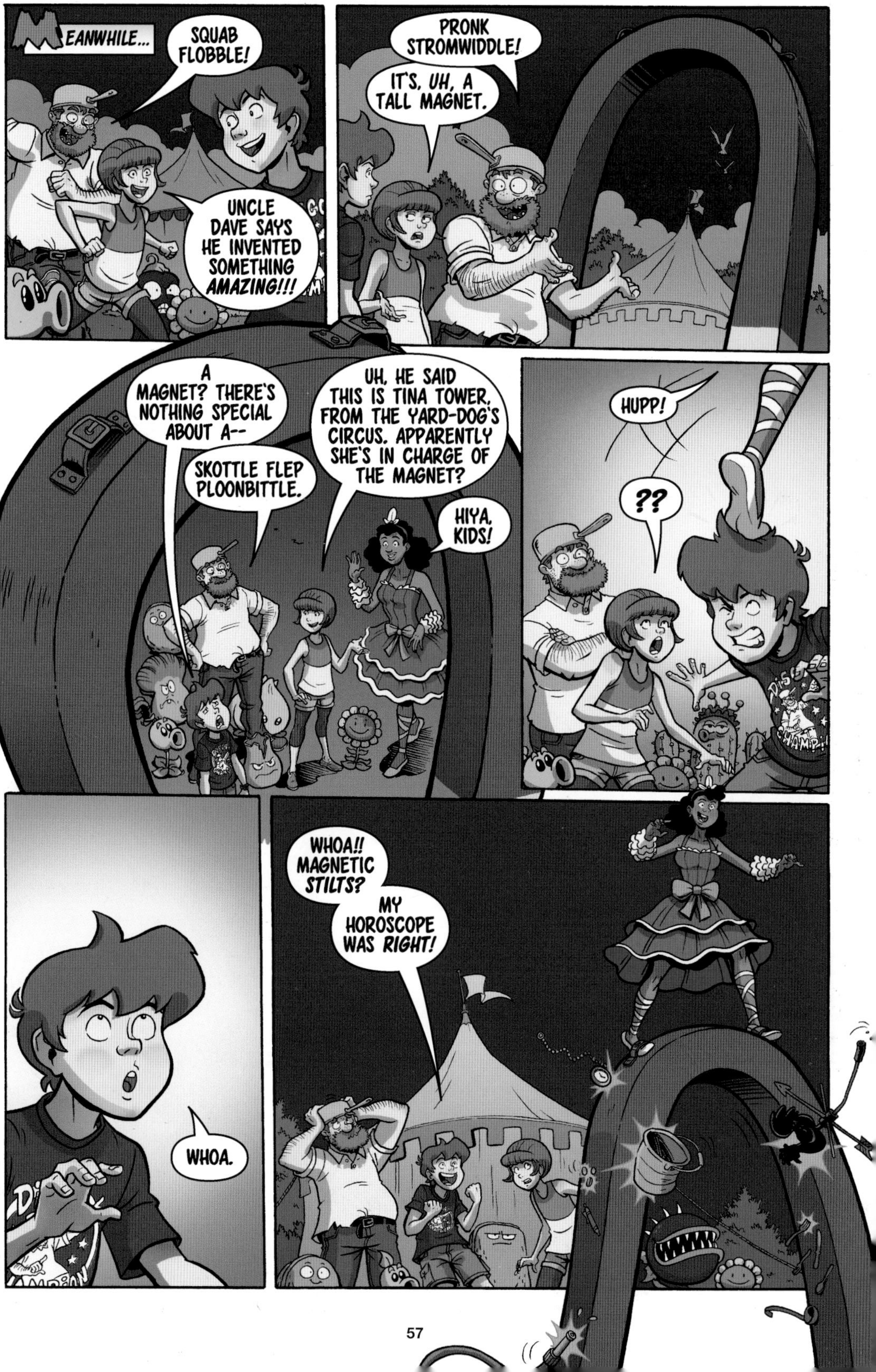
MEANWHILE...
SQUAB FLOBBLE!
UNCLE DAVE SAYS HE INVENTED SOMETHING AMAZING!!!
PRONK STROMWIDDLE!
IT'S, UH, A TALL MAGNET.
A MAGNET? THERE'S NOTHING SPECIAL ABOUT A--
SKOTTLE FLEP PLOONBITTLE.
UH, HE SAID THIS IS TINA TOWER, FROM THE YARD-DOG'S CIRCUS. APPARENTLY SHE'S IN CHARGE OF THE MAGNET?
HIYA, KIDS!
HUPP!
??
WHOA.
WHOA!! MAGNETIC STILTS?
MY HOROSCOPE WAS RIGHT!

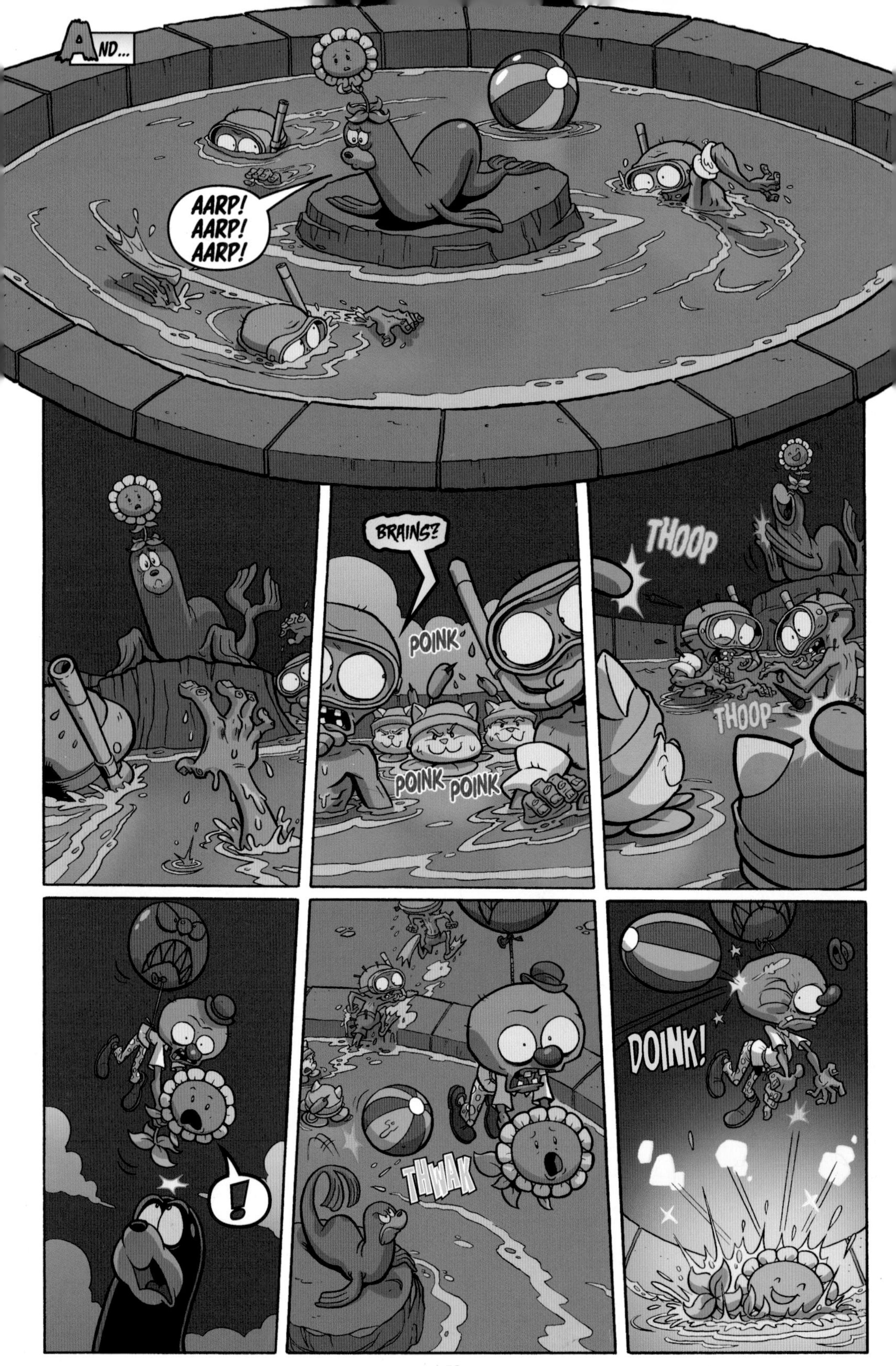
AND...
AARP! AARP! AARP!
BRAINS?
POINK
POINK POINK
THOOP
THOOP
!
THWAK
DOINK!

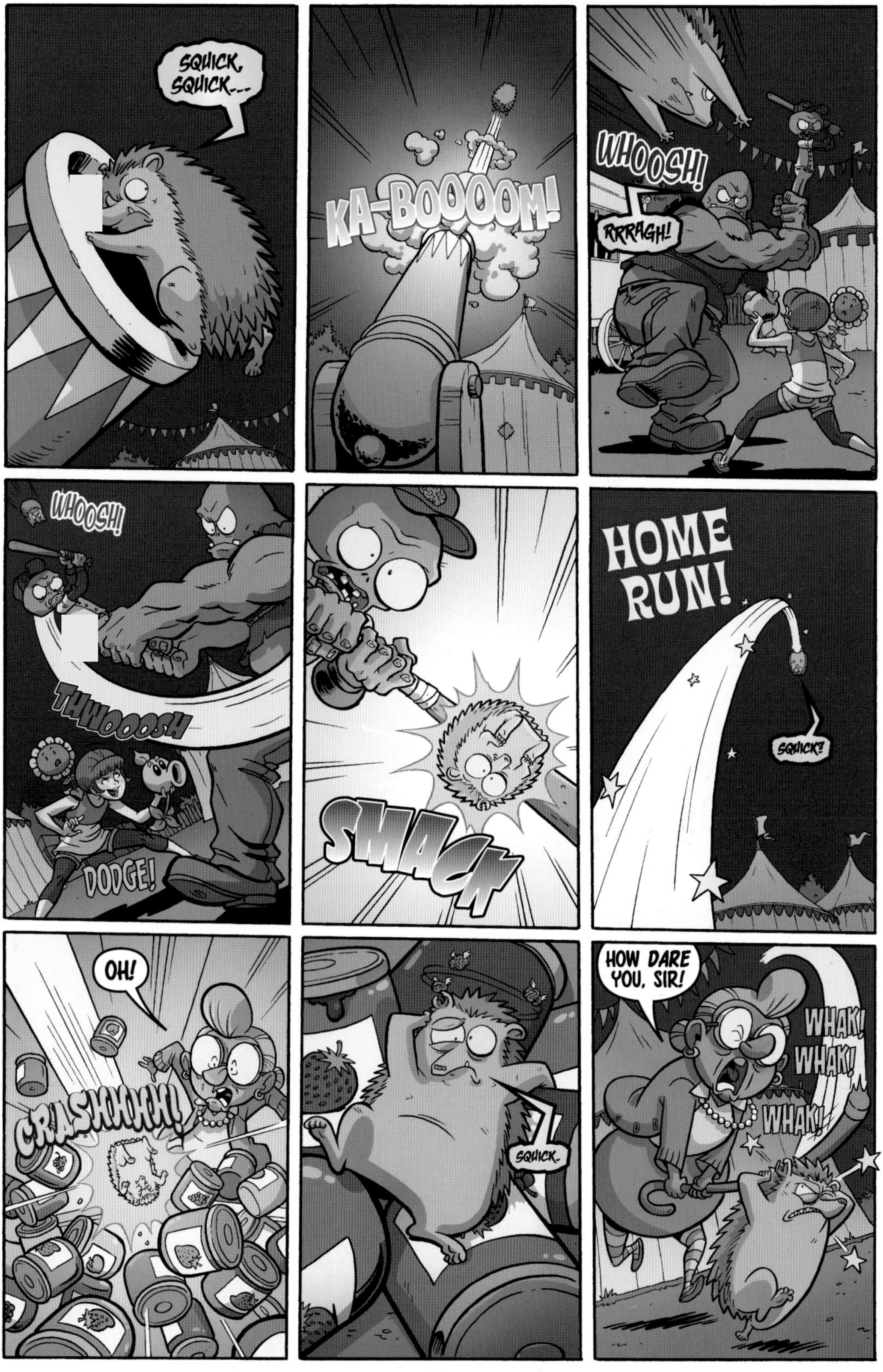
SQUICK, SQUICK...
KA-BOOOOM!
WHOOSH!
RRRAGH!
WHOOSH!
THWOOOSH
DODGE!
SMACK
HOME RUN!
SQUICK?
OH!
CRASHHHH!
SQUICK.
HOW DARE YOU, SIR!
WHAK!
WHAK!
WHAK!

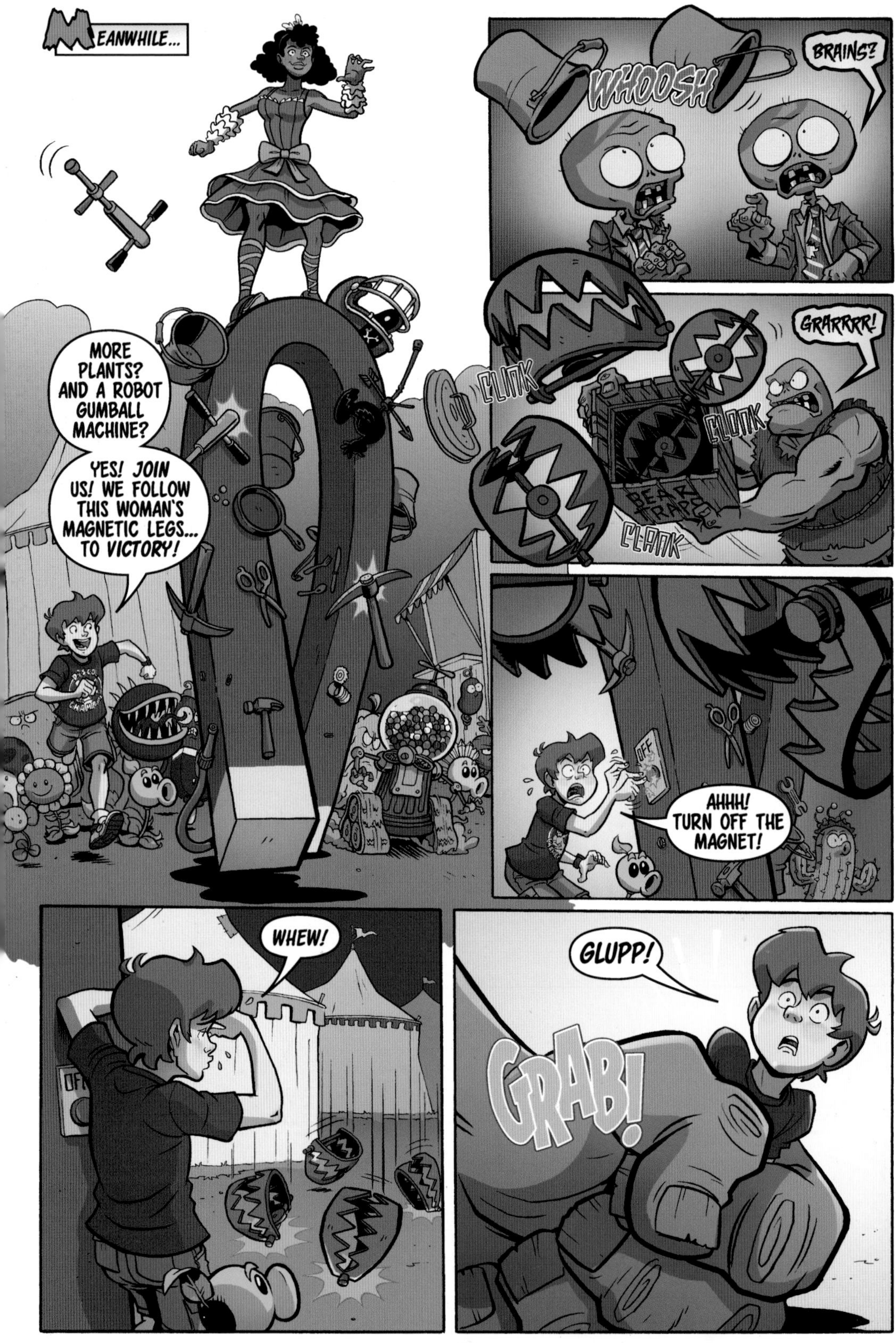
MEANWHILE...
WHOOSH
BRAINS?
MORE PLANTS? AND A ROBOT GUMBALL MACHINE?
YES! JOIN US! WE FOLLOW THIS WOMAN'S MAGNETIC LEGS... TO VICTORY!
CLINK
GRARRRR!
CLONK
CLANK
AHHH! TURN OFF THE MAGNET!
OFF
WHEW!
GLUPP!
GRAB!

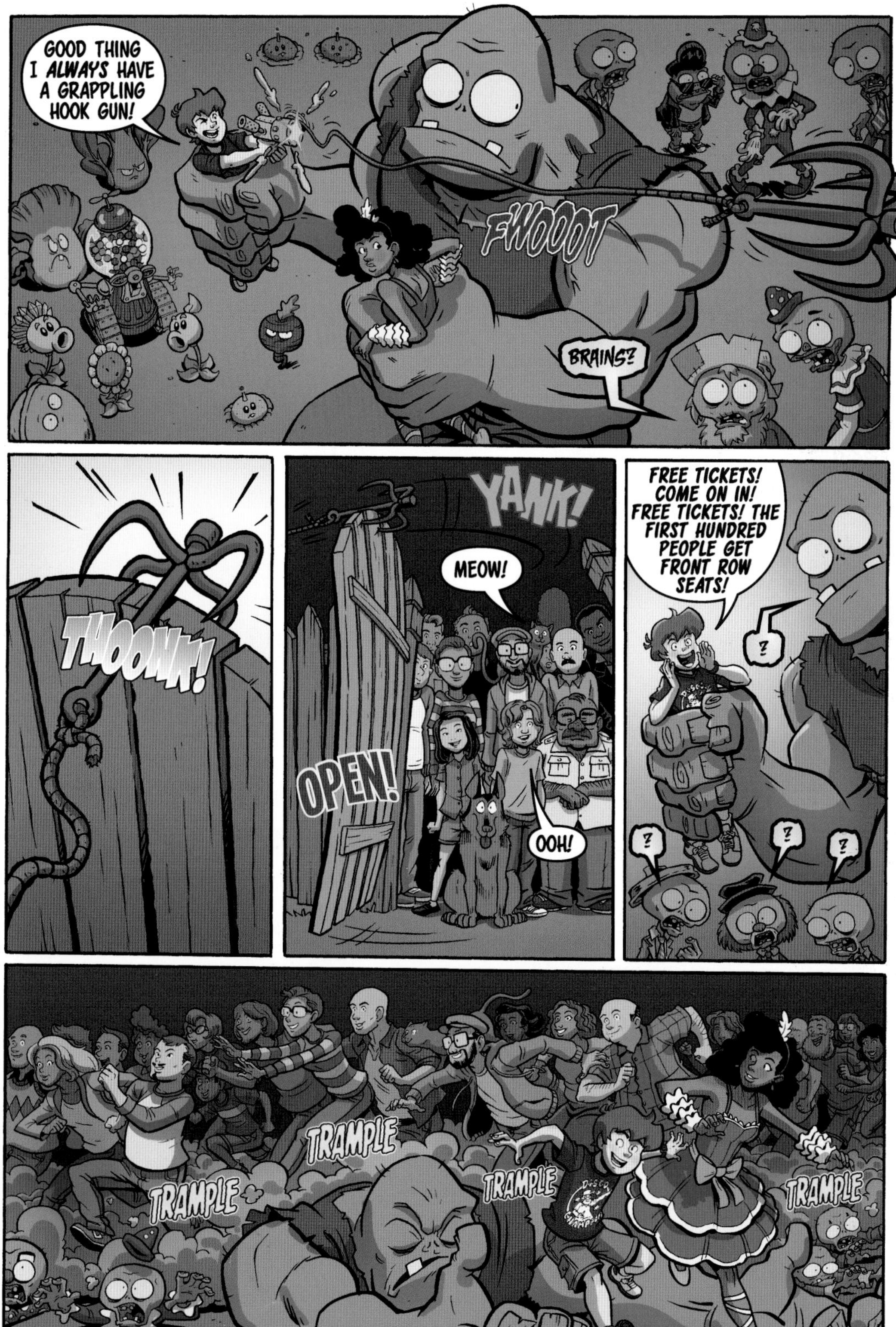
GOOD THING I ALWAYS HAVE A GRAPPLING HOOK GUN!
FWOOOT
BRAINS?
THOONK!
YANK!
MEOW!
OPEN!
OOH!
FREE TICKETS! COME ON IN! FREE TICKETS! THE FIRST HUNDRED PEOPLE GET FRONT ROW SEATS!
?
?
?
?
TRAMPLE
TRAMPLE
TRAMPLE
TRAMPLE

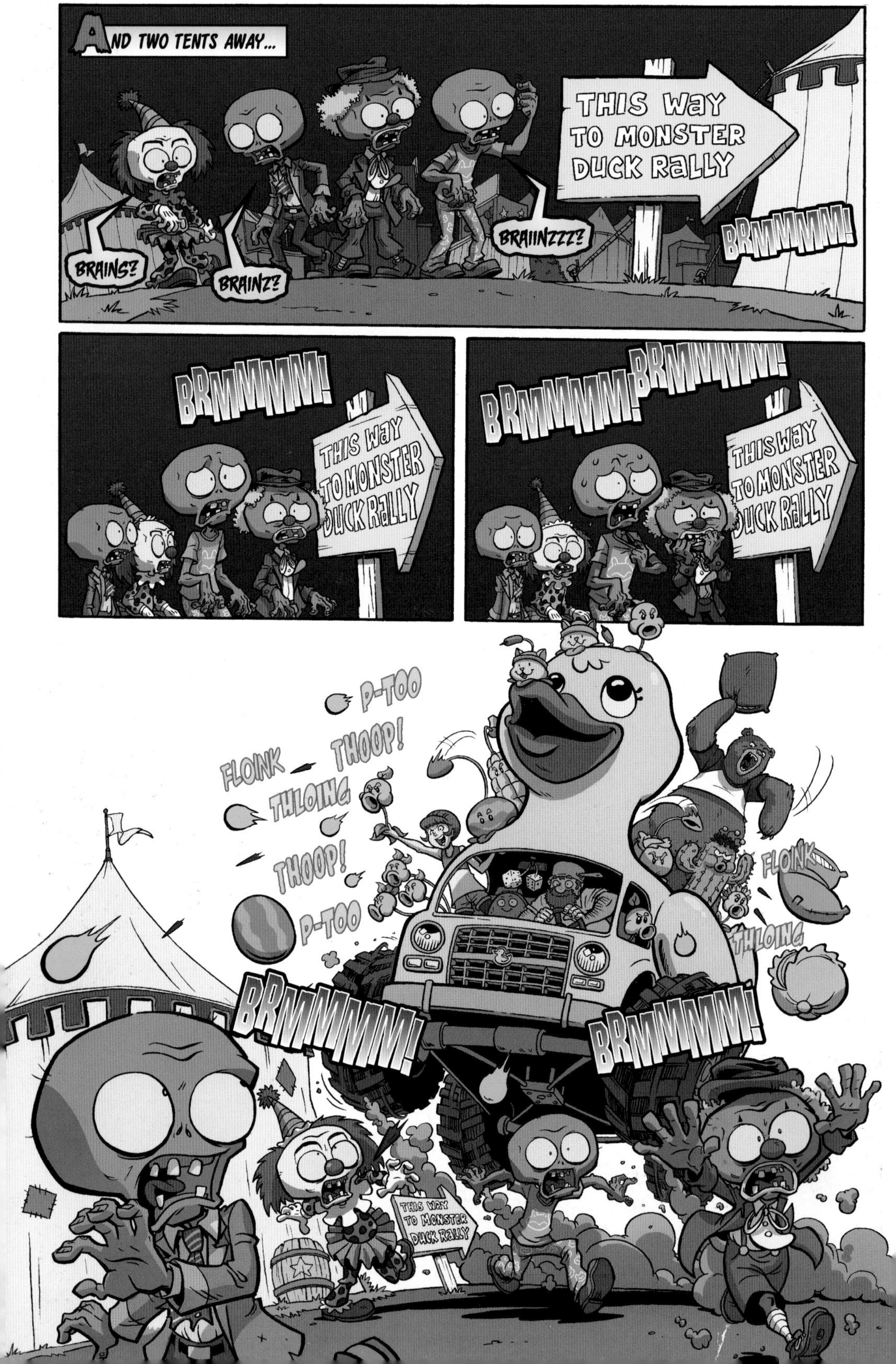
AND TWO TENTS AWAY...
THIS WAY TO MONSTER DUCK RALLY
BRAINS?
BRAINZ?
BRAIINZZZ?
BRMMMM!
BRMMMM!
THIS WAY TO MONSTER DUCK RALLY
BRMMMM! BRMMMM!
THIS WAY TO MONSTER DUCK RALLY
P-TOO
THOOP!
FLOINK
THLOING
THOOP!
P-TOO
FLOINK
THLOING
BRMMMM!
BRMMMM!
THIS WAY TO MONSTER DUCK RALLY

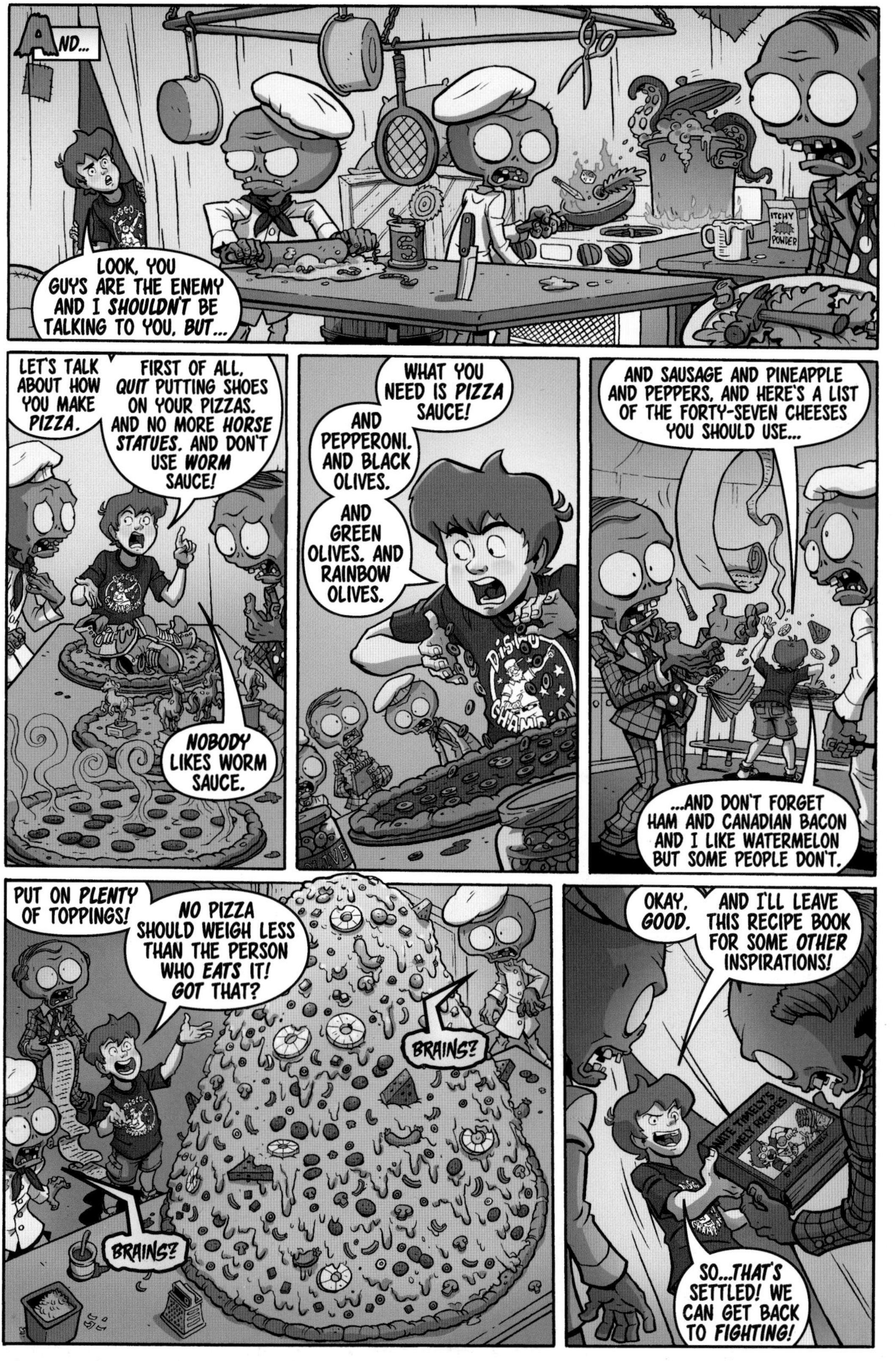
AND...
LOOK, YOU GUYS ARE THE ENEMY AND I SHOULDN'T BE TALKING TO YOU, BUT...
ITCHY POWDER
LET'S TALK ABOUT HOW YOU MAKE PIZZA.
FIRST OF ALL, QUIT PUTTING SHOES ON YOUR PIZZAS. AND NO MORE HORSE STATUES. AND DON'T USE WORM SAUCE!
NOBODY LIKES WORM SAUCE.
WHAT YOU NEED IS PIZZA SAUCE!
AND PEPPERONI. AND BLACK OLIVES.
AND GREEN OLIVES. AND RAINBOW OLIVES.
AND SAUSAGE AND PINEAPPLE AND PEPPERS, AND HERE'S A LIST OF THE FORTY-SEVEN CHEESES YOU SHOULD USE...
...AND DON'T FORGET HAM AND CANADIAN BACON AND I LIKE WATERMELON BUT SOME PEOPLE DON'T.
PUT ON PLENTY OF TOPPINGS!
NO PIZZA SHOULD WEIGH LESS THAN THE PERSON WHO EATS IT! GOT THAT?
BRAINS?
BRAINS?
OKAY, GOOD.
AND I'LL LEAVE THIS RECIPE BOOK FOR SOME OTHER INSPIRATIONS!
NATE TIMELY'S TIMELY RECIPES
SO...THAT'S SETTLED! WE CAN GET BACK TO FIGHTING!

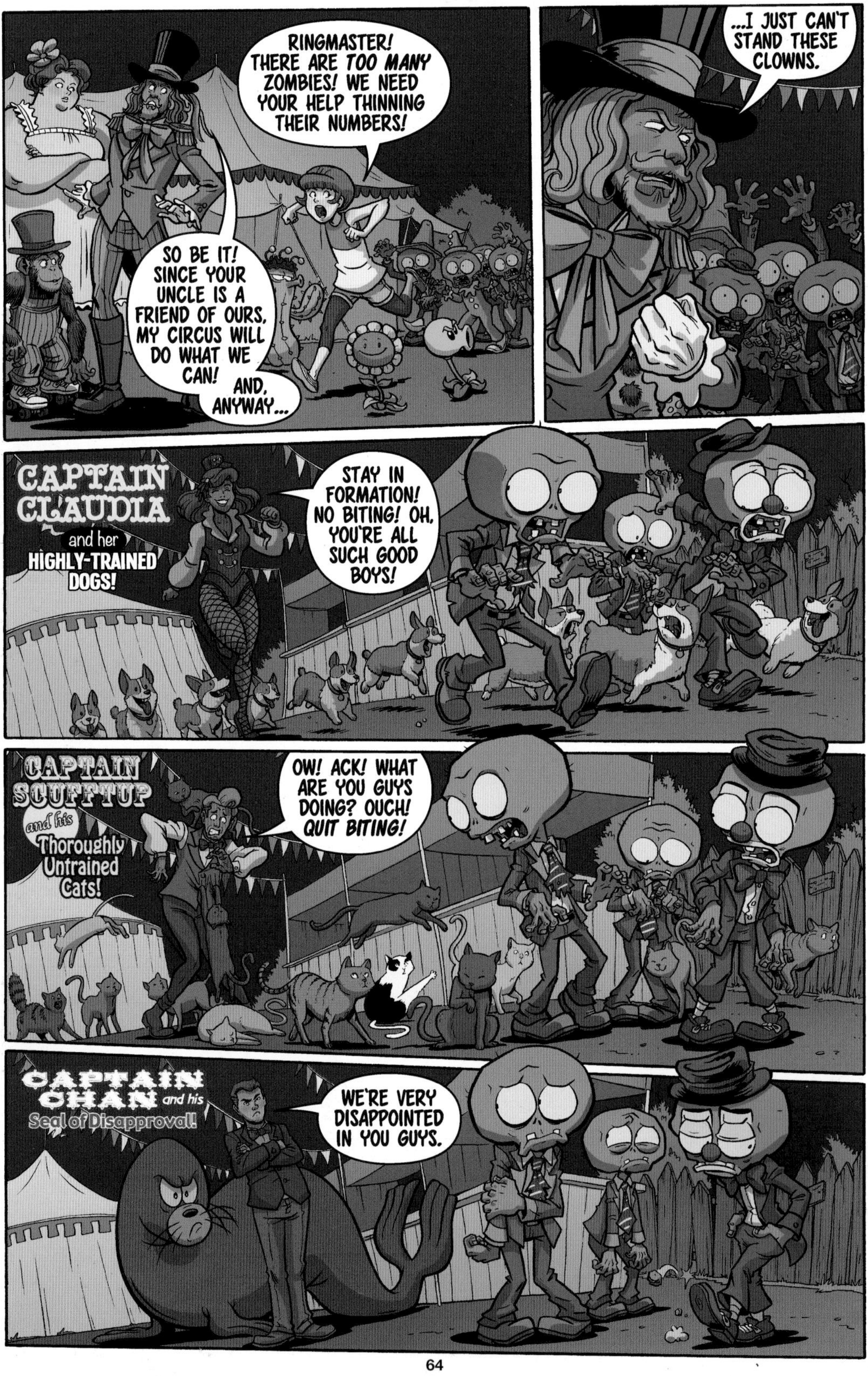
RINGMASTER! THERE ARE TOO MANY ZOMBIES! WE NEED YOUR HELP THINNING THEIR NUMBERS!
SO BE IT! SINCE YOUR UNCLE IS A FRIEND OF OURS, MY CIRCUS WILL DO WHAT WE CAN!
AND, ANYWAY...
...I JUST CAN'T STAND THESE CLOWNS.
CAPTAIN CLAUDIA and her HIGHLY-TRAINED DOGS!
STAY IN FORMATION! NO BITING! OH, YOU'RE ALL SUCH GOOD BOYS!
CAPTAIN SCUFFTUP and his Thoroughly Untrained Cats!
OW! ACK! WHAT ARE YOU GUYS DOING? OUCH! QUIT BITING!
CAPTAIN CHAN and his Seal of Disapproval!
WE'RE VERY DISAPPOINTED IN YOU GUYS.

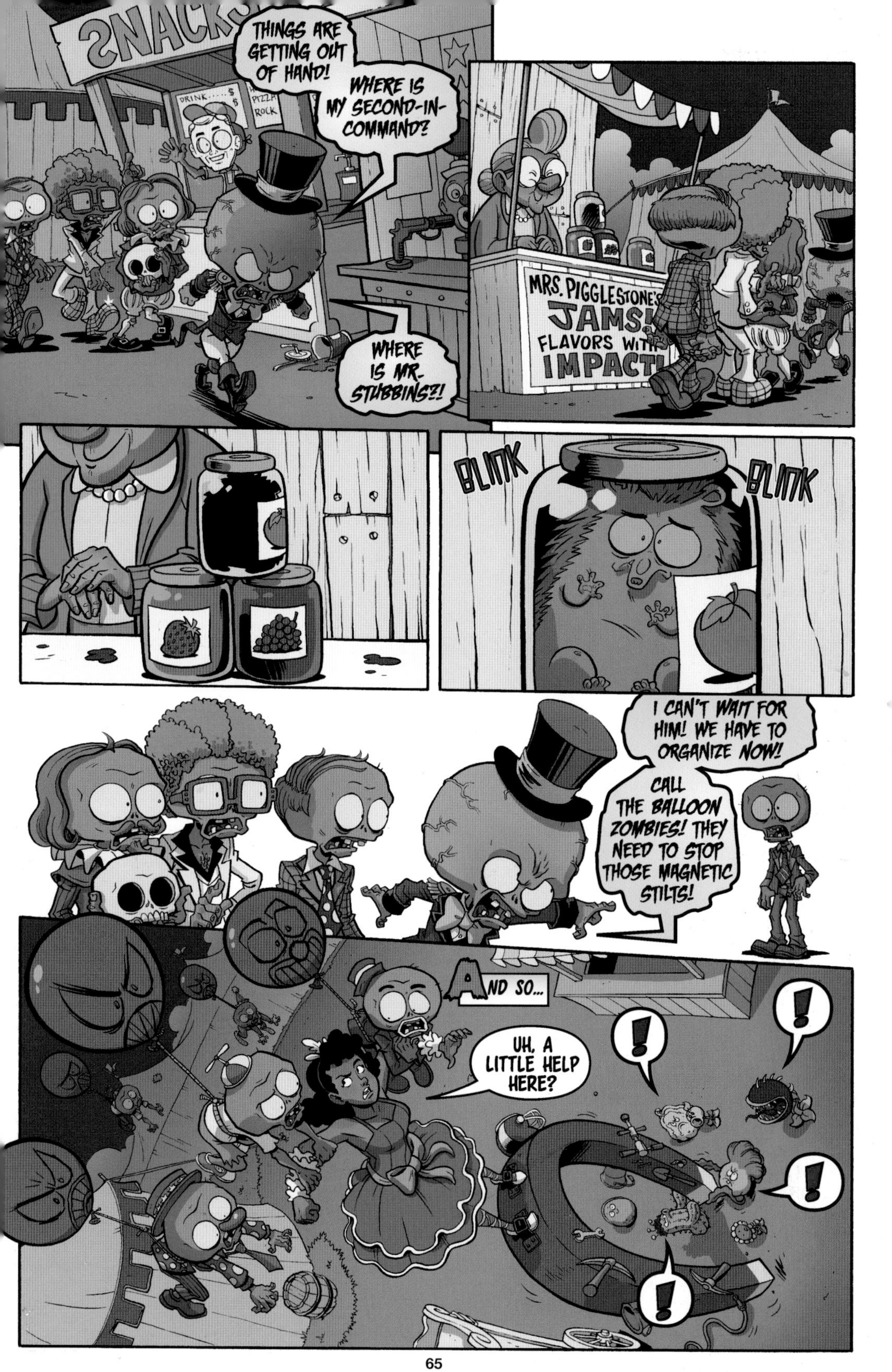
SNACKS
DRINK
PIZZA ROCK
THINGS ARE GETTING OUT OF HAND!
WHERE IS MY SECOND-IN-COMMAND?
WHERE IS MR. STUBBINS?!
MRS. PIGGLESTONE'S JAMS! FLAVORS WITH IMPACT!
BLINK
BLINK
I CAN'T WAIT FOR HIM! WE HAVE TO ORGANIZE NOW!
CALL THE BALLOON ZOMBIES! THEY NEED TO STOP THOSE MAGNETIC STILTS!
AND SO...
UH, A LITTLE HELP HERE?
!
!
!
!

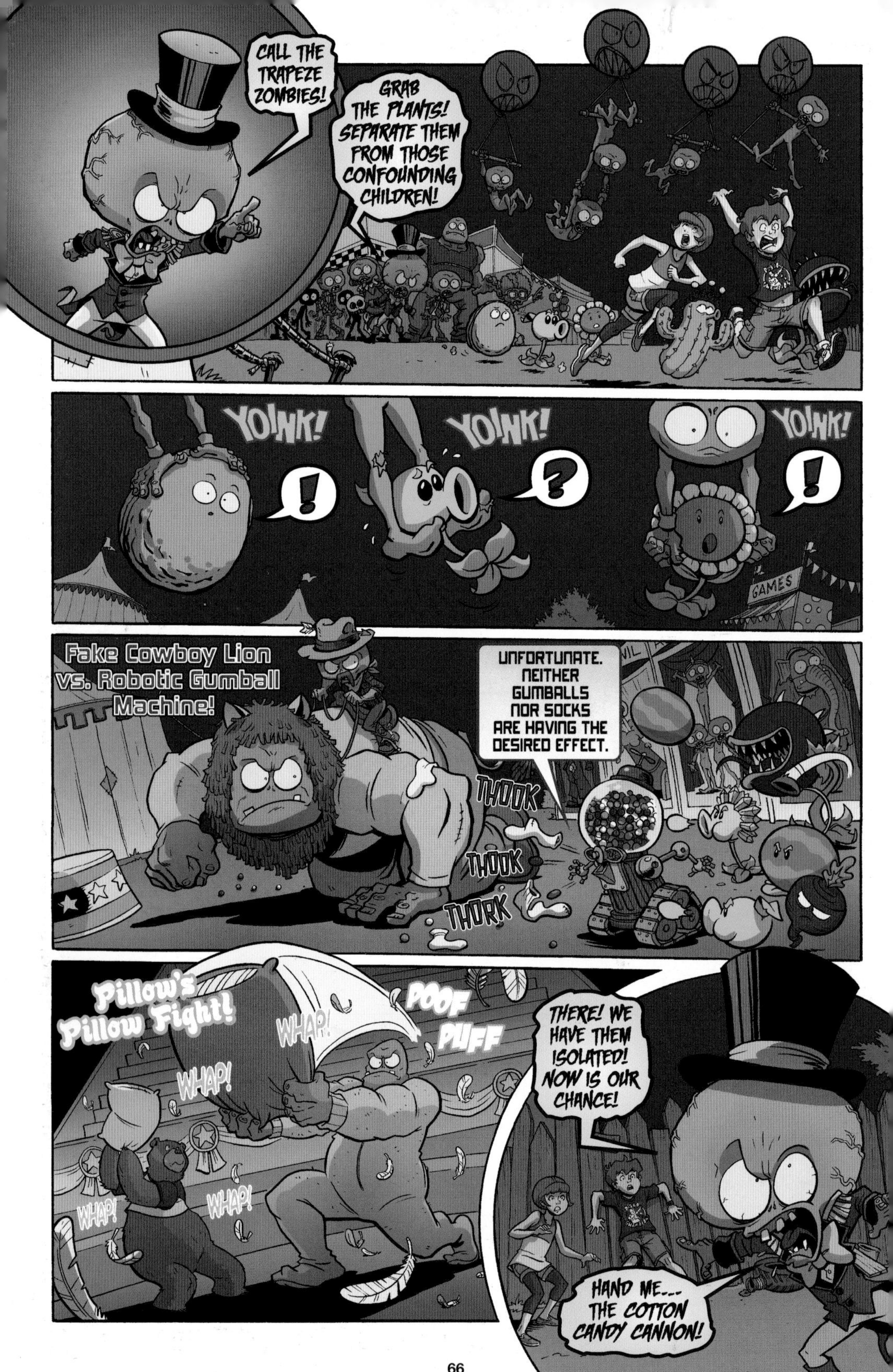

CALL THE TRAPEZE ZOMBIES!
GRAB THE PLANTS! SEPARATE THEM FROM THOSE CONFOUNDING CHILDREN!
YOINK!
!
YOINK!
?
YOINK!
!
GAMES
Fake Cowboy Lion vs. Robotic Gumball Machine!
UNFORTUNATE. NEITHER GUMBALLS NOR SOCKS ARE HAVING THE DESIRED EFFECT.
THOOK
THOOK
THORK
Pillow's Pillow Fight!
POOF
PUFF
WHAP!
WHAP!
WHAP!
WHAP!
THERE! WE HAVE THEM ISOLATED! NOW IS OUR CHANCE!
HAND ME... THE COTTON CANDY CANNON!

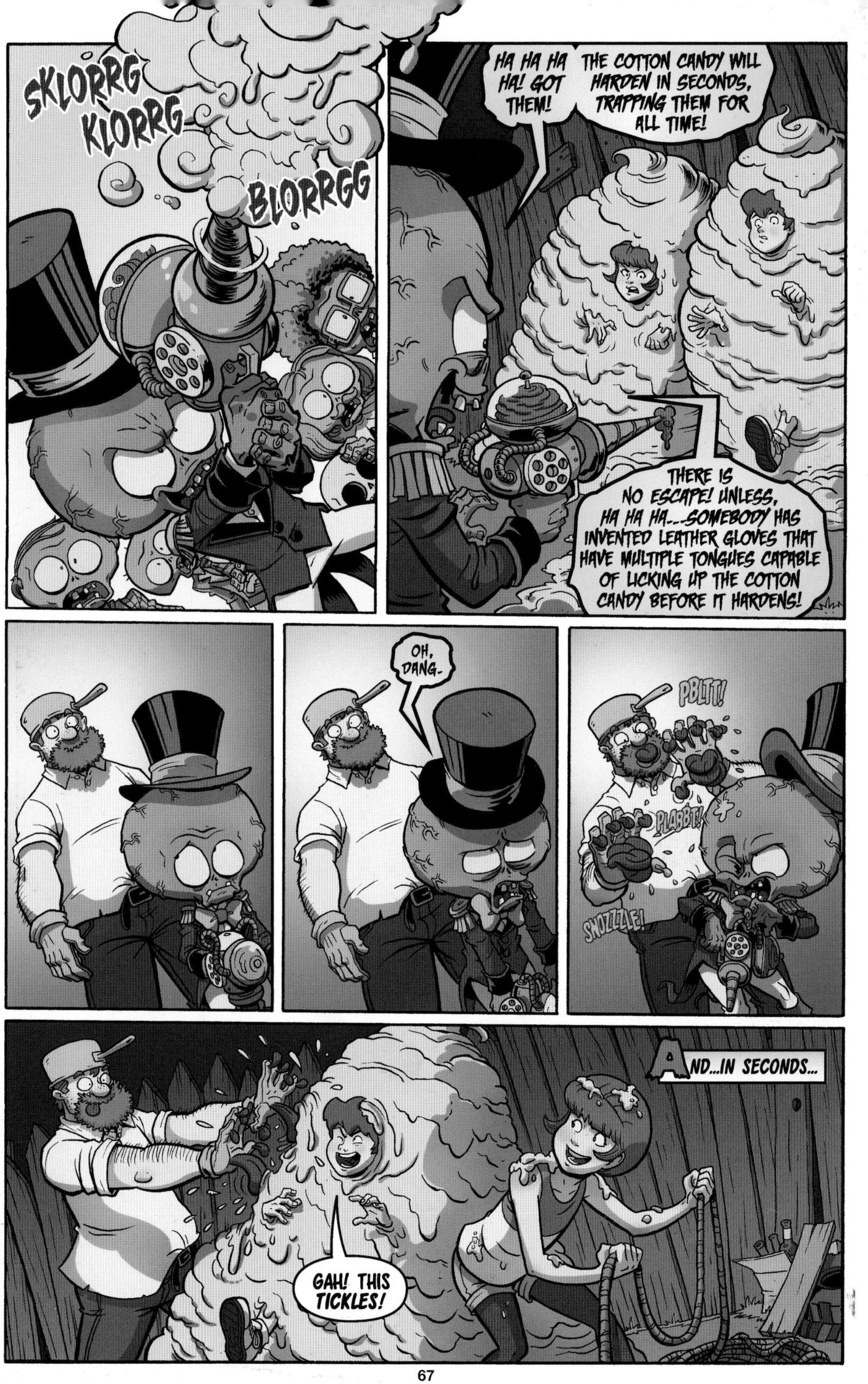
SKLORRG
KLORRG
BLORRGG
HA HA HA HA! GOT THEM!
THE COTTON CANDY WILL HARDEN IN SECONDS, TRAPPING THEM FOR ALL TIME!
THERE IS NO ESCAPE! UNLESS, HA HA HA... SOMEBODY HAS INVENTED LEATHER GLOVES THAT HAVE MULTIPLE TONGUES CAPABLE OF LICKING UP THE COTTON CANDY BEFORE IT HARDENS!
OH, DANG.
PBLTT!
PLABBT!
SNOZZZLE!
AND...IN SECONDS...
GAH! THIS TICKLES!

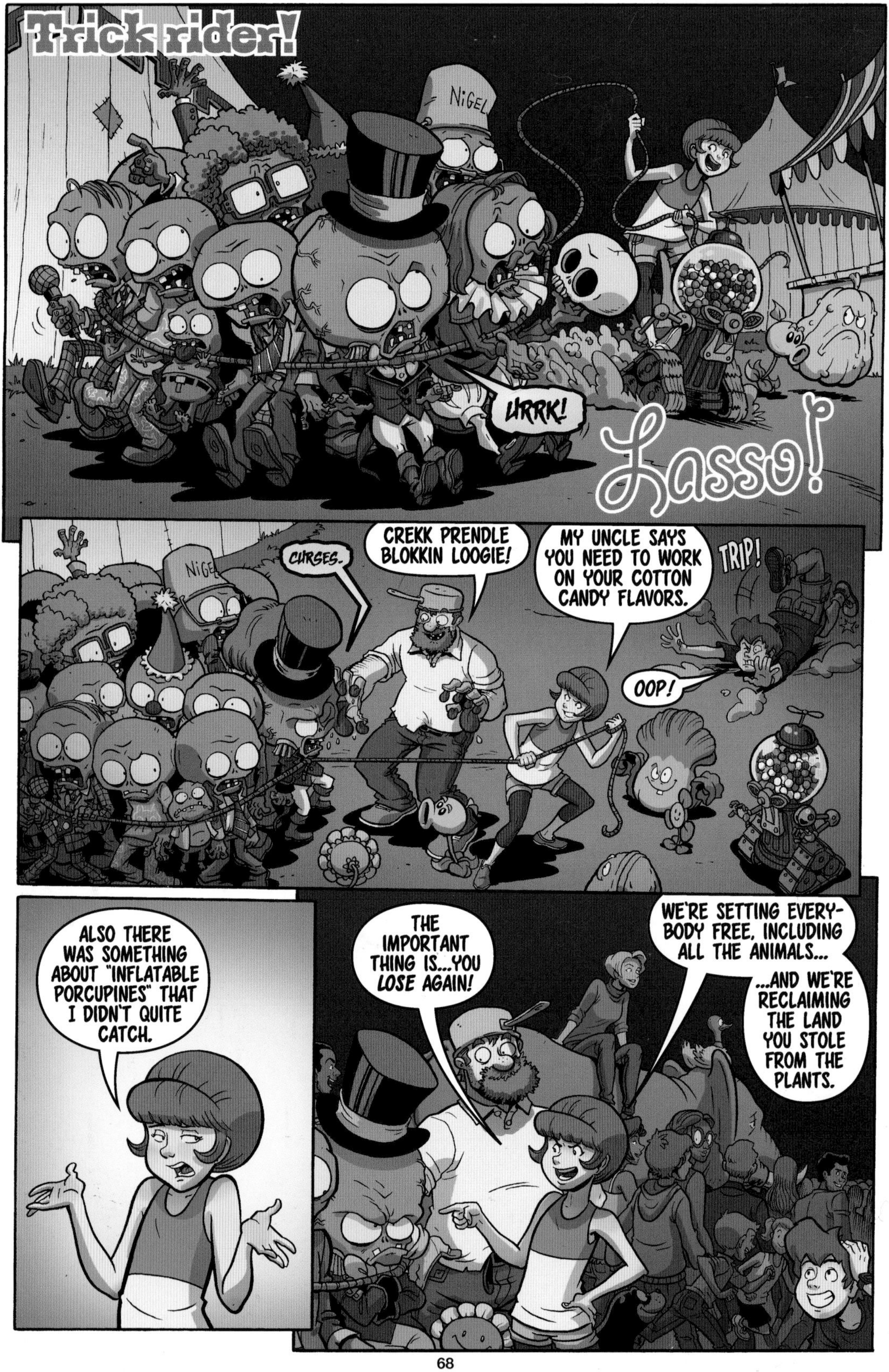
Trick rider!
NiGEL
URRK!
Lasso!
NiGEL
CURSES.
CREKK PRENDLE BLOKKIN LOOGIE!
MY UNCLE SAYS YOU NEED TO WORK ON YOUR COTTON CANDY FLAVORS.
TRIP!
OOP!
ALSO THERE WAS SOMETHING ABOUT "INFLATABLE PORCUPINES" THAT I DIDN'T QUITE CATCH.
THE IMPORTANT THING IS...YOU LOSE AGAIN!
WE'RE SETTING EVERY-BODY FREE, INCLUDING ALL THE ANIMALS...
...AND WE'RE RECLAIMING THE LAND YOU STOLE FROM THE PLANTS.

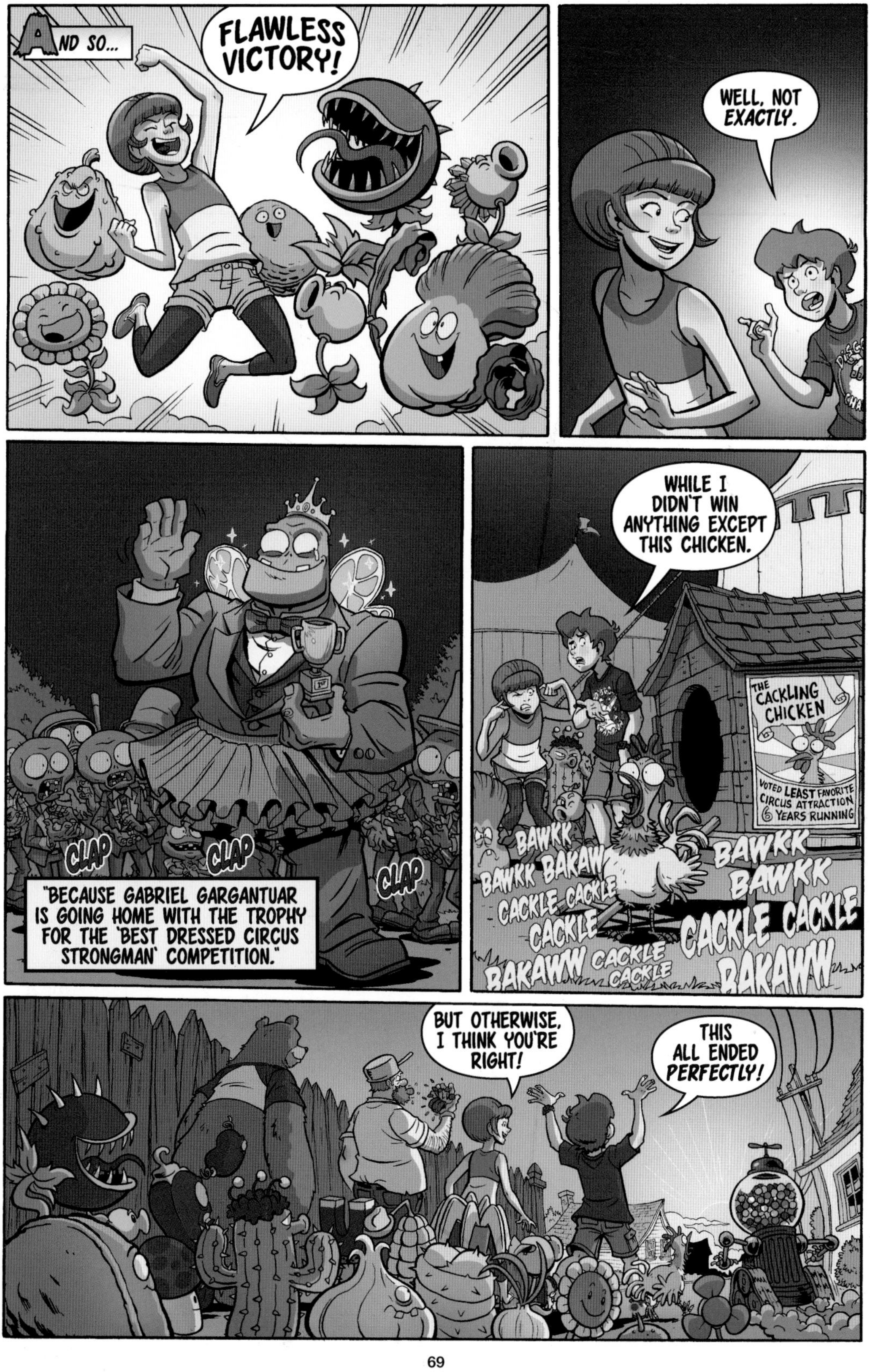
AND SO...
FLAWLESS VICTORY!
WELL, NOT EXACTLY.
CLAP
CLAP
CLAP
"BECAUSE GABRIEL GARGANTUAR IS GOING HOME WITH THE TROPHY FOR THE 'BEST DRESSED CIRCUS STRONGMAN' COMPETITION."
WHILE I DIDN'T WIN ANYTHING EXCEPT THIS CHICKEN.
THE CACKLING CHICKEN
VOTED LEAST FAVORITE CIRCUS ATTRACTION 6 YEARS RUNNING
BAWKK BAWKK BAKAW CACKLE CACKLE CACKLE BAKAWW CACKLE CACKLE
BAWKK BAWKK CACKLE CACKLE BAKAWW
BUT OTHERWISE, I THINK YOU'RE RIGHT!
THIS ALL ENDED PERFECTLY!

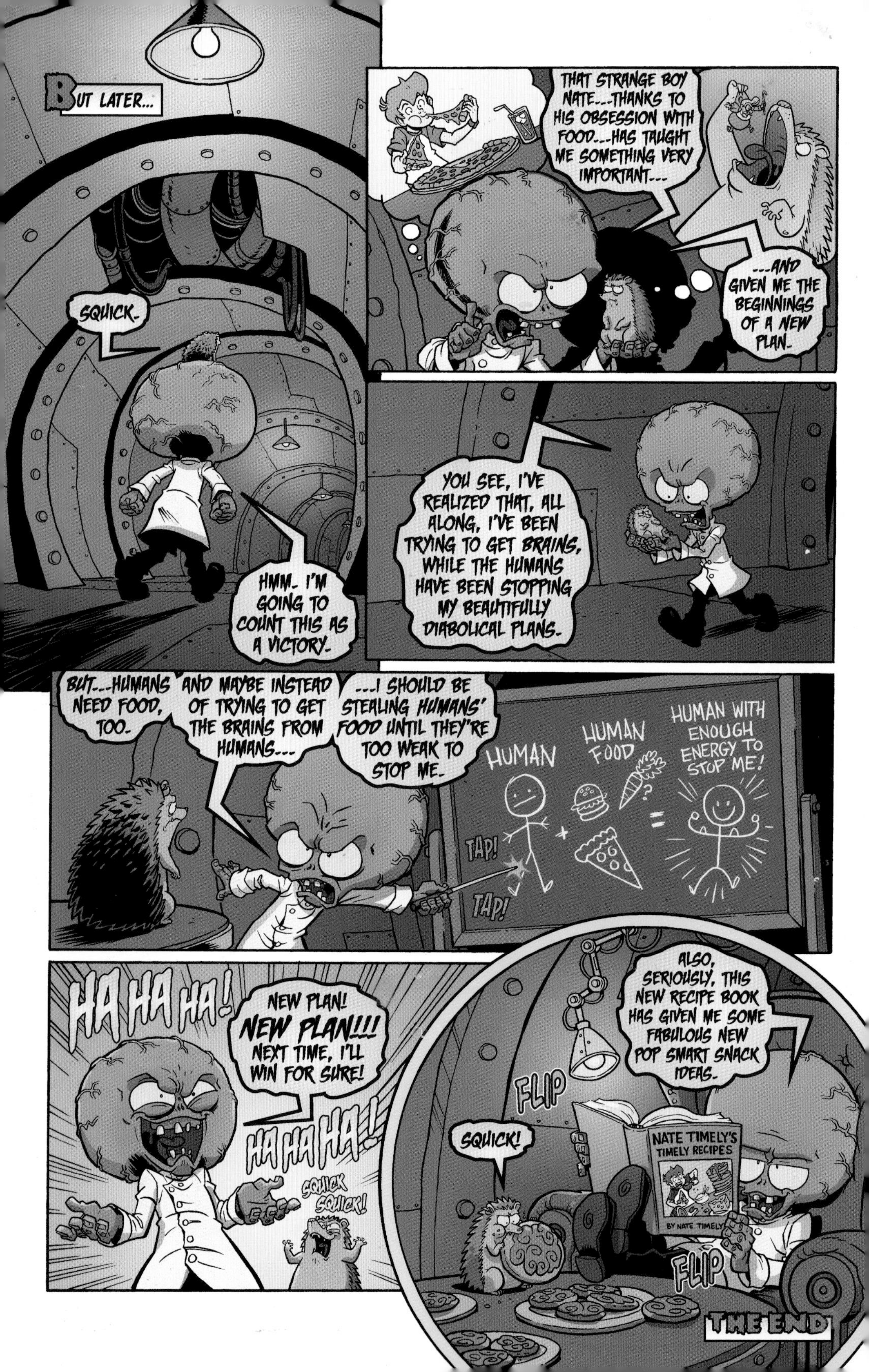
BUT LATER...
SQUICK.
HMM. I'M GOING TO COUNT THIS AS A VICTORY.
THAT STRANGE BOY NATE...THANKS TO HIS OBSESSION WITH FOOD...HAS TAUGHT ME SOMETHING VERY IMPORTANT...
...AND GIVEN ME THE BEGINNINGS OF A NEW PLAN.
YOU SEE, I'VE REALIZED THAT, ALL ALONG, I'VE BEEN TRYING TO GET BRAINS, WHILE THE HUMANS HAVE BEEN STOPPING MY BEAUTIFULLY DIABOLICAL PLANS.
BUT...HUMANS NEED FOOD, TOO.
AND MAYBE INSTEAD OF TRYING TO GET THE BRAINS FROM HUMANS...
...I SHOULD BE STEALING HUMANS' FOOD UNTIL THEY'RE TOO WEAK TO STOP ME.
HUMAN
HUMAN FOOD
HUMAN WITH ENOUGH ENERGY TO STOP ME!
TAP!
TAP!
HA HA HA!
NEW PLAN! NEW PLAN!!! NEXT TIME, I'LL WIN FOR SURE!
HA HA HA!
SQUICK SQUICK!
ALSO, SERIOUSLY, THIS NEW RECIPE BOOK HAS GIVEN ME SOME FABULOUS NEW POP SMART SNACK IDEAS.
FLIP
SQUICK!
NATE TIMELY'S TIMELY RECIPES
BY NATE TIMELY
FLIP
THE END

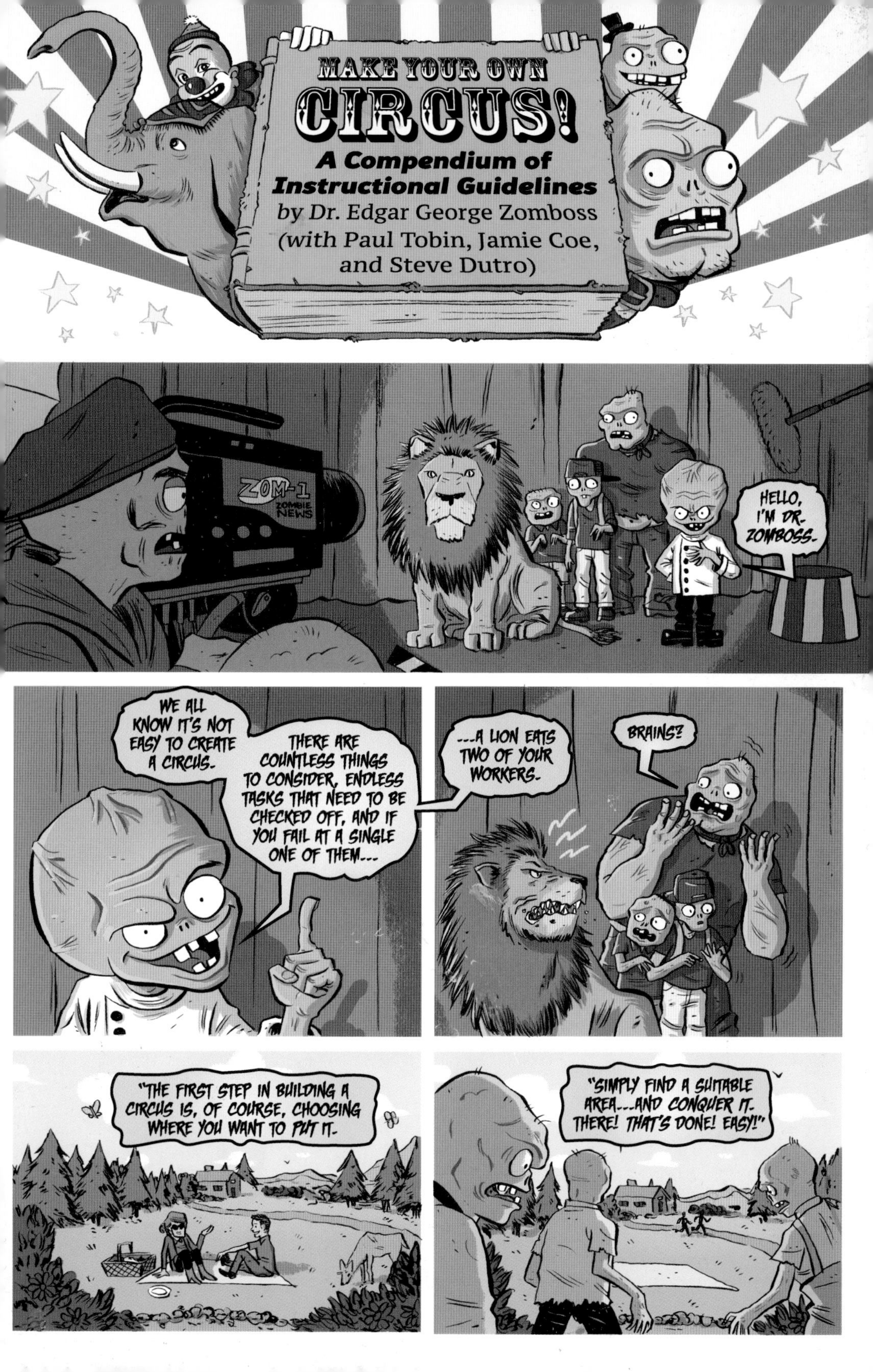
MAKE YOUR OWN
CIRCUS!
A Compendium of Instructional Guidelines
by Dr. Edgar George Zomboss (with Paul Tobin, Jamie Coe, and Steve Dutro)
ZOM-1 ZOMBIE NEWS
HELLO, I'M DR. ZOMBOSS.
WE ALL KNOW IT'S NOT EASY TO CREATE A CIRCUS.
THERE ARE COUNTLESS THINGS TO CONSIDER, ENDLESS TASKS THAT NEED TO BE CHECKED OFF, AND IF YOU FAIL AT A SINGLE ONE OF THEM...
...A LION EATS TWO OF YOUR WORKERS.
BRAINS?
"THE FIRST STEP IN BUILDING A CIRCUS IS, OF COURSE, CHOOSING WHERE YOU WANT TO PUT IT.
"SIMPLY FIND A SUITABLE AREA...AND CONQUER IT. THERE! THAT'S DONE! EASY!"

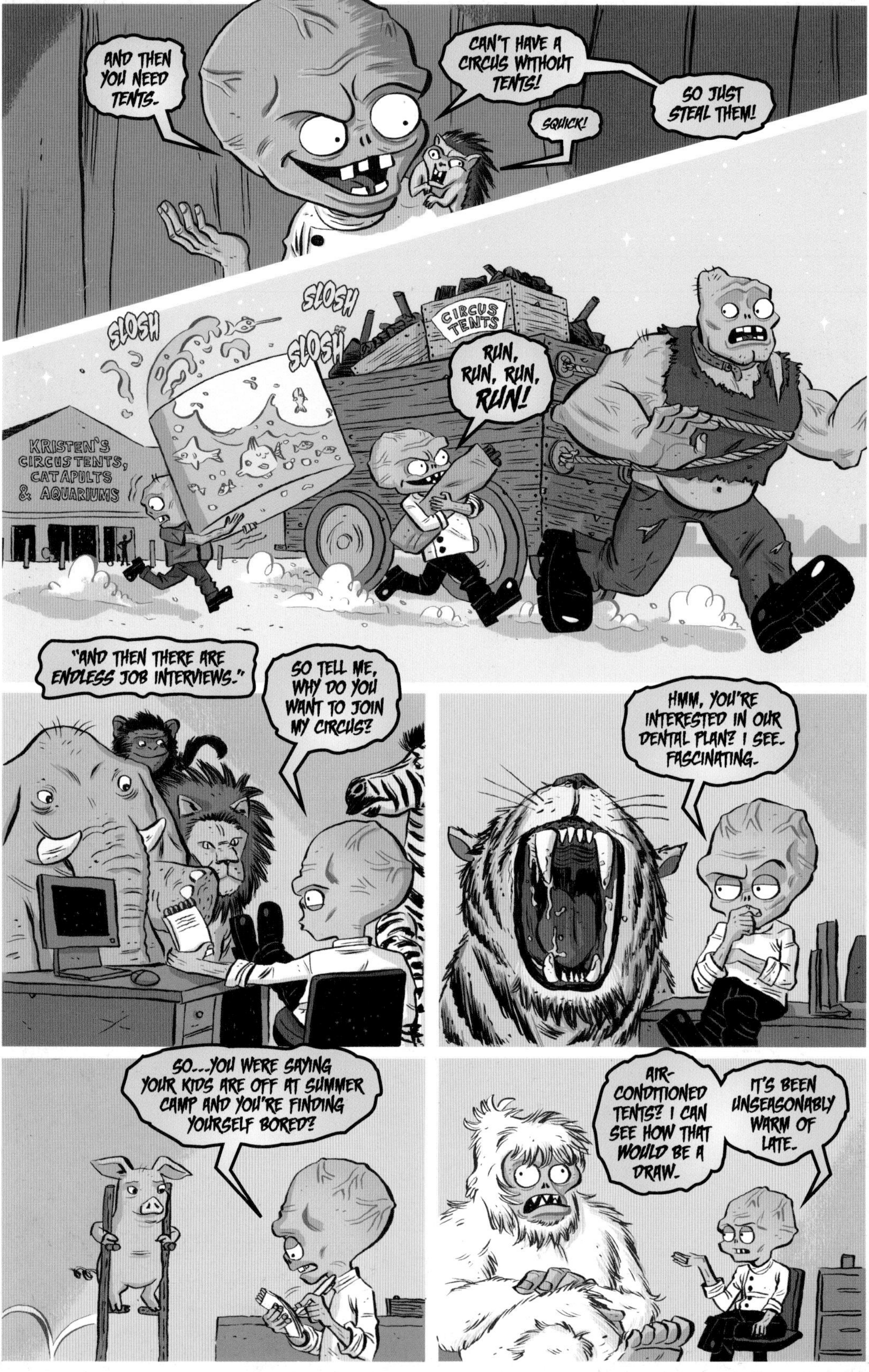

AND THEN YOU NEED TENTS.
CAN'T HAVE A CIRCUS WITHOUT TENTS!
SO JUST STEAL THEM!
SQUICK!
SLOSH
SLOSH
SLOSH
CIRCUS TENTS
RUN, RUN, RUN, RUN!
KRISTEN'S CIRCUSTENTS, CATAPULTS & AQUARIUMS
"AND THEN THERE ARE ENDLESS JOB INTERVIEWS."
SO TELL ME, WHY DO YOU WANT TO JOIN MY CIRCUS?
HMM, YOU'RE INTERESTED IN OUR DENTAL PLAN? I SEE. FASCINATING.
SO...YOU WERE SAYING YOUR KIDS ARE OFF AT SUMMER CAMP AND YOU'RE FINDING YOURSELF BORED?
AIR-CONDITIONED TENTS? I CAN SEE HOW THAT WOULD BE A DRAW.
IT'S BEEN UNSEASONABLY WARM OF LATE.

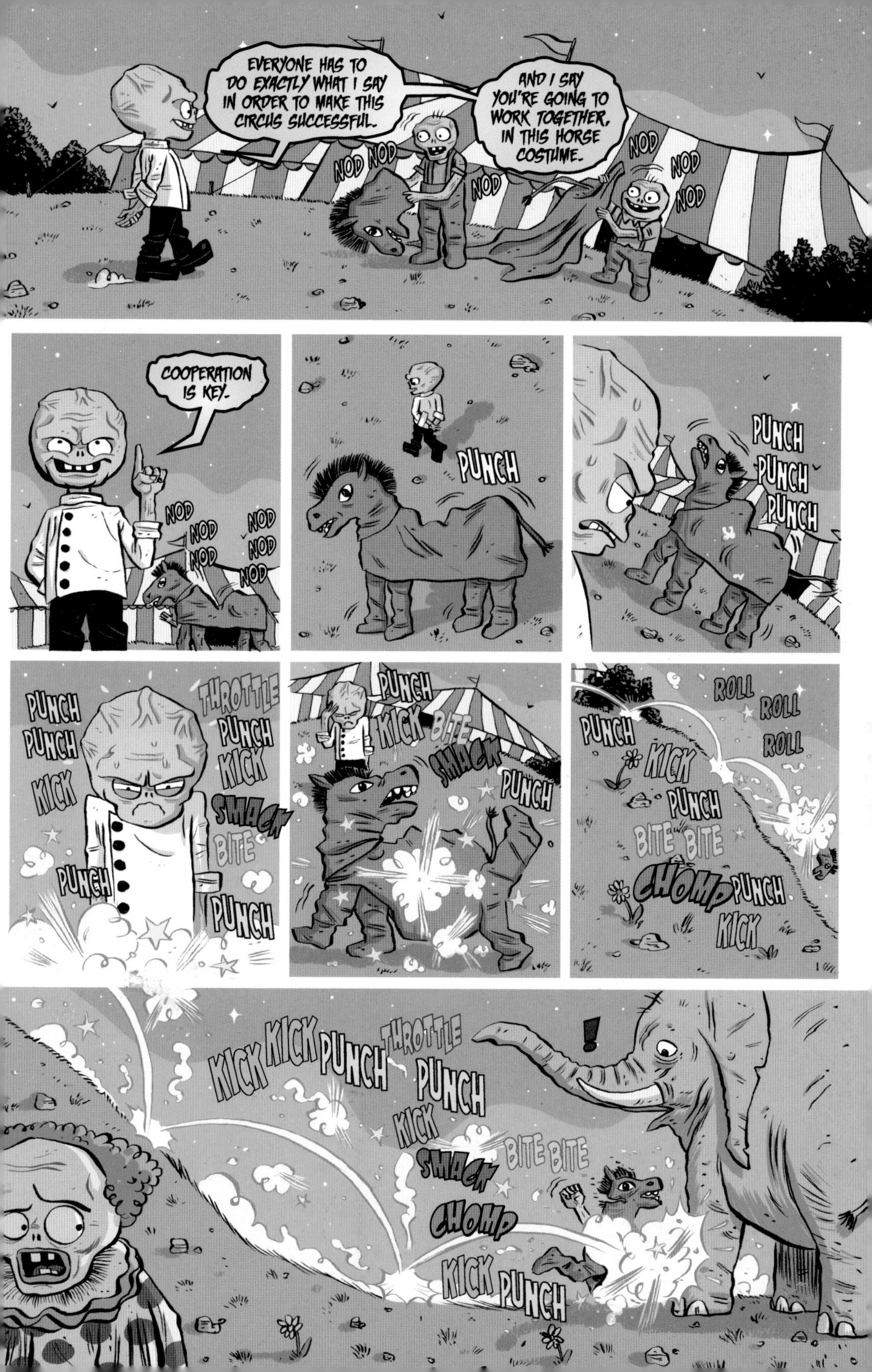

EVERYONE HAS TO DO EXACTLY WHAT I SAY IN ORDER TO MAKE THIS CIRCUS SUCCESSFUL.
AND I SAY YOU'RE GOING TO WORK TOGETHER, IN THIS HORSE COSTUME.
NOD NOD
NOD
NOD
NOD
NOD
COOPERATION IS KEY.
NOD
NOD
NOD
NOD
NOD
NOD
PUNCH
PUNCH
PUNCH
PUNCH
PUNCH
PUNCH
KICK
THROTTLE
PUNCH
KICK
SMACK
BITE
PUNCH
PUNCH
PUNCH
KICK
BITE
SMACK
PUNCH
ROLL
ROLL
ROLL
PUNCH
KICK
PUNCH
BITE BITE
CHOMP
PUNCH
KICK
KICK KICK PUNCH THROTTLE
PUNCH
KICK
SMACK
BITE BITE
CHOMP
KICK PUNCH
!

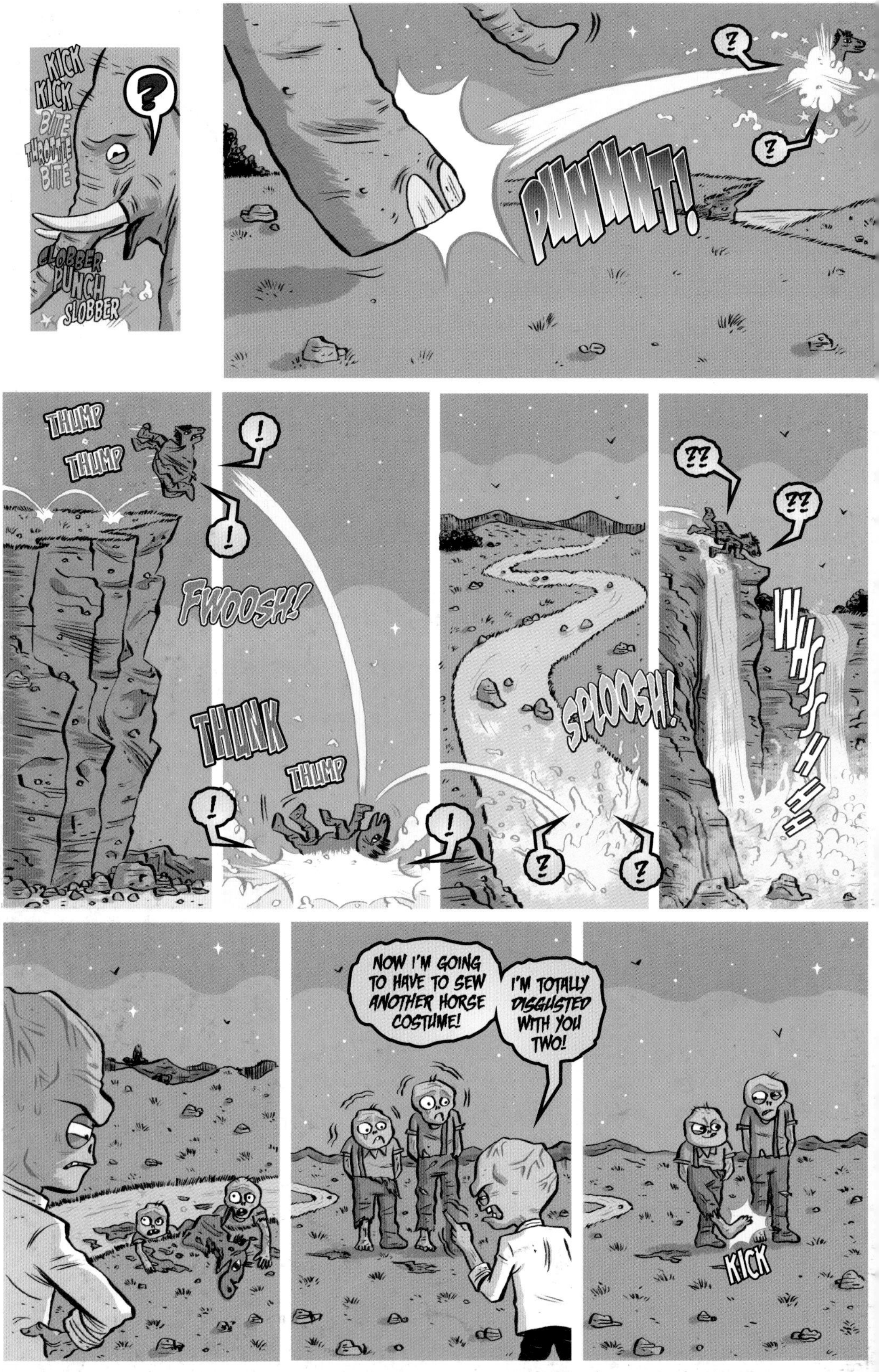
KICK
KICK
BITE
THROTTLE
BITE
CLOBBER
PUNCH
SLOBBER
?
PUNNNT!
?
?
THUMP
THUMP
!
!
FWOOSH!
THUNK
THUMP
!
!
SPLOOSH!
?
?
??
??
WHSSSHHHH
NOW I'M GOING TO HAVE TO SEW ANOTHER HORSE COSTUME!
I'M TOTALLY DISGUSTED WITH YOU TWO!
KICK

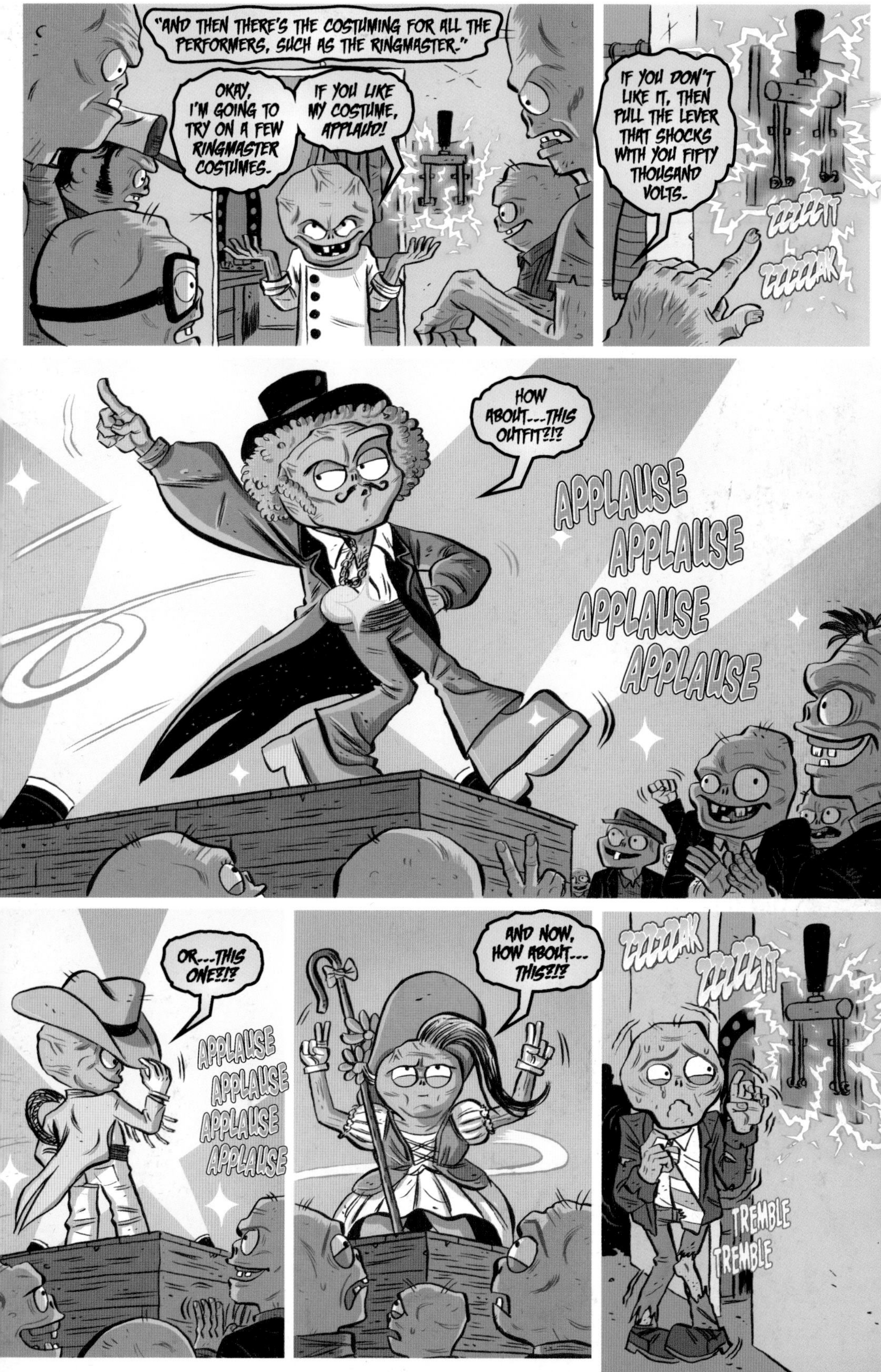
"AND THEN THERE'S THE COSTUMING FOR ALL THE PERFORMERS, SUCH AS THE RINGMASTER."
OKAY, I'M GOING TO TRY ON A FEW RINGMASTER COSTUMES.
IF YOU LIKE MY COSTUME, APPLAUD!
IF YOU DON'T LIKE IT, THEN PULL THE LEVER THAT SHOCKS WITH YOU FIFTY THOUSAND VOLTS.
ZZZZZTT
ZZZZZAK
HOW ABOUT---THIS OUTFIT?!?
APPLAUSE
APPLAUSE
APPLAUSE
APPLAUSE
OR---THIS ONE?!?
APPLAUSE
APPLAUSE
APPLAUSE
APPLAUSE
AND NOW, HOW ABOUT--- THIS?!?
ZZZZZAK
ZZZZZTT
TREMBLE
TREMBLE

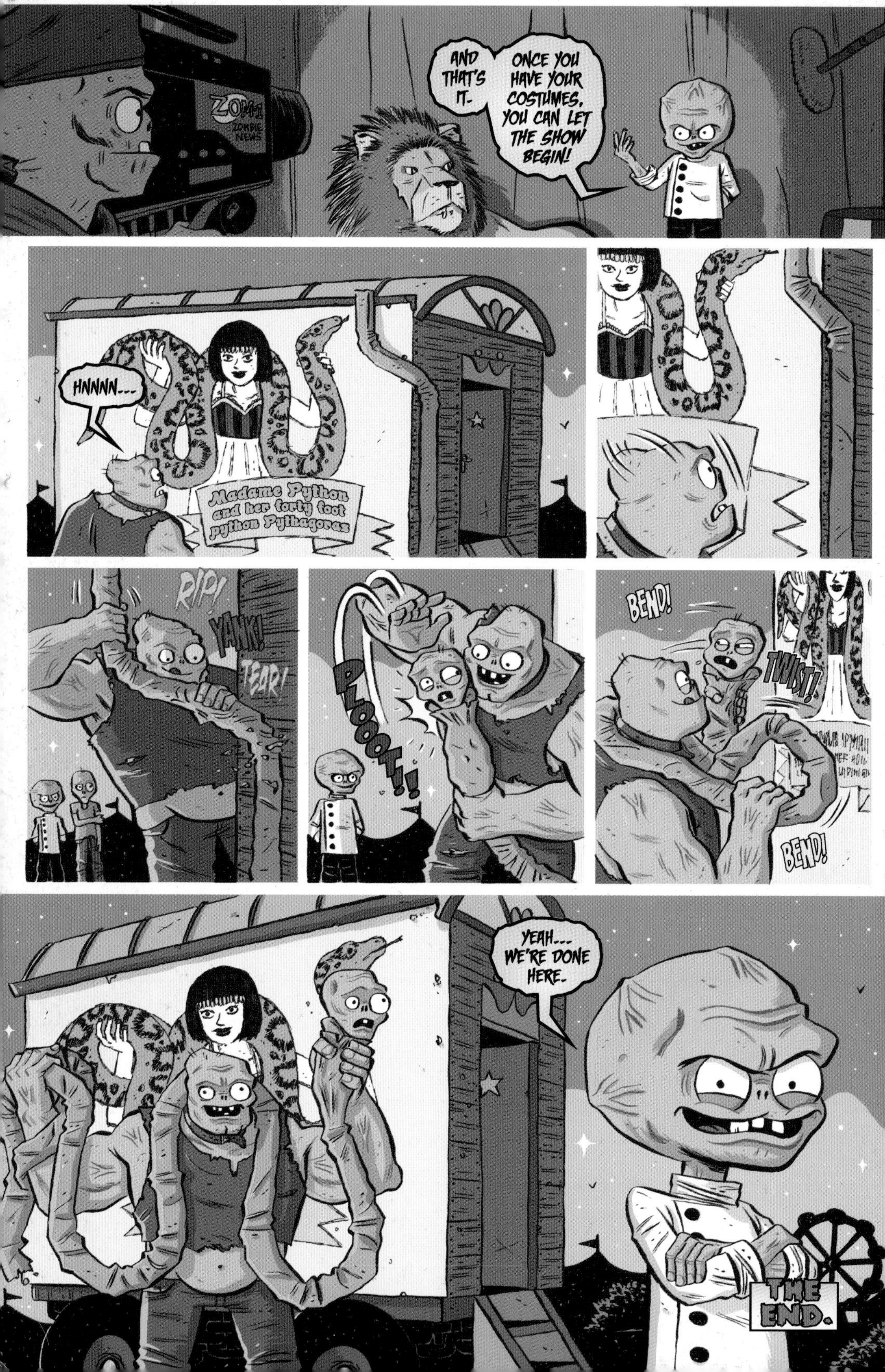
ZOM-1
ZOMBIE NEWS
AND THAT'S IT.
ONCE YOU HAVE YOUR COSTUMES, YOU CAN LET THE SHOW BEGIN!
HNNNN...
Madame Python and her forty foot python Pythagoras
RIP!
YANK!
TEAR!
PLOOOOT!!
BEND!
TWIST!
BEND!
YEAH... WE'RE DONE HERE.
THE END.

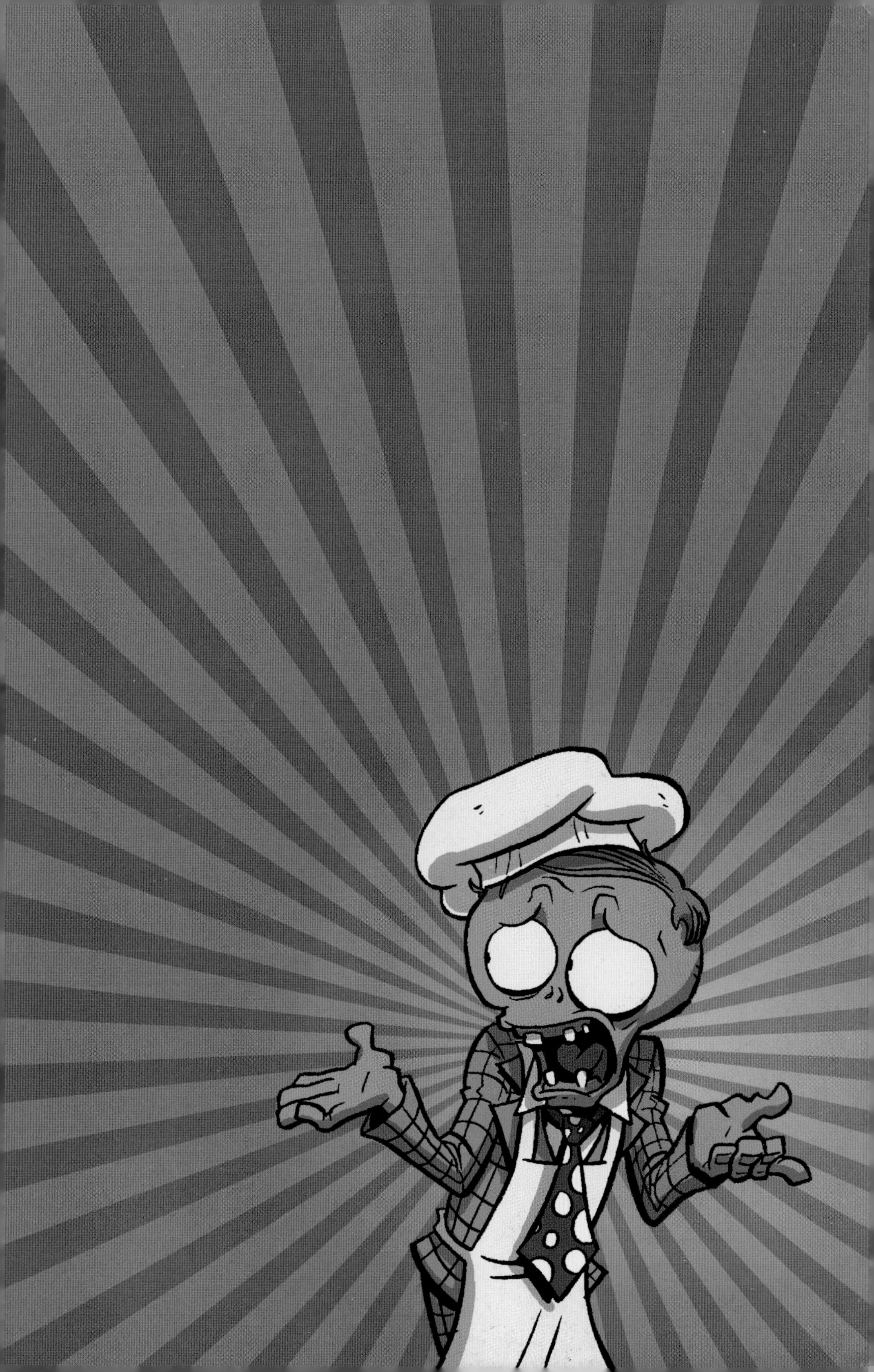

PLANTS VS. ZOMBIES: THE GREATEST SHOW UNEARTHED
COVER PENCILS BY JACOB CHABOT

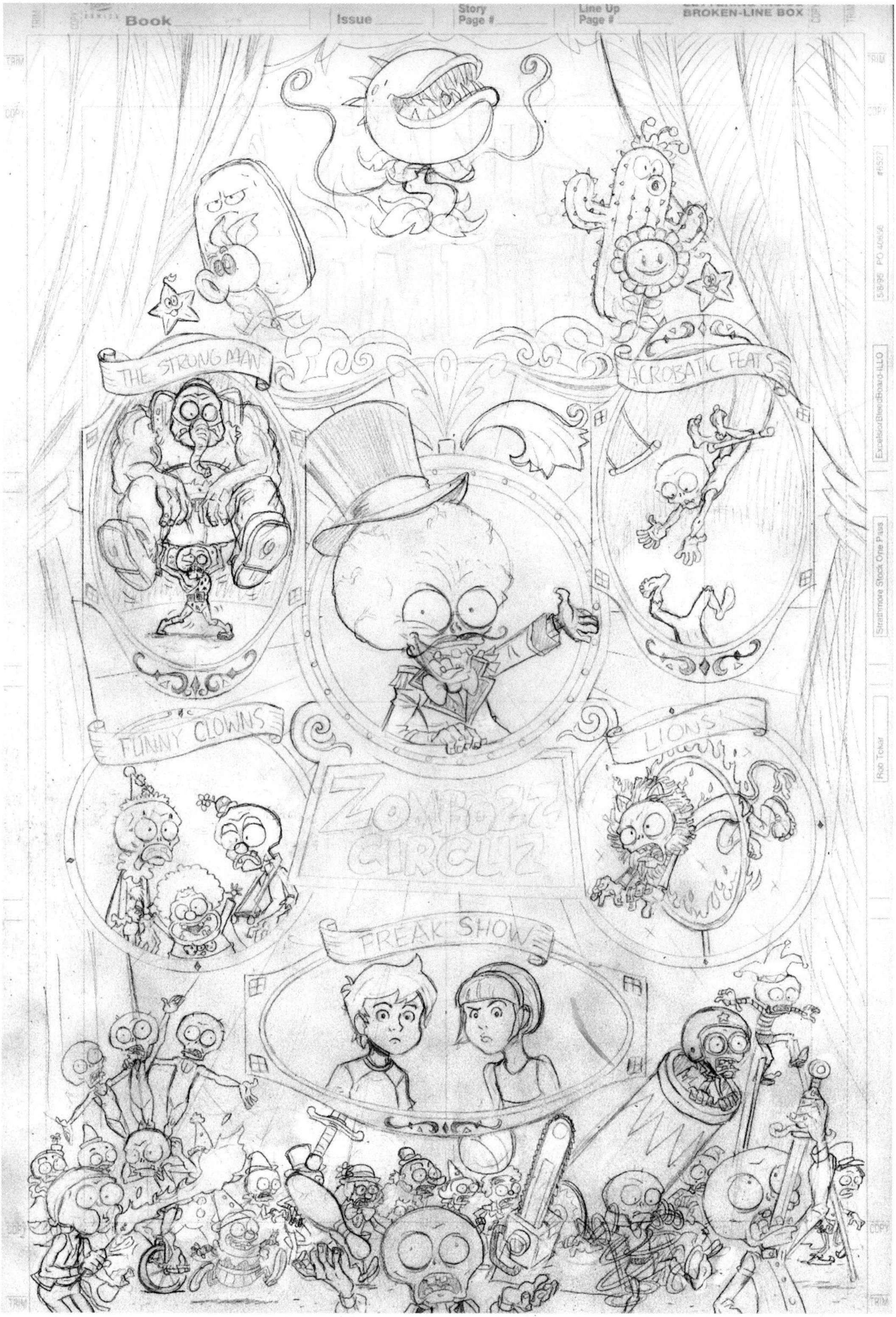
Book
Issue
Story Page #
Line Up Page #
BROKEN-LINE BOX
THE STRONG MAN
ACROBATIC FEATS
FUNNY CLOWNS
LIONS!
FREAK SHOW

PLANTS VS. ZOMBIES: THE GREATEST SHOW UNEARTHED
COVER INKS BY JACOB CHABOT

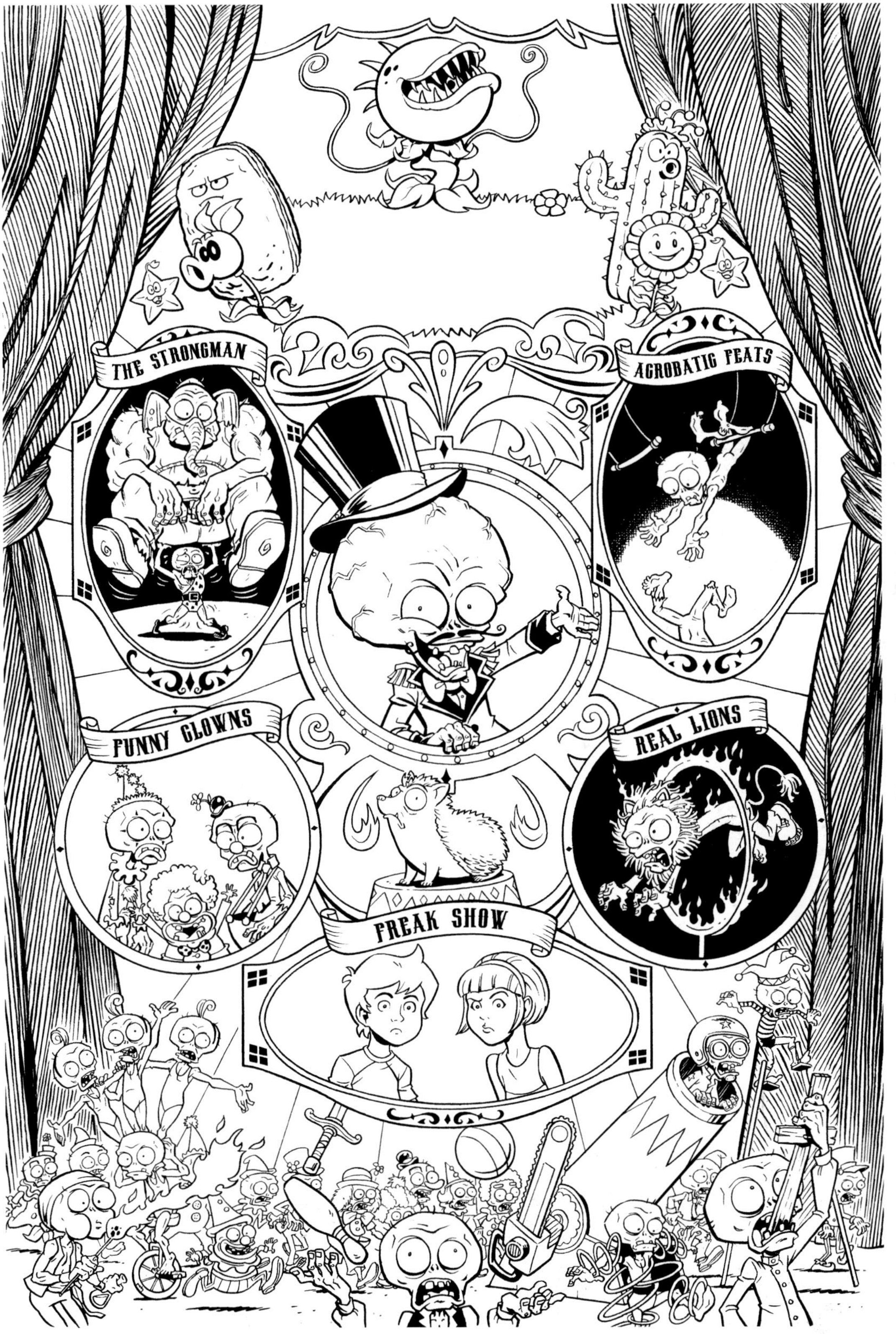
THE STRONGMAN
ACROBATIC FEATS
FUNNY CLOWNS
REAL LIONS
FREAK SHOW

PENCIL ART FROM *THE GREATEST SHOW UNEARTHED* PAGES 22-25 BY ARTIST JACOB CHABOT!

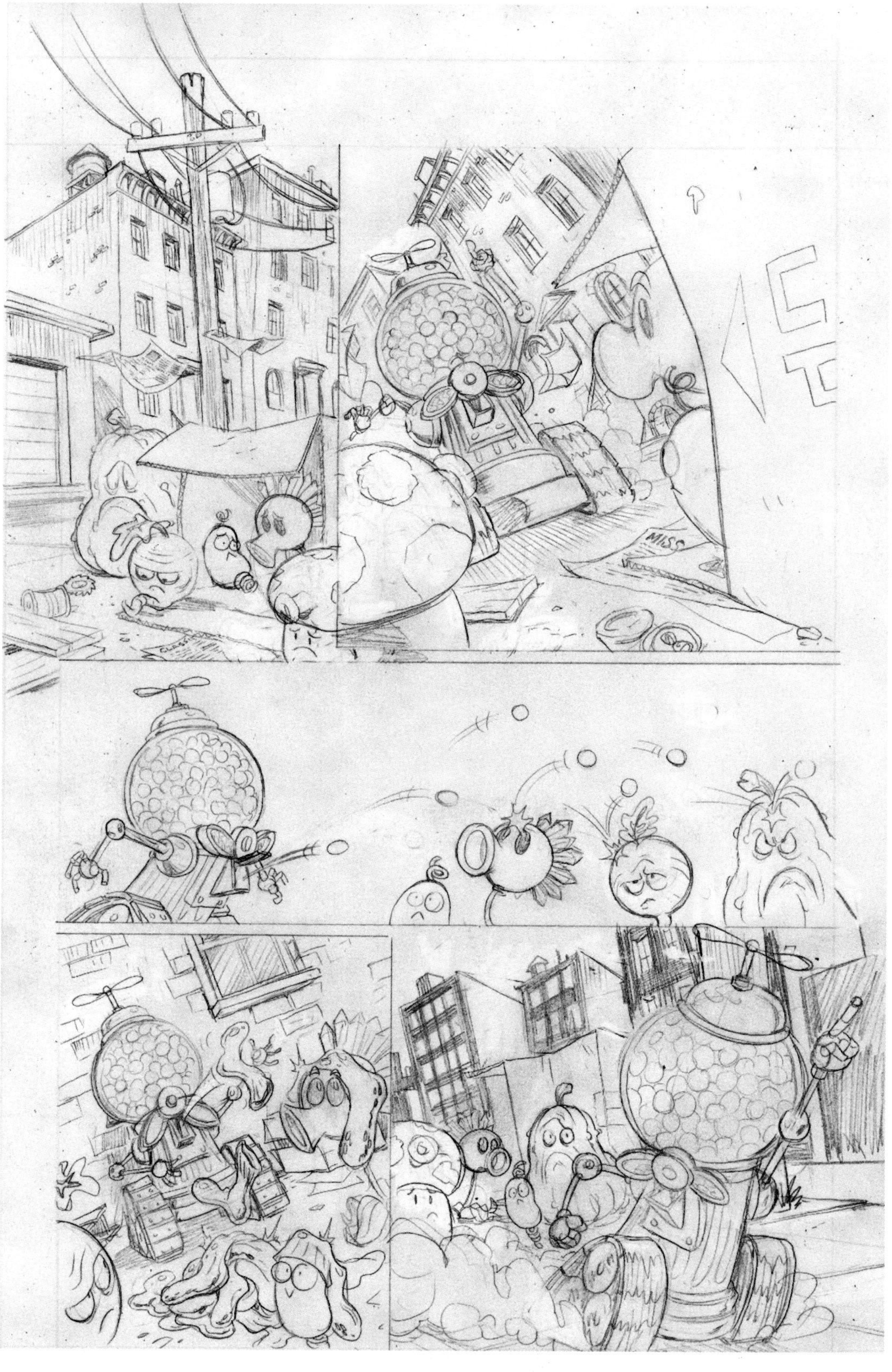

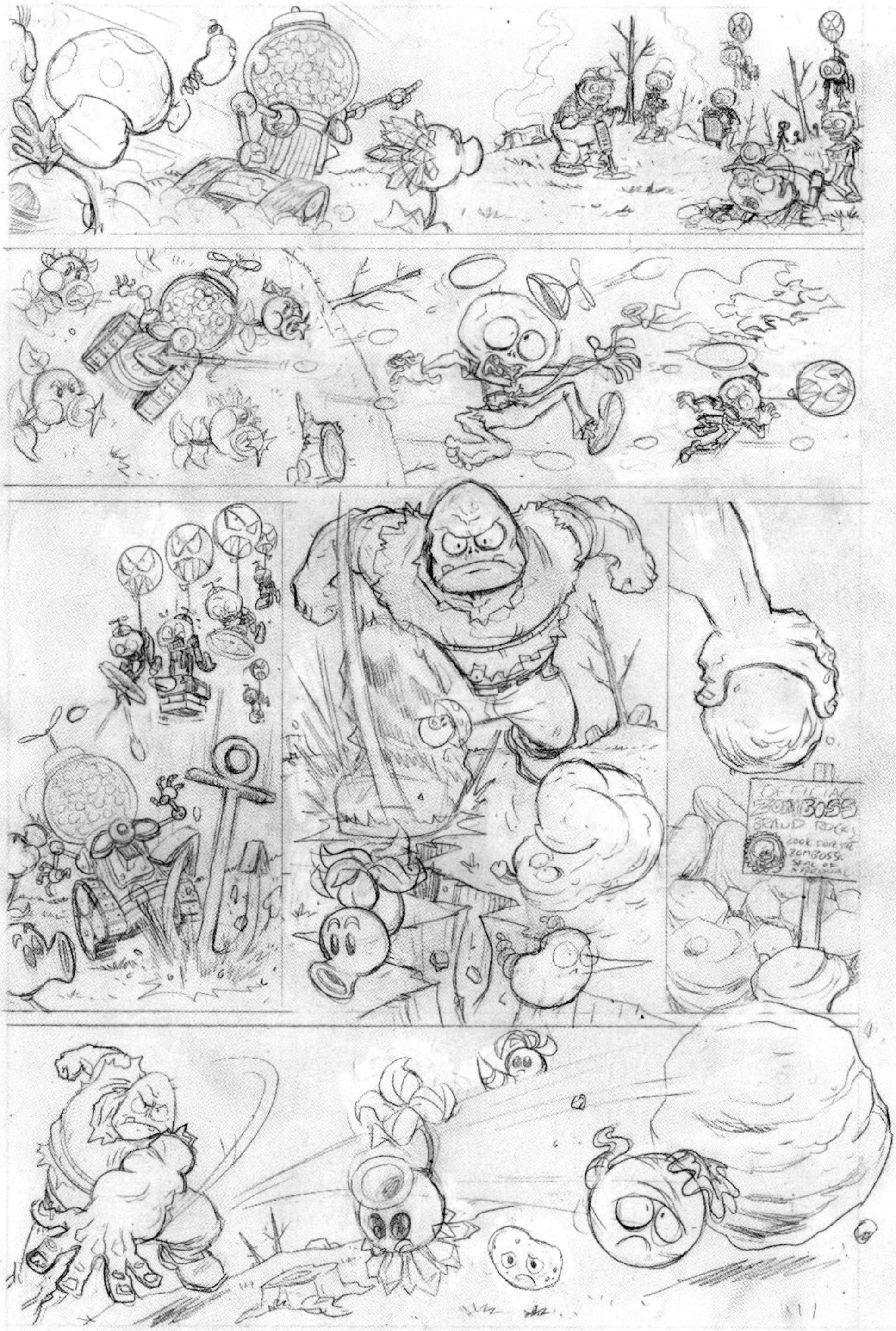
OFFICIAL
ZOMBOSS
BRAND ROCKS

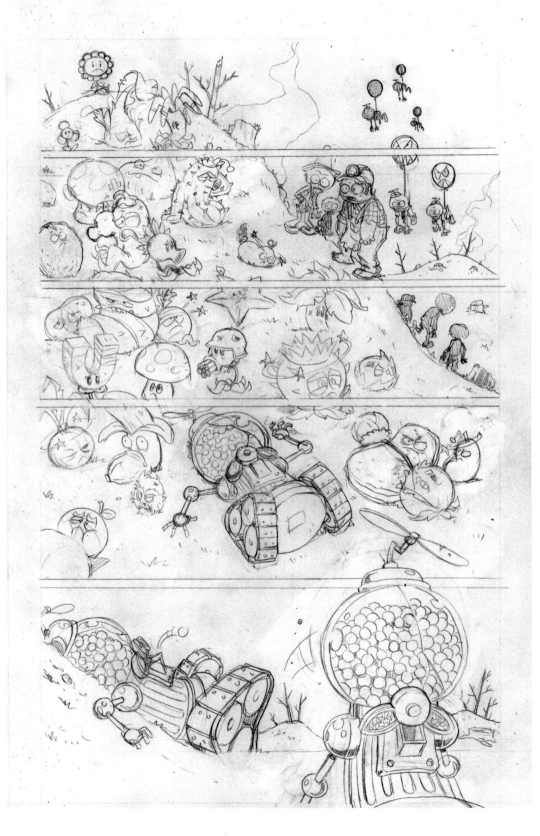

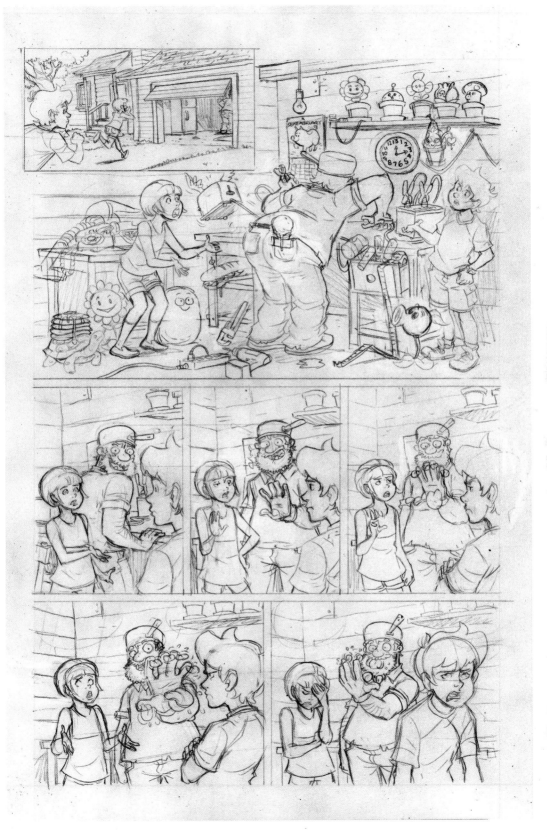

CREATOR BIOS

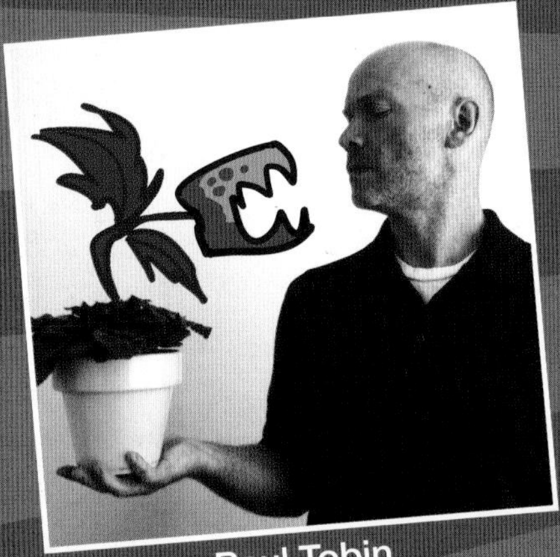

Paul Tobin

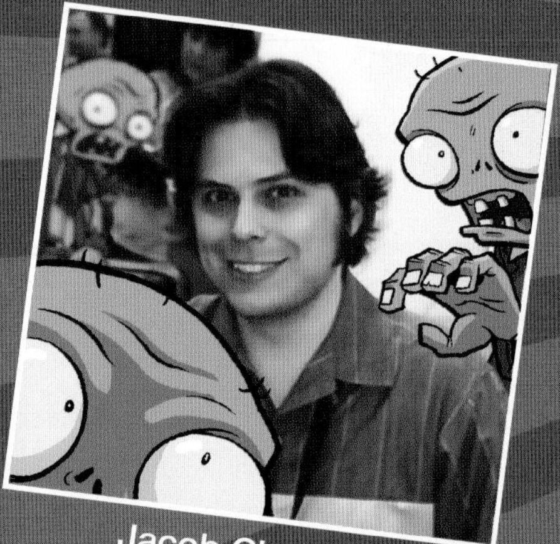

Jacob Chabot

PAUL TOBIN enjoys that his author photo makes him look insane, and he once accidentally cut his ear with a potato chip. He doesn't know how it happened, either. Life is so full of mystery. If you ask him about the Potato Chip Incident, he'll just make up a story. That's what he does. He's written hundreds of stories for Marvel, DC, Dark Horse, and many others, including such creator-owned titles as *Colder* and *Bandette*, as well as *Prepare to Die!*—his debut novel. His *Genius Factor* series of novels about a fifth-grade genius and his war against the Red Death Tea Society debuted in March 2016 with *How to Capture an Invisible Cat*, from Bloomsbury Publishing, and continued in early 2017 with *How to Outsmart a Billion Robot Bees*. Paul has won some Very Important Awards for his writing but so far none for his karaoke skills.

JACOB CHABOT is a New York City–based cartoonist and illustrator. His credits include work for *SpongeBob Comics*, *Simpsons Comics*, Marvel Comics, *Hello Kitty*, and his own Eisner-nominated book *The Mighty Skullboy Army* (published by Dark Horse Comics). He also has almost all the achievements in *Plants vs. Zombies Garden Warfare*, and if he could stop drawing for a minute, maybe he could finish them all!

Matt J. Rainwater

Steve Dutro

Residing in the cool, damp forests of Portland, Oregon, **MATT J. RAINWATER** is a freelance illustrator whose work has been featured in advertising, web design, and independent video games. On top of this, he also self-publishes several comic books, including *Trailer Park Warlock*, *Garage Raja*, and *The Feeling Is Multiplied*—all of which can be found at MattJRainwater.com. His favorite zombie-bashing strategy utilizes a line of Bonk Choys with a Wall-nut front guard and Threepeater covering fire.

STEVE DUTRO is an Eisner Award-nominated comic-book letterer from Redding, California, who can also drive a tractor. He graduated from the Kubert School and has been lettering comics since the days when foil-embossed covers were cool, working for Dark Horse (*The Fifth Beatle*, *I Am a Hero*, *Planet of the Apes*, *Star Wars*), Viz, Marvel, and DC. He has submitted a request to the Department of Homeland Security that in the event of a zombie apocalypse he be put in charge of all digital freeway signs so citizens can be alerted to avoid nearby brain-eatings and the like. He finds the *Plants vs. Zombies* game to be a real stress-fest, but highly recommends the *Plants vs. Zombies* table on *Pinball FX2* for game-room hipsters.

ALSO AVAILABLE FROM DARK HORSE!

THE HIT VIDEO GAME CONTINUES ITS COMIC BOOK INVASION!

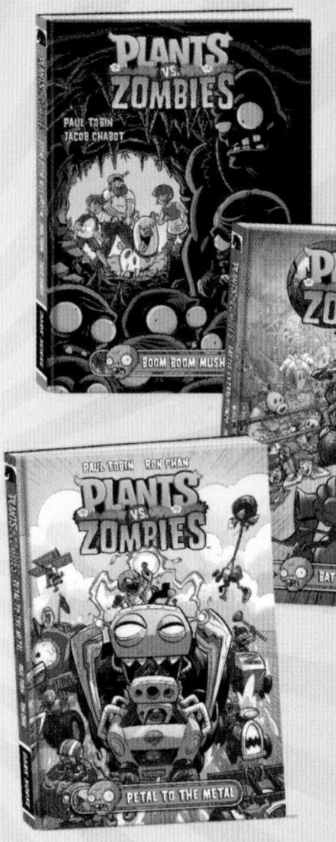
PLANTS VS. ZOMBIES
PAUL TOBIN
JACOB CHABOT
BOOM BOOM MUSH
PLANTS VS. ZOMBIES
BATTLE EXTRAVAGONZO
PAUL TOBIN
RON CHAN
PLANTS VS. ZOMBIES
PETAL TO THE METAL

PLANTS VS. ZOMBIES: LAWNMAGEDDON
Crazy Dave—the babbling-yet-brilliant inventor and top-notch neighborhood defender—helps young adventurer Nate fend off a zombie invasion that threatens to overrun the peaceful town of Neighborville in *Plants vs. Zombies: Lawnmageddon*! Their only hope is a brave army of chomping, squashing, and pea-shooting plants! A wacky adventure for zombie zappers young and old!
ISBN 978-1-61655-192-6 | $9.99

THE ART OF PLANTS VS. ZOMBIES
Part zombie memoir, part celebration of zombie triumphs, and part anti-plant screed, *The Art of Plants vs. Zombies* is a treasure trove of never-before-seen concept art, character sketches, and surprises from PopCap's popular Plants vs. Zombies games!
ISBN 978-1-61655-331-9 | $9.99

PLANTS VS. ZOMBIES: TIMEPOCALYPSE
Crazy Dave helps Patrice and Nate Timely fend off Zomboss's latest attack in *Plants vs. Zombies: Timepocalypse*! This new standalone tale will tickle your funny bones and thrill your brains through any timeline!
ISBN 978-1-61655-621-1 | $9.99

PLANTS VS. ZOMBIES: BULLY FOR YOU
Patrice and Nate are ready to investigate a strange college campus to keep the streets safe from zombies!
ISBN 978-1-61655-889-5 | $9.99

PLANTS VS. ZOMBIES: GARDEN WARFARE
Based on the hit video game, this comic tells the story leading up to the events in *Plants vs. Zombies: Garden Warfare 2*!
ISBN 978-1-61655-946-5 | $9.99

PLANTS VS. ZOMBIES: GROWN SWEET HOME
With newfound knowledge of humanity, Dr. Zomboss strikes at the heart of Neighborville . . . sparking a series of plant-versus-zombie brawls!
ISBN 978-1-61655-971-7 | $9.99

PLANTS VS. ZOMBIES: PETAL TO THE METAL
Crazy Dave takes on the tough *Don't Blink* video game—and challenges Dr. Zomboss to a race to determine the future of Neighborville!
ISBN 978-1-61655-999-1 | $9.99

PLANTS VS. ZOMBIES: BOOM BOOM MUSHROOM
The gang discover Zomboss' secret plan for swallowing the city of Neighborville whole! A rare mushroom must be found in order to save the humans aboveground!
ISBN 978-1-50670-037-3 | $9.99

PLANTS VS. ZOMBIES: BATTLE EXTRAVAGONZO
Zomboss is back, hoping to buy the same factory that Crazy Dave is eyeing! Will Crazy Dave and his intelligent plants beat Zomboss and his zombie army to the punch?
ISBN 978-1-50670-189-9 | $9.99

PLANTS VS. ZOMBIES: LAWN OF DOOM
With Zomboss filling everyone's yards with traps and special soldiers, will he and his zombie army turn Halloween into their scarier Lawn of Doom celebration?!
ISBN 978-1-50670-204-9 | $9.99

PLANTS VS. ZOMBIES: THE GREATEST SHOW UNEARTHED
Dr. Zomboss believes that all humans hold a secret desire to run away and join the circus, so he aims to use his "Big Z's Adequately Amazing Flytrap Circus" to lure Neighborville's citizens to their doom!
ISBN 978-1-50670-298-8 | $9.99

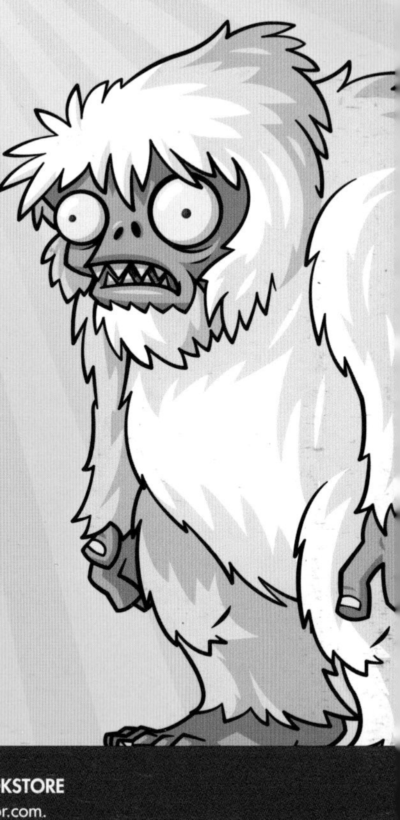

AVAILABLE AT YOUR LOCAL COMICS SHOP OR BOOKSTORE
To find a comics shop in your area, visit comicshoplocator.com.
For more information or to order direct visit **DarkHorse.com** or call 1-800-862-0052

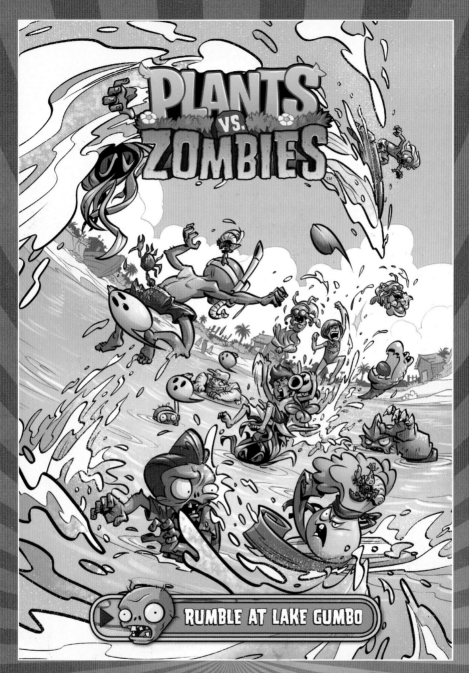

RUMBLE AT LAKE GUMBO

**PLANTS VS. ZOMBIES: RUMBLE AT LAKE GUMBO
—DIVING IN JUNE 2018!**

Calling all Cat-Tail Commanders and Spudmarines, the battle for clean water begins! As soon as Dr. Zomboss discovers Lake Gumbo near Neighborville, Gargantuars start posing on Muscle Beach, volleyballs bounce off bungee zombies, and Zomboss uses a giant underwater drill to stir up and pollute the lake! Neighborhood defenders Nate, Patrice, and Crazy Dave spot trouble and grab all the Tangle Kelp and Party Crabs they can to quell another zombie attack!

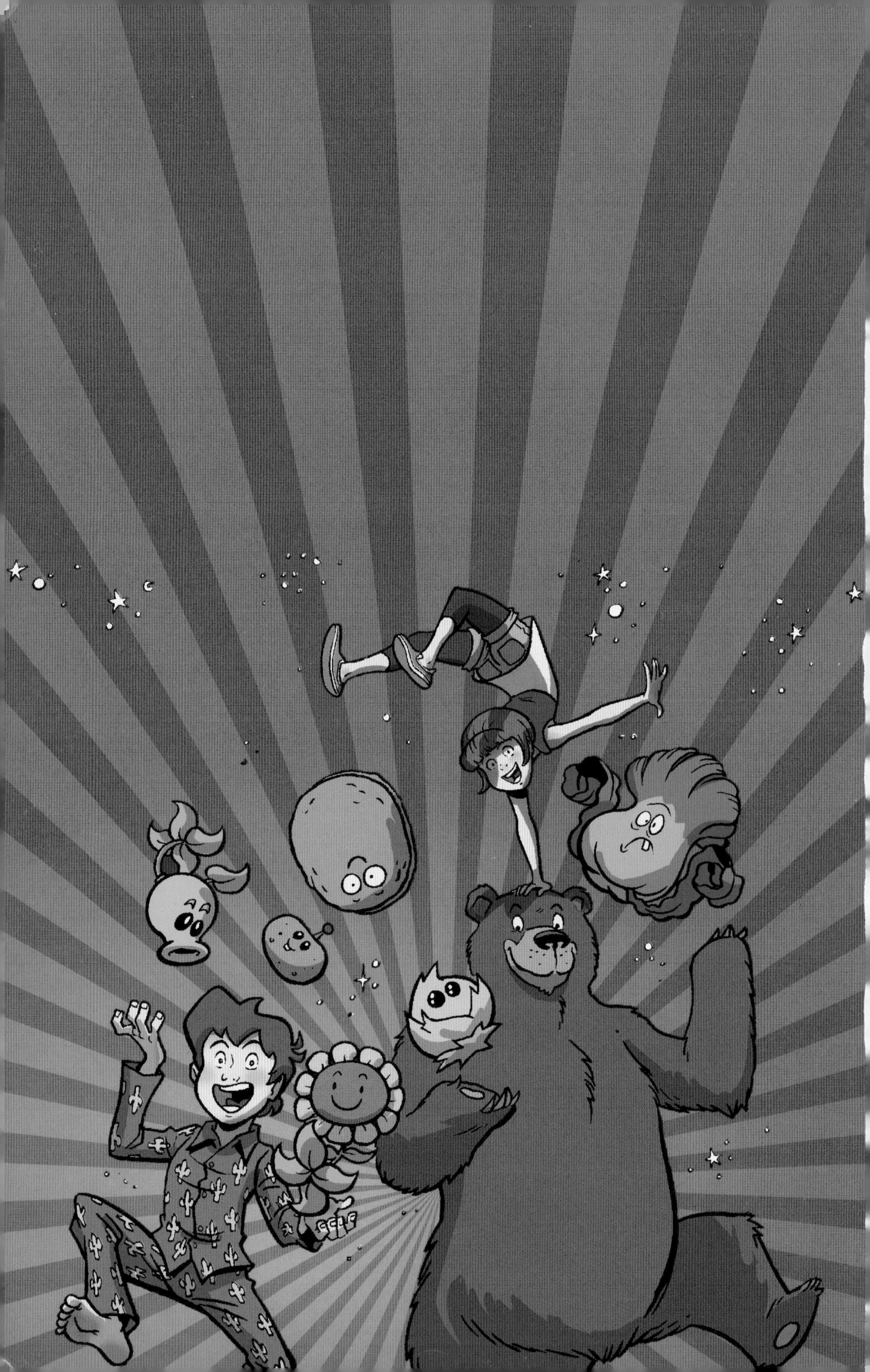